## Bay of Blood

"This elegant, insightful murder m[...][...]le
mystery unfolds with an homage t[...] at
inspired Canada's legendary Grou[...] a
seasoned writer..." —Suzanne Bar[...] ......ui of *Likely Stories*

"In Eva Naslund, we discover a sleuth who is sympathetic,
vulnerable, and smart. *Bay of Blood* is an exciting new entry in the
world of detective fiction."
—Ken Haigh, author of *Under the Holy Mountain*

"*Bay of Blood* is a whodunit with soul. Detective Eva Naslund is a
gem. She's both logical and intuitive, both tough and approachable."
—Patrick Tilley, retired RCMP Detective

"Hold on to your hats because author Andy Potter wastes no time
diving in to a fast-paced plot that holds the reader's attention with
chilling police work detail and a perplexing lineup of persons of
interest, all of whom seem to be prime suspects."—James White

## The Color Red

"The complex investigation includes many possible suspects... Potter
makes Bourque, who gave up a career in organic chemistry to hunt
killers, a credible lead readers will root for. Fans of intelligent
procedurals will hope for a long series run."—*Publishers Weekly*

"*The Color Red* stands out as a gripping, intelligent, and well-written
detective story. An excellent start to what promises to be a must-
read series." —Jane Bwye, author of *Breath of Africa*

"Potter is writing at the top of his form with the launch of his new
detective series set in Cape Cod. Ancient Balkan grudges collide
with no-nonsense Yankee detectives in this exceptionally well-
written mystery."
—Caroline Woodward, author of *Alaska Highway Two-Step*

"*The Color Red* is a captivating eddy of old world and new, east and
west, masculine and feminine, fed on a healthy menu of well-cooked
dishes of revenge. Potter's language is accurate and elegant, and his
characters are on point. A superb read."
—S.M. Collins, author of *To Be Human Again*

"*The Color Red* is a smart, fast-paced mystery by a master craftsman
of the genre who knows how to weave complex ideas into a riveting
storyline. Detective Bourque is one unique officer of the law, willing
to 'dance with the devil' when need be." —Lesley Choyce, author of
*The Unlikely Redemption of John Alexander MacNeil*

A. M. Potter Bibliography

Bay of Blood (2019)
The Color Red (2023)

# SILVER MOON RISING

## Book Two in the
## Detective Bourque Series

## by A.M. Potter

STARK
HOUSE

**Stark House Press • Eureka California**

SILVER MOON RISING

Published by Stark House Press
1315 H Street
Eureka, CA 95501, USA
griffinskye3@sbcglobal.net
www.starkhousepress.com

ISBN: 979-8-88601-100-5

Book text and cover design by Mark Shepard, shepgraphics.com
Cover photo by Tolga Ahmetler
Proofreading by Bill Kelly

First Stark House Press Edition: September 2024

Sail forbidden seas ~ Herman Melville

Whoever loves being alone must be
either a beast or a God ~ Plato

DEDICATION

To John:
The best kind of man, a man
of both principle and pleasure.

# Map of Cape Cod
## Massachusetts

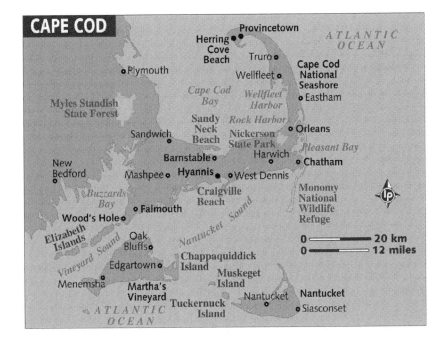

# Chapter 1

## Woods Hole, Massachusetts, USA. October 19th

Daniel Fitzgerald surveyed the early night sky. Mars ruled the eastern quadrant; Saturn and Jupiter governed the south. A full moon cast Vineyard Sound in a cold metallic light. His nostrils quivered, catching the scent of land. The ferry was nearing Woods Hole. A claxon sounded, followed by an announcement for passengers to prepare to disembark.

From the corner of his eye, he saw a short wide man join him at the deck rail. They were alone. The man abruptly ran at him, barreling into his back, pinning his chest against the rail.

Fitzgerald felt a knife being driven into his left side. He reacted immediately, elbowing the man in the stomach. The man pulled the knife out, calmly drove it in again, and tipped Fitzgerald over the rail. His heart skipped a beat. He plunged headfirst into Vineyard Sound like a diving bird.

## Chapter 2

**DAY ONE: Cape & Islands Detective Region, Massachusetts State Police. October 20th**

Detective Lieutenant Ivy Bourque boarded the *Islander* just after midnight. An enormous silver moon outshone the constellations, demoting them to minor dignitaries. In the ferry's main passageway, a man approached her, blocking the light behind him. She recognized him instantly: State Trooper Donnelly, who, at six-five, topped 240 pounds.

"Looks like some simple math," Donnelly said. "One young buck plus one abandoned car equals Studly sleeping it off." He grinned. "Maybe with someone's wife. But that's my first impression. What if the car wasn't abandoned? You know what those TV detectives say: there could be *foul play*."

"Oh yeah." Bourque smiled. "Have you heard the rumors?"

He shook his head.

"You'd make a fine detective. A real one."

"Never. I'm a foot soldier. I like it that way."

"Ditch the uniform. Wear your own suits."

"I like uniforms." He winked. "So does my wife."

Bourque had been called to the ferry on a missing-person initiated by the ship's skipper. The abandoned car's sole occupant, Daniel John Fitzgerald, had boarded on Martha's Vineyard. She'd scanned his background. Home address near Chilmark, on the quiet side of the Vineyard—up-island, as it was known. He was "New England Royalty," which complicated matters. Royalty of any kind always did. They wanted answers yesterday. Fitzgerald's grandfather was a first cousin of Joseph Fitzgerald Sr., father of three famous sons: a Massachusetts governor, a State Attorney General, and a State senator.

"Let's visit the skipper," she said to Donnelly.

"Lead on, Lieutenant Macduff."

*Macduff?* A new Donnellyism? This time with a Shakespearean reference. The trooper might be obtuse but he was never stale.

Although the October air was crisp, the air inside the ship was close and heavy. Bourque and Donnelly mounted a confined metal stairwell, ascending four levels to the skipper's cabin. The nameplate on the door read Captain Brock Macey. A gruff voice called them in.

She switched on her duty phone's audio recorder. Macey's cabin was as confined as the stairwell. There was scarcely enough room for a bunk, a small adjoining bathroom or head, as nautical types called it, and a desk and chair, occupied by Macey. The only concession to his rank was a large storage locker.

The captain was a wide man with bushy eyebrows and wavy white hair. His eyes held the blue-grey of the North Atlantic. She pegged him at sixty-plus. His hands were huge; his fingers, thick and muscular. He wore a blue officer's blazer that was too tight in the shoulders.

"I have news," he curtly said. "I called the Coast Guard to upgrade the incident from a missing passenger to a man overboard." He paused. "They have powerful searchlights. Then there's the moon. Full moon, fast find."

Bourque hoped so. Vineyard Sound had cooled abruptly in the past week. She swam in it every morning until late October—these days wearing a wetsuit. "Why did you think Mr. Fitzgerald was missing?" she asked.

"The abandoned car. I figured he'd been drinking or met someone. The usual. Then a seaman found blood on the aft viewing deck and I went to take a look. Just me," he added. "I kept others away in case it was a crime scene. On the other hand, maybe the young man hit his head and fell overboard."

Bourque didn't respond. The captain seemed to be familiar with crime scenes. "Who found the blood?"

"Sam Carson. He's due back in the morning."

"Please give me his home address." There'd be security cameras onboard but at the beginning of an investigation she focused on witnesses. She watched the captain carefully as he wrote on a piece of paper. His demeanor was unruffled. "How many passengers did you have on your last crossing?"

Macey referred to a laptop. "One hundred and twenty-six, a quiet run."

"How many crew?"

"The usual. Twelve plus myself. And the three service-staff who run the snack bar and giftshop."

"For now, the aft deck is off limits to everyone, including you and your crew. I need someone to take me to the abandoned car."

"Seaman Balan will escort you."

Outside the cabin, she spoke quietly to Donnelly. "Secure the aft deck."

□ □ □

Bourque descended three levels preceded by Balan, a tall glum seaman who didn't say a word, let alone look at her. His face was spectral; his narrow body, insubstantial.

On the car deck, he pointed to a clunker. The vehicle surprised her. Fitzgerald drove a beat-up Ford station wagon, about two decades old. She thanked Balan and excused him. Judging by his dark yet sparse hair, he could be any age from forty to sixty. He brought to mind Lurch, the lugubrious butler from the Addams family. His dirt-brown overalls looked like a prison jumpsuit. He stopped fifteen yards away, not disguising the fact he was watching her.

Ignoring Lurch, she pulled a hooded clean-suit, shoe covers, and gloves from her crime scene bag and donned them. Beginning at the driver's front side, she paced methodically clockwise. Rust everywhere. Both front doors were locked; the windows, shut tight. She walked on. The passenger side backdoor was another matter. It had been crudely jimmied open. Hiding her reaction from Lurch, she surreptitiously assessed the jimmy. The work of a crowbar. The call-out was now a criminal investigation—even before she'd inspected the blood on the deck. The captain hadn't mentioned a break-in.

She phoned for a trooper to guard the car and waved Lurch over, wanting to keep him occupied elsewhere. "Please get the captain."

Lurch gone, she scanned the ship's high sidewall, seeing a security camera covering the car. She'd requisition the videotape. Using her phone, she snapped photos of the jimmied door, then opened it and began a crime scene search. Despite her thoroughness, it didn't take long to examine the entire backseat area. There was nothing there. She opened the driver's door from the inside, careful to preserve evidence.

The front-seat area was no different. She popped the glove compartment. Empty with the exception of a faded manual. No sign of the owner anywhere. She unlocked the rear hatch door. Other than a spare tire and flat repair kit, the area was bare. She felt and sounded for hidden compartments. There were none.

She heard bootsteps and turned to watch Macey and Balan head her way. Seeing the sailors walk side-by-side, she observed a story of opposites. It was almost comical. Macey was short and unusually wide; Balan, tall and unusually thin.

"How can I help you?" Macey asked.

"Fitzgerald's car was broken into. I'm surprised your crew didn't report that to you."

"Not surprising at all," he replied, his voice instantly gruffer. "A different team unloads the vehicles. The unloading super said the car was empty. That's all I got from him."

"No mention of a jimmied backdoor?"

"He probably didn't see it. Given the quiet run, the car didn't block off any vehicles. The unloaders worked around it."

Macey seemed to have seen distrust in her face. She hadn't hidden her thoughts well enough. "I understand." Although she had more questions, she decided to keep them sheathed for now. "You'll be docked until further notice. Please remain in your cabin. I'll need to speak with you again."

# Chapter 3

**Woods Hole, Massachusetts**

Bourque briefed the trooper sent to guard the car and hurried to the aft deck. Heat still radiated from the ferry's engines. The smell of diesel hung in the air. A swathe of moonlight bisected the harbor, leading away from the ship toward the open sea.

At the deck, Donnelly waved her to the stern rail. She liked working with Donnelly. A grin was never far from his face but, at his size, people didn't mess with him. He'd once played for the New England Patriots, making him a local hero. He knew the Vineyard, having been stationed on it until the previous year. Beyond that, he understood New Englanders: which dogs to lean on, which ones to let sleep.

Given the moon, the viewing deck was awash in silver. As it always did, especially in the fall, the full moon tugged at Bourque's blood and quickened her mind. She stepped purposefully forward, sweeping the deck with her flashlight. At the stern rail, she spotted a pool of blood the size of a halved grapefruit—small for a head wound. Blood hadn't spread to the edge of the deck and dripped overboard, shrinking the pool's size. The splatter pattern resembled the spurting caused by a stab wound, not the wide-angle spray found with blunt force trauma, such as when a person's head hit the deck. Which discounted Macey's story about Fitzgerald hitting his head.

Continuing her inspection, she noticed the stern rail's lower safety line was about four inches above the deck. The human body was surprisingly flexible, especially when young, but Fitzgerald couldn't have rolled under a four-inch gap. Adult heads were too wide for that.

Bourque examined the scene for signs of a struggle or a body being dragged. Nothing. As she stepped back, she noticed an anomaly. To her right, a narrow swathe of deck near the blood pool looked too clean. Someone had backed away along the rail wiping the deck as they went. Although they'd masked potential shoeprints and blood or other DNA carriers, they'd left a trail. Maybe they weren't worried about that.

Walking toward the ship's funnel, she distanced herself from a possible listener. On a still night, her voice would carry. Something told her Balan could be eavesdropping near the aft deck. She peered east over Vineyard Sound. The October constellations spun placidly through the night, following their timeworn tracks. The water was flat and motionless. However, her mind was spinning. It was too soon to impute guilt, but not too soon to form suspicions. She knew the New England coast, having sailed it frequently. Some people believed local ferry skippers were second-tier captains. Not her. Macey was an old seadog, wily and capable. He appeared to be cooperative, even helpful, yet she wasn't sure about him. Ditto for Balan.

Pulling out her phone, she called Central's forensic department. "Logistics," a deep male voice answered. "Bradley."

*Loverboy Bradley*, she thought, friend of all single gals. "Hello, Bradley. Bourque, Cape and Islands. We need a full MU in Woods Hole." MU being a Mobile Unit: three forensic officers deployed with a lab trailer that doubled as a bunk house.

"For you, Ivy, I'll send the best."

□ □ □

Bourque entered Macey's cabin to find him working on a crossword puzzle.

"Captain," she began, "the aft viewing deck is a crime scene. I need to impound your boots and clothes."

"Oh?"

"We want to eliminate you as a suspect. I also need to fingerprint you and take DNA. Standard procedure," she explained. "We don't want to confuse your biosignature with anyone else's."

"I see. All right."

After processing Macey's bio matter, she handed him an evidence sack and pointed to his washroom. In due course, he reappeared wearing loafers and a landlubber's suit smelling of mothballs. "Please call Seaman Balan," she said.

Macey raised Balan on a two-way radio.

The seaman materialized in an instant, as if from thin air. She suspected he'd been in the passageway outside. Listening in? Awaiting orders?

"Mr. Balan," she stated, "I need your clothes and boots. Use the captain's washroom."

Balan said nothing but complied.

She turned to Macey. "Please get someone to bring him a fresh jumpsuit and boots."

Later, as she took Balan's fingerprints, he remained studiously mute. She'd encountered fish that were more talkative.

□ □ □

Bourque disembarked from the *Islander* and sat at a picnic table under a loading light. Instantly, three seagulls landed nearby, screeching madly. The Three Terrors, she sardonically dubbed them. The loading area smelled of congealed tar. The night had cooled down, signaling the ascendence of autumn. Week by week, New England seemed to be drawing inward. Its citizens were huddling closer together, preparing for the first cold snap. She zipped up her fleece jacket and resumed her background search of Daniel Fitzgerald. The Terrors settled in.

An hour on the internet told her Fitzgerald had severed his family's longtime connection to the Democratic Party. While politics was fascinating to many people, she took after her recently departed father, a Boston homicide superintendent. In his view, whereas the police acted to serve and protect, politicians acted to serve and project—those who bothered to serve. Regardless, all politicians spent hours projecting themselves, believing publicity led to power.

Fitzgerald was thirty-three and single. After finishing a Ph.D. in History at Harvard, he'd moved to Washington D.C. and taken a political right turn. He'd joined the GOP, the Republican Party, starting as a youth vote organizer, advancing to the Young Republicans executive team, and then contributing to numerous conservative publications, primarily *The New American* and *National Review*.

A few years later, he'd returned to Massachusetts to become a speech writer for Republican Governor Karri Laker. While Bourque had little interest in politics, Laker's persona and presence were ubiquitous. You couldn't get away from the woman.

Bourque continued digging. Fitzgerald's star kept rising—and then precipitously fell. Three years ago, he'd quit the Republican Party and started writing biting exposés of Laker and her followers, extended pieces for *The Washington Post*. In response, Laker berated him on social media. Fitzgerald was a turncoat, a hack who deserved to be jailed.

Bourque checked out Fitzgerald's social media sites. The guy was handsome: athletic, ardent blue eyes, an apparently genuine smile. Over 20,000 Instagram followers; 1,000+ posts, mostly about politics. He was the president of a non-profit called Right Whales First, RWF, a group protecting Atlantic and Pacific right whales supported by, among others, Greenpeace.

She googled RWF. Their goal was clear: control all ship traffic in whale feeding grounds. They'd held numerous protests, a few ending in confrontations between pro- and anti-protection factions, which included fishermen and shipping companies.

Bourque sat back. Politics. Left wing, right wing, centrist—it wasn't on her radar. Until now, she realized.

She changed tack and googled the *Islander*. Capacity 1,200 passengers. At 255 feet, it was the largest ferry operating out of Woods Hole, a vessel which could unload vehicles from either end, meaning it had two bridges, the fore bridge being used for navigation. She studied the sightlines. The aft viewing deck wasn't visible from the fore bridge; hence the ship's navigation crew couldn't see the crime scene. If Macey were involved, that made sense. He wouldn't want them to see anything. In late October, the ship made seven crossings a day. Although there'd only been 126 passengers on the previous crossing, she had a lot of potential perps.

Her duty phone crooned Elvis Costello. "Watching the detectives. Watching the de—"

"Detective Lieutenant Bourque," she answered, "State Police."

"Morning, Lieutenant. Captain Milhous, U.S. Coast Guard. The man overboard has been recovered."

*Recovered*, she noted, not rescued—which meant dead. So much for finding the misper alive and returning home to find her man in bed, naked. Not happening tonight. "Did you ID the body?" she asked.

"Yes. Daniel Fitzgerald. His driver's license was in a pants pocket. Come to the *Hammerhead*. We're at the Coast Guard jetty in Woods Hole."

Bourque knew the location, a few hundred yards away. As she walked, her boots echoed sharply on the pavement. She saw no one. However, out beyond the ambient glow of the terminal, the night sky was alive. The Big Bear and the Swan—Ursa Major and Cygnus—dominated the north. If the moon were the sun, its declension would announce the day was almost done. As it was, it indicated there were about two hours of deep night left. She'd seen no signs of life on the *Islander* other than a light shining in a cabin amidship. From her study of the ferry's layout, she knew it was Macey's cabin.

Approaching the jetty, she recognized the USCG Cutter *Hammerhead*, an iconic vessel that had saved hundreds of shipwrecked sailors. It was built to withstand ocean storms yet top twenty-five knots, to deliver both stability and speed—the sweet spot for rescue craft.

Captain Milhous met her at the gangway and waved her aboard. Milhous was a common Quaker name. Fittingly, the man wore a Quaker beard, long and flowing, but with his upper lip shaved. Bourque liked the looks of him. His eyes were piercing. The beard might be a bit archaic but he was definitely handsome. He was also married. Big wedding ring. Not that she was looking for herself, but her best friend Gigi Lambert, an FBI agent, would drive anywhere to get her short-and-curlies tickled by a rustic-looking hunk. They were hard to come by in D.C., Gigi's current post.

"Where did you find Fitzgerald?" Bourque asked.

"At the easternmost point of Nonamesset Island, floating in a foot of water."

"When was that?"

Milhous referred to his watch. "Twenty-one minutes ago. Oh-four-fifty-one."

As he led her aft, she did a quick calculation. Knowing the *Islander* made its last departure from the Vineyard at 2130 and that it passed Nonamesset half an hour later, she deduced Fitzgerald had gone overboard around 2200, which meant he'd been in the water roughly seven hours.

When they reached the stern deck, Milhous pointed to a corpse lying atop a body bag.

Bourque bent down and studied Fitzgerald. He was a fit young man: well-muscled, about 190 pounds, roughly six feet tall. His face had been tanned in the photos she'd seen; now it was blueish-grey. Dark brown hair was plastered to his head. His eyes were open, the whites the color of moonstone. Traces of foam oozed from his nose and mouth. He wore hiking pants and a long-sleeve shirt, both khaki-colored. Her gaze stopped under his left armpit. The shirt was ripped. She bent closer. There were two puncture wounds in his side, near his heart, the kind made by a wide knife. Given the blood splatter pattern she'd seen earlier, she wasn't surprised. Unless Fitzgerald had knifed himself—intending to commit suicide—he'd been assaulted.

She addressed Milhous. "A medical examiner will be coming to process the body. In the meantime, I want to mention a few things."

Milhous nodded. "Just so you know, the crew had medical gloves on when they retrieved him."

"Good. Please don't cover the corpse directly. We need to maintain as much forensic integrity as possible. In addition, don't talk about the death to anyone except your commander, until further notice. Advise your crew as well. Next-of-kin considerations, as well as crime scene considerations."

"Understood."

Bourque was pleased to find Milhous cooperative. As a detective, she'd learned it was always better to clearly state what you required, especially with men. To borrow a Donnellyism, men weren't slow learners, they were fast forgetters. Especially, she knew, in the presence of women.

# Chapter 4

Walking back to the *Islander*, Bourque phoned her boss, Captain Peabody, to set the required machinery in motion. "Bourque here," she said when he picked up. "We have a dead body in Woods Hole."

"The Fitzgerald boy?" Peabody's voice was fast and high-pitched, like a whistling teakettle.

"Yes."

"Another one. That family, they're a tragedy still happening."

She agreed with Peabody, which was unusual. It didn't seem shocking that a new misfortune had befallen the luckless Fitzgeralds. Beyond that, from what she'd seen, the latest tragedy wasn't just a death, it was a murder. "It's a suspicious death," she told Peabody. "Man overboard. Knifing."

He sighed.

She didn't respond. Peabody's typical reaction to suspicious deaths. His main concern was what an investigation would cost. She could almost hear his brain whirring: how many officers would be needed, how many person-hours racked up. Recently, he'd evolved a tad. He thought in terms of *person*-hours now, not man-hours.

"I'll call the med examiner and forensic team," he finally said. "And send two more troopers to secure the scene."

"Please send them to the aft deck."

"Don't say I don't support you."

Rare, Bourque thought as she disconnected. Peabody was already loosening his purse strings. Royalty had that effect.

When the troopers arrived, she'd take Donnelly with her to question Sam Carson. In the meantime, she continued to her car and looked him up, a potentially valuable person-of-interest, aka POI. Carson was forty-four, widowed, and had a clean sheet.

□ □ □

As Donnelly sat in Bourque's car, she turned to him. "Fitzgerald's body was found."

"Where?"

"Off Nonamesset Island. Looks like murder," she said as she

drove. "Knife wounds to the heart."

"Damn knives. And guns." Donnelly shook his head grimly. "Damn them all."

She nodded. Donnelly felt it when people died or were injured. It was another thing she liked about him.

He pulled a thermos from his jacket. "My wife made coffee," he said. "Decaf, black."

"Sounds good." Marty, her man, had convinced her to switch to decaf.

Donnelly poured two cups.

"Hot," she said after taking a sip, "and very sweet."

"Just like me."

She chuckled. She'd walked into that one.

"Did you see that moon, Lieutenant? Bizarre color. Reminded me of a knife blade. Which gave me the willies. *Don't go around tonight,*" he sang in an eerie baritone, "*it's bound to take your life.* 'Bad Moon Rising.' Do you know it?"

She nodded. "Credence Clearwater Revival. My father played their albums."

"Are you saying I'm old?"

She winked. "We're about the same age, but a lady never tells."

Sam Carson lived on Falmouth's Inner Harbor. As with most small Cape harbors, other than the tides, little changed from day to night and night to day again. To the southeast, the sky had shed its blackness. The Milky Way was a fading delta. Night was losing its grip. Outside Carson's tidy bungalow, bamboo grass rustled in the predawn breeze. A wide granite walkway led to the front door. Not what Bourque expected. Carson's place was trendy, almost posh. She rang the doorbell.

"Coming!" a loud friendly voice called.

The man who answered the door regarded Donnelly with deference. "Morning, Trooper." His gaze shifted to Bourque. Being a non-uniformed cop, she was wearing a cobalt fall jacket and moss-green Dockers. To Peabody's chagrin, her auburn hair wasn't regulation. It was long and wavy and loose. She could tell the POI wasn't sure what to think of her.

"Detective Lieutenant Bourque, State Police," she said. "Are you Sam Carson?"

"Yes, Mam."

No need for the *Mam*, she thought, offering her hand. Carson shook it, his handshake firm and easy. He wore an *Islander* jumpsuit, the dirt-brown number she'd seen on Balan. In other respects, he was the opposite of Balan: short and wide with a walrus moustache and light brown hair. She recognized his cologne: Old Spice. Her father had worn it. He used to say the best way to crack a case was to get people talking. He claimed the main reason murders went unsolved was out of his control: *dead people didn't talk*.

She gestured to her sidekick. "This is Trooper Donnelly. We have some questions for you."

"Sure. Come in."

Carson's bungalow was built railroad-style. He led them down a long hall to an airy kitchen at the back. Sliding glass doors opened onto a deck facing the harbor. Close by, a dozen sailboat masts rose above an old warehouse lining the shore, their accompanying hulls unseen, as if the masts were trees rooted in the water.

Bourque sat across from Carson, covertly activating her phone's audio recorder. "How long have you crewed on the *Islander?*"

"Quite a while." He stopped to think. "Eleven years now. Started when I left the container ships. Needed something closer to home, what with my wife Donna passing. The boys needed more 'attention,' they called it." He shook his head. "One was a handful, let me tell you."

"Where are they now?"

"Boston, both at Harvard. I paid the whole ticket," he proudly said.

Expensive, Bourque reflected, like the granite walkway. She looked for deviations from the norm; a ferry crewman who was a big spender threw up a red flag. "How long has Brock Macey captained the ferry?" she asked.

"Not long," Carson replied. "Eight years."

"Do you like him?"

"Well, you don't have to like a captain. Some of the container skippers were downright cruel. As for Macey, we're not best friends, if that's what you're asking."

"I understand you found blood on the aft viewing deck."

"Yes. As soon as I saw it, I called Macey. I didn't go near it."

That remained to be seen. "The passenger's body was recovered," she offhandedly said. Carson's eyes told her he'd already heard the news. In port towns, it was impossible to keep a death on the water quiet for long, yet she had to try. "Please keep that to yourself for now."

"Will do. By the way, I admire you officers. You have a hard job."

"The passenger was a man named Daniel Fitzgerald. Do you recognize the name?"

Carson nodded. "I knew him a bit, casual-like. He was a regular the last few summers."

"How did you meet?"

"He came up to me on the aft deck one evening and started talking."

"When was that?"

"Let me think." Carson scanned the masts outside. "It was June, two summers ago."

"What did you talk about?"

"The Cape, fishing, maritime history. He liked to hear about my time on the big ships."

"Did he talk about himself?"

Carson shook his head. "Not once. He was old-fashioned in that way. I took to him from the start. I'm sad to hear the news. Terrible for his family. If Dan—he told me to call him Dan—ever ran for the State House or Senate, I'd support him. We need better people in Boston."

"Why were you on the aft deck?"

"I'd just had a smoke. Can't quit." He pointed self-deprecatingly to his chest pocket. It held a packet of Camels. "The old man, the skipper, that is, hates us smoking so I always go near the aft bridge deck."

"Did you and Mr. Fitzgerald ever meet off the ship?"

"No."

"Ever direct message each other or talk on the phone?"

"No."

"We need to take your prints and DNA. Standard procedure." She gestured at his jumpsuit. "We'll take that too." He could have worn it yesterday; it could have latent blood.

Back in her car with Donnelly, Bourque broached the subject of Carson. "What do you think of him?" she asked.

"Friendly, but that could be a facade. He was almost obsequious. Suspicious mind, Lieutenant. I can't lose it."

"I've said it before. You'd make a ..."

"No thanks. You know what I say: The first day of a homicide case is murder. So are the rest of them."

She grinned wryly. As she turned the ignition key, her phone trilled. "Watching the detectives—"

"Morning, Bourque," a relaxed voice said when she answered. "Eller here. Central is sending me your way."

"Good to hear." She'd assumed Central would assign one of their roving detectives to the case. She was glad it was Victor Eller. Although even-tempered, he could do an intimidating bad cop, which is what she wanted in a partner: a stoic who read the riot act when it was called for.

"Got any leads?" he asked.

"Too early to say."

"We're flying blind?"

"Half-blind."

"But not dumb. Not you, Bourque."

Huh, Eller was dishing out compliments before the game got going. "I'll email you the audio of my first interviews."

"Thanks. Can't wait to work with Peabody," he deadpanned.

"Who can?"

# Chapter 5

Bourque and Donnelly returned to the ferry terminal to see the sun peeking above the Atlantic. The transition from predawn to dawn had come suddenly. The sky was now pale blue from east to west.

She released Donnelly to take a break. Having done hundreds of surveillances as a Boston undercover operative, she knew all about long nightshifts. After hours of peering into the dark, your brain went dead.

She was beginning to fade. Her glucose was low; her melatonin, high. When it spiked, the body's chemistry couldn't fight it. Before becoming a cop, she'd studied OC, organic chemistry, a field based on the transmutability of carbon. She found OC overly theoretical. Conversely, tracking down murderers was tangible—clear and present, sometimes dangerous—which is what she wanted in a job. Homicides didn't unsettle her. All life was death. Ashes to ashes, carbon to carbon.

Bourque drove to the *Hammerhead* to meet with the med examiner. Dr. Andre Wozniak was waiting for her on the cutter's stern deck. As usual, regardless of the weather and his weight, the med examiner wore a tight three-piece suit. His face was red. His nose was redder. He'd had a long love affair with Polish vodka. According to Donnelly, Wozniak had recently downgraded his love to a friendship.

"I skipped breakfast," he announced. "I hope you appreciate that, Detective."

"I do."

The corners of his mouth lifted into a smile. "Always swimming pools or boats with you. Always water."

"Blame it on the Cape."

"Oh?"

"It's surrounded by water on three sides. Admittedly, not four."

"Can't argue with geography," he genially said and studied Fitzgerald's body. "Looks like a wet drowning," he soon pronounced. "But we need an autopsy to confirm that." He regarded Bourque benevolently. "*You* know the difference between a wet drowning and a dry drowning. Tell me."

At times, Wozniak made her feel like a school girl. "In a dry drowning," she stated, "death results from throat spasms, not from water blocking the airway. In a wet drowning, water enters the lungs." She pointed at Fitzgerald's mouth and nose. "That foam signals water entered the lungs. The victim became immersed while still breathing."

"Very good. However, as you can see, there isn't much foam, and there isn't much blood in it. Which suggests the victim didn't inhale much water. The less inrushing water, the less the lungs bleed." Wozniak's eyes moved down the body. He stopped at Fitzgerald's chest, parted the slit in his shirt, and indicated the wounds under his left armpit. "Consider the knife incisions. They could offer an explanation for the dearth of foam. What do you think?"

"They might," she said. "Given the wound locations—the aortic region—perhaps the victim's heart failed. It stopped pumping blood when he was in the sound."

"I agree. Quite possibly. *Aortic region*. Well, Detective, you won't have to call me out next time." Wozniak chuckled and bent closer. "The smaller of the two wounds isn't exactly small," he related, "but it's lower down the torso, between the fifth and sixth ribs. The larger wound is between the fourth and fifth. To inflict a mortal wound, you aim between those ribs."

Bourque nodded. She was familiar with the vulnerable area between the fourth and fifth ribs.

"Do you know how long the body was in the sound?" he asked.

"Roughly seven hours. The current water temperature is fifty-four."

"How long has he been on the ship?"

"About two-and-a-half hours."

Wozniak turned back to the body. "Let's see if we can establish time of death. I'll deploy the usual hat trick."

Wozniak's *hat trick* was lividity, rigor mortis, and algor mortis. Lividity, aka blood pooling, turned a body purple and pink. Rigor mortis, or body stiffening, usually became fully established in twelve hours. Algor referred to a body turning cold. With no blood flowing, the temperature of a body found in cold water, like the ocean off Cape Cod, dropped by an average of three degrees Fahrenheit each hour. On land, it dropped about two degrees. The triumvirate predicted PMI, post-mortem interval. If the team could place a suspect at a crime scene during the PMI window, they had opportunity; they could probe for motive.

Wozniak noted that lividity and rigor were inconclusive, then drew a liver thermometer from his medical bag and pierced Fitzgerald's right side. "Seventy-two-point-nine Fahrenheit," he read. "Given that ninety-eight-point-six is the norm, and that the victim was here two-and-a-half hours, algor suggests he spent approximately seven hours in the sound, which corresponds to your estimate, Detective. I like it when the numbers line up. Well, two of them."

The med examiner stood. "I'd rule a PMI of nine to eleven hours, making the estimated time of death about ten p.m. last night. *Estimated* being the salient word. But you know that. I'll deliver my report this afternoon. In my view, the wounds weren't self-inflicted. You can certainly stab yourself under the armpit, but the entry angles are close to ninety degrees, which indicates the kind of wounds inflicted by another person. I surmise the victim was attacked. He was alive when he entered Vineyard Sound, but then drowned. Cause of death: Drowning. Means: Homicide."

□ □ □

Bourque returned to the *Islander* and parked her car, an eight-year-old Mazda 3. After tilting the driver's seat back, she covered herself with a space blanket, shut her eyes, and tried to still her mind. It didn't cooperate. Instead, it settled on a troubling detail. Other than Carson, who'd discovered the blood, Macey had kept everyone away from it. If his prints and/or DNA were found at the scene, it wouldn't be abnormal—giving him a potential alibi.

She inhaled deeply, counted to five, exhaled, and repeated the cycle until her body began to relax. However, tired as she was, sleep still eluded her. What about Balan? Was he collaborating with Macey? The silent tar knew the ship, which meant he knew when and where he could attack Fitzgerald. On the other hand, he didn't look strong enough to do it. She shut her eyes tighter but the case wouldn't let go. What about Carson? As Donnelly said, Carson was almost obsequious. He could be scamming them, pretending he liked Fitzgerald. He admitted to finding the blood, which put him in the vicinity of the attack. Did he have a motive?

She shook her head. Stop the wheels, she told herself. Get some sleep.

□ □ □

Bourque's phone alarm buzzed an hour later. Checking her hair in the rearview mirror, she heard her mother's voice: *Brush it or put a lid on it.* Meaning a hat. Bourque hated hats. She pulled a hairbrush from the glove compartment. Head down, she shook her long hair forward, brushed it for twenty seconds, then tossed it back and drew it in a ponytail. She had her father's thick auburn hair. A lot of men said she looked like Uma Thurman. Bourque didn't know about that. However, she knew one thing: she didn't want people to think she was a cop. In her eyes, a good strategy for a police detective was to avoid looking like one. With her competent manner and quick movements, people often pegged her as a thirty-something paramedic or doctor.

On a whim, she added lipstick—Dusty Rose—State-Police-approved. Toilet complete, she left her car, chewing a mint. Dusty Rose didn't hide coffee breath. The sky said summer, but the air temperature didn't. It was fifty-two degrees.

Bourque entered a local bakery and bought two chocolate croissants. Lipstick or not, she probably looked like death warmed over. She certainly felt like it.

Eating on a bench near the terminal, she surveyed the morning. The air smelled of late-blooming flowers: asters and chrysanthemums. The trees looked thinner than a week ago; their leaves, less vibrant. Autumn ascending. A blue jay vacated a nearby maple, bursting into flight, splitting the sky like a blue shooting star. Quintessential Cape Cod, an elemental world, dominated by the sea and sky.

After devouring both croissants, she felt reinvigorated. She thought of the abandoned Ford. The carjacking wasn't committed with finesse. Same for the obvious cleanup on the aft deck. The murder could be the work of locals. Then again, the victim wasn't a true local. He had three addresses—on Martha's Vineyard, in Groton, Massachusetts, and Washington D.C.—making him a half-islander at best, the kind locals had been ignoring for centuries. Why would they target him? She considered a different perspective. Fitzgerald's body had been found off Nonamesset Island. Pulling out her phone, she checked the ferry's course. It came within 500 yards of Nonamesset. There'd been virtually no drift. Ergo, the victim was likely assaulted as the ferry passed the island. Although it was uninhabited, someone nearby might have seen the assault, whether on a boat or the mainland. She emailed a reminder for Peabody to get the public involved.

With the day warming up, she began making case notes, the least favorite part of her job. Like any detective, she was saddled with reams of paperwork. Halfway through her notes, she heard a vehicle skidding into the terminal parking lot and looked up to see Eller's elongated black Ford Explorer. It brought to mind a hearse, which, given his job, was appropriate. In twenty-six years as a detective, he'd worked over 300 homicides. In her nine years— four with the Boston Police Department, five with the State Police—she'd worked ninety-plus. They'd recently solved a double murder in East Falmouth. Jumping out of his hearse, he strode toward her.

Eller was a tall, fit man with a close brush cut. His eyes said *don't cross me*. He kept his home life to himself: a wife, two kids, a tumbledown bungalow near Holyoke, far from Central. Although in his mid-fifties, he moved like a much younger man. He wore a natty charcoal suit and an indigo-blue tie.

"Well Bourque, looks like it's up to us again."

"*Again*," she kidded.

"The Dynamic Duo." Eller smiled. "Just got Central's roadmap," he said. "They requisitioned a passenger list from the Steamship Authority, the *Islander*'s owners. Central's going to track down the passengers. Most live in the Northeast. That helps. Fifteen were commercial operators. All trucks, no buses. The rest were car passengers. Landon's on the way," he added. "He and I will handle the crew."

"Good." Detective Rick Landon was ex-Boston police, early-thirties. "Let's jump in my car. I'll take you to the body."

□   □   □

On the Coast Guard cutter, the detectives donned CS gear and walked to the corpse. Eller knelt beside it and blew out his cheeks, seemingly lost in thought.

"The lower wound was probably the first one," he eventually said. "The perp realized it was off-base, so they struck again, between the fourth and fifth ribs. I'd say they were professional."

He paused. "Looks like one perp. What do you think?"

"One, with perhaps an accessory or two in the shadows. The attack was carried out in a relatively public place in a tight time window. The fewer people involved, the better. Did you have time to listen to my Macey interviews?"

"Yes. All of your interviews, in fact. Don't tell Peabody I drive and listen. That chump would arrest me for driving and breathing."

"He'd arrest anyone."

Eller chuckled and stood. "I think Macey needs a few visitors."

Bourque and Eller reached Macey's cabin to find it shut and locked. As she was knocking on the door, the captain opened it. He seemed to have been sleeping in his suit. It was rumpled and still smelled of mothballs. However, he looked rested. His hair was brushed; his eyes, bright.

Eller smiled. "Here's the man of the hour. I'm Detective Lieutenant Eller. Are you feeling refreshed, Captain?"

"Yes, thank you for asking."

Bourque noted Eller and Macey seemed to like each other instantly. Not unusual, she knew, for New England men. It was the Northeast's egalitarian ethic. Macey courteously ushered Eller in, chatting about hockey, saying the Bruins would go places this season. A moment later, Balan appeared, unfolded two wooden chairs for the detectives and wordlessly departed.

"I have a few questions," Eller began. "Do you think Mr. Fitzgerald went overboard on his own?"

"That's what I originally thought," Macey replied. "However, I understand the situation better this morning. It's possible someone pushed him."

"Assaulted him as well?"

"Possible."

"We'll be interviewing all of your staff. Is last night's crew onboard now?"

"Yes."

"What's their rotation?"

"The same as mine. In summer and fall, we're on six days and off one."

"All day?"

Macey nodded. "Roughly fifteen hours, but they get lengthy breaks in port."

Long hours aboard, Bourque deemed, regardless of the breaks.

Plenty of opportunity.

Eller stood. "Please call the first eight staff members to the main passenger lounge in an hour."

"By all means. I want to sail as soon as possible," Macey stated. "It's a matter of public service. People count on us."

"They do," Eller conceded. "But you have to give us time to work our magic."

Eller followed Bourque off the *Islander*, swaying slightly as they stood by the Mobile Unit. "Great sea legs," she kidded.

"Oh yeah, like a puppy on an ice patch. What can I say? I was born in Kansas." He pensively regarded the ferry. "You know what's bothering me," he related. "The murder at sea. Why kill Fitzgerald aboard a ferry? We have the passenger and crew list. It's almost a closed-box."

"The perp could have snuck aboard."

"True. And, admittedly, you can toss the body overboard. But it'd probably wash ashore in a matter of days. In this case, it only took hours."

"Could have been weeks," she said.

"Still, makes more sense to kill him on land. Or weigh his body down."

"I'm guessing the perp didn't have time. *Guessing* being the operative word. And why was Fitzgerald driving a clunker? He had money, or his family does. Was there some kind of familial breach?"

"Hold those thoughts," Eller said. "You're heading home. Don't bother arguing. Get some sleep."

No argument there.

"By the way, I'm aware Macey might be playing me, but that's a two-way street. I'm playing him. He was a bit prickly on your audiotapes. But prickly doesn't mean he's a perp. I think we have other *tars* to feather."

She shook her head indulgently. "You're worse than Donnelly."

"One day I'll be better."

"Them's fighting words."

## Chapter 6

Bourque watched enviously as Marty poured himself an after-
dinner whiskey. *Uisce beatha,* he called it, Irish for whiskey. Good
thing she liked wordy guys. Once a Navy Seal, Marty was now a
magazine journalist, a freelancer who wrote long pieces about
history informing the present. To her, his house was fascinating.
Its old floorboards were worn butter-smooth by countless feet.
Among other things, he collected East Coast memorabilia: sea
chests, ships-in-bottles, old sextants, chronometers.

He took a sip of whiskey and smiled. "What about you? Not
even a small one?"

"Not even." Being French-Canadian on her father's side, she
had a more 'European' attitude to alcohol than Peabody did. A
glass of wine with meals wouldn't torpedo her sense of duty.
However, a Kilbeggan whiskey or two was another thing—
regrettably. They'd had a great dinner, Marty's specialty: linguine
with langoustines, vermouth, garlic, and cherry tomatoes. He'd
opened a crisp white wine. The pasta had been preceded by her
favorite hors d'oeuvre, olives. He'd arrayed two platters, one packed
with plump orbs chock-full of marinated red peppers, almonds, or
gherkins; the other with spherical delights from Greece, Spain,
and the Lebanon, ranging from pale gold-green to pitch-tar black,
from devil-tongued spicy to baby-mouth mild. She loved them all,
yet had a definite favorite: black olives from Heraklion, Crete,
perfectly spherical, suspended in rosemary-scented oil.

Now, post-feast, she sighed heavily and screwed her mind to
the job. The first forty-eight hours of a murder case were crucial.
Even after years as a detective, she still found it jarring to move
from 'normal' life to case life, from convivial person to focused
homicide cop. Luckily, she had her father's example to turn to.
He'd been the same person at work that he was at home.

"Where're you off to?" Marty asked.

She smiled cryptically. She never talked "business" with Marty.
Some cops chatted privately with their partners about work but
she didn't. It was a professional decision. It was also a sign of love.
Why burden him with grim details? Having served in the Middle

East, Marty could certainly handle death but she didn't bring it to him.

"I packed you a snack," he said. "Olives and smoked gouda."

She kissed him on the cheek. "The best combo ever. Gotta go."

"If you need a nightcap later, I'll spill a little whisky into a thermos." He winked, announcing a friendly dig. "Not that your captain would approve."

How did he know that? He'd only met Peabody twice.

Marty seemed to have read her mind. "I've become more observant, courtesy of a certain female detective."

"Oh? Who?"

"Not Nancy Drew."

□ □ □

Bourque drove along Surf Drive ignoring the speed limit. Peabody wouldn't be happy but, hell, the road was virtually deserted. She arrived in Woods Hole just after 1930. The *Islander* hadn't sailed that day. The Mobile Unit was still processing the dual crime scenes, the aft deck and the abandoned vehicle.

Central had ordered the team to proceed with extreme thoroughness, leaving Peabody fuming. In his view, they were dawdling, wasting time and, more abhorrently, money. Bourque conceded parsimony had its place—she hated people who padded expense accounts—but a murder investigation wasn't one of them. You didn't cut corners, especially in the beginning.

She pulled out her phone and called Eller.

"Bourque here," she said when he answered. "I'm back at the terminal."

"Good. I identified a POI who requires a second interview immediately, a Ruby Halliday. I held her back. She might be more involved than she let on. She runs the giftshop on the *Islander*. Can you handle her?"

"Sure."

"By the way, I'm at the Inn on the Sound in Falmouth, Suite Three-oh-one. I don't want to drive back and forth from Holyoke every day."

"Did you run your little outpost by Peabody?"

"Forget Peabody. Central secured the internet connectivity. Drop by when you're done."

Sitting in her car, Bourque watched the videotape of Halliday's first interview on her laptop. The POI was twenty-six, a Cape local, and a recent postgraduate from NYU with a M.A. in Psychology. She wore no makeup. Her long red hair was haphazardly yet stylishly piled atop her head. She claimed to have talked to Fitzgerald six times during the summer. He'd visited the previous evening but, apparently, she didn't have time to chat. It was inventory night at the shop.

Bourque exited her car and walked toward the ship. The harbor looked silver, as if it were leaching light from the moon. When she entered the giftshop, an elegant young woman glanced up from a book. Halliday was much more attractive in person than on tape. Bourque's first impression was man-magnet. The POI's designer jacket was fitted at the waist, accentuating her chest. Her pale skin was silky, resembling the inside of a lily. Her blue eyes stood out like sapphires. Her hair was carmine-red. Tight jeans made her long, slim legs look even longer, as did her footwear, a pair of polished knee-high boots.

She strode gazelle-like to Bourque and gracefully shook her hand. "Ruby Halliday."

"Lieutenant Bourque, Cape and Islands. Let's have a chat." Bourque pointed to two stools. "I understand you knew Mr. Fitzgerald," she began.

"I wouldn't say I knew him well," Halliday quickly replied. "But I'll do what I can to help you." Her voice was fluid and likeable. "He was so nice. I can't believe it."

Bourque kept quiet.

"Such a good guy. No," Halliday corrected herself, "not a guy. A man." Her eyes looked resolute. Suddenly, they misted over. Her calm demeanor broke; her chest heaved. She started sobbing. "So kind," she eventually whispered, "so intelligent."

Bourque studied Halliday's face. Loss and rapture. She seemed to have been smitten by Fitzgerald. "Would you like a break?" Bourque asked.

Halliday shook herself and wiped away her tears. "I'm okay," she insisted. "Sorry, it's a shock." She forced a smile. "Please, go ahead."

"How many times did you chat with Mr. Fitzgerald?"

The POI sat straight up. "I've been thinking about that. I told the other officers we spoke six times, but it was eight. We met twice for coffee in Woods Hole. And we talked six times aboard the ship."

"Over what time period?"

"About four months. I started working here in mid-May but we met in June." Halliday smiled. A half-second later, her gaze was ultra-serious. "We got along so well."

Bourque found Halliday's eyes suspicious. They changed so quickly. "You talked eight times in four months?"

"That's right. I was usually busy. We could only talk when there were no customers."

Bourque noted the POI spoke like a mature woman, not a youngster. No *I went, like, you know.* "What did you two talk about?"

"Everything. History, science, politics, poetry. I love poetry, so did he. We were like long-lost friends. We couldn't stop talking."

"What kind of politics?"

"Mostly American. He tried to convince me of the benefits of federalism." Halliday shook her head. "Like anyone could. It's a mess. He referred to our country as a *trial balloon, born aloft by noble ideals, then punctured by schisms.* Schisms, indeed. Everyone is a partisan. If you want less government waste, you're a fascist. If you want more health care, you're a communist. To borrow Lincoln's phrase, we're a house divided. And that's at our best," she added.

"Did you two always agree?"

Halliday let out a pretty sniffle. "Of course not. He was upper crust. I'm a fisherman's daughter."

"Did you fight?"

"Oh no. We *debated.* Wait. Do you suspect me?"

"We suspect everyone, Ms. Halliday, until we know not to."

Halliday nodded thoughtfully. "I can understand that."

"Tell me about your chats at the café."

"They were the same. We talked like houses on fire."

"Were they dates?" Bourque asked.

"Dates?" Halliday waved a hand disparagingly. "He had a girlfriend. Well, an ex."

"Did he mention her name?"

"No."

"Why did he talk to you?"

"I don't really know."

Taking in Halliday's appearance, Bourque had some idea. "Did he mention what he was doing on the Vineyard?"

"No."

"Did he speak about being in any fights?"

"No."

"Did he speak of any enemies?"

"No."

Bourque leaned forward. A long *no*-train, which sometimes masked a yes. "Were you more than friends? I'll put that directly. Did you sleep with him?"

Halliday shook her head forcefully.

"I trust you're telling me the truth."

"Of course I am. He was a grand salmon. I'm a measly small fry. I didn't expect more."

"You have a master's degree in psychology Why are you working here?"

"I'm taking a gap year." Halliday smiled eagerly. "I'm going to Europe after Christmas."

□ □ □

Eller's top-floor suite overlooked Vineyard Sound. Bourque entered it to find him typing awkwardly on his laptop, deploying his usual four-finger pecking. She plopped herself down in an easy chair.

"You look relaxed," he said.

"The waterside lifestyle." She pulled out her snack pack and offered him some olives.

He wrinkled his nose.

Your loss, she thought, munching a perfect Heraklion olive.

"Central got a call from a Chase Heaney, who claims to be Fitzgerald's friend. He's in South Boston. We've been ordered to see him first thing in the morning."

She did a mock-salute.

Eller grinned. "After Heaney, Peabody's sending me to the crime lab in Maynard. He wants you to take the *Islander* and search Fitzgerald's cottage. The ferry's been released to sail at noon."

"I'll be there," she said.

"What's the news on young Ruby Halliday?" Eller asked.

"I wouldn't write her off."

"That's two of us. I just got a report from Central's morgue. They found something interesting in the vic's clothes: a flash drive.

E-Forensics is drying it out. They tell me if USB drives get wet, they're fine unless you power them up before they're dry. To be safe, the tech heads are going to store it in silica gel for two days. That little USB might reveal what Fitzgerald was up to. Might even tell us why he was killed."

"I'm not holding my breath."

"Ye of little faith. With luck, you'll find some useful possessions on the island. I called the Vineyard barracks and ordered a lockdown on his cottage, although it might be too late for that. If someone swept his car, the cottage could be cleaned out."

Unfortunate, she thought, but true.

## Chapter 7

**DAY TWO: Falmouth, Massachusetts. October 21st**

A lot of Cape Cod police officers kept golf clubs or fishing rods in their cars. Bourque kept a wetsuit. She owned two. While one was drying, the other was in her trunk, ready for her next swim. Leaving Marty's place on Menauhant Road at dawn, she pulled on a wetsuit and walked across to Bristol Beach.

The air was sweet yet salty. Mercury hovered low over the ocean. The eastern horizon cradled the sun. She closed her eyes to seal the morning inside her. The Cape had been formed 23,000 years ago, after the last Ice Age, long before her Pilgrim ancestors arrived. A retreating glacier had deposited millions of tons of rock and sand, which were sculpted by the sea into a massive sandbar, one of the largest glacial peninsulas on Earth. She admired the Cape's impassiveness. Storms roared in off the Atlantic, hurling waves against its beaches, but the Cape paid them no heed. If the vast sandbar had a purpose, it was to have no apparent purpose. It was sufficient unto itself. She found solace in that notion.

Bourque waded in at the strand. In addition to her wetsuit, she was wearing neoprene boots, gloves, and a full hood. Crawling leisurely offshore, she let her core body temperature warm the water that had permeated her suit. A mile later—she'd been training herself—she headed back to land. It was the kind of swim she loved, a full wakeup.

Afterward, gazing out at the ocean from shore, she saluted her move to Cape Cod. Her maternal grandfather, who'd run a dairy farm near Salem, used to own an old beach cottage on the Cape, not that he had much time for it. However, his daughter—Bourque's mother—did, which is how Bourque had come to join the Cape & Islands Detective Unit. As a girl, she'd sailed dinghies off South Yarmouth all summer. Later, after joining the State Police, she'd applied for an open detective's post in Barnstable, where the Cape & Islands Unit was housed.

In the 1950s, Grandpa had left his farm behind every year for a short fishing trip on the Cape, availing himself of local guide-boats, wooden cruisers that took anglers out to the Atlantic. At the height of their popularity, most Cape ports had wooden guide-boats. Now there were none. Her grandpa, too, was gone, as was her father. Although she wasn't often given to introspection, she was disposed to it after swimming. The sub-marine world stirred her mind. In some sense, she'd traversed a boundary. Moving from land to water was like crossing the River Styx to the Underworld, the domain of death. Although death was mysterious, to her, murders weren't. She felt born to work on them. She wanted to solve cases not only for the State, but for the victim's loved ones. Closure set them free. They began to live again.

### South Boston, Massachusetts

Chase Heaney owned a rundown frame house off Columbia Road near M Street Beach. Bourque estimated the house hadn't been painted in thirty years. It brought to mind a derelict schooner. The roof sagged like a caved-in sterncastle; the walls resembled a water-logged hull. Conversely, the neighboring triple-deckers were fully restored, exemplars of the new Southie, a district "in transition."

When she knocked on the front door, a long-haired, bearded man answered. He looked like a biker, if bikers wore neon cargo shorts and purple Guess hoodies.

"Chase Heaney?" she asked.

"Who's asking?" He grinned crookedly. "I know. The police."

"Yep. Detectives Bourque and Eller, State Police. I'm the B."

"Surely not 'B' for bitch." His voice was gravelly yet good-humored. "Not with your looks."

"Don't let appearances deceive you. What's on your mind, Mr. Heaney?"

"Dan Fitzgerald's murder."

To Bourque's ear, the POI had what her father called an upgraded Southie accent. Her research told her that although raised in South Boston, Heaney had lived out-of-state for years. He'd completed a B.A. in English at the University of Oregon and worked crab boats in Alaska. He'd done two stints in jail, both six months for damaging property. He reminded her of Paul Watson of Greenpeace, a tougher-looking, younger Watson with hefty shoulders and neck tattoos.

While it was rare for a perp to invite the police to their residence, it wasn't unheard of. Eller suspected Heaney might be trying to lead them down a garden path. He was Southie bred and buttered. For a lot of locals, playing the cops was their birthright, a sacrament holier than Sunday communion.

Heaney led the detectives to a dingy living room crammed with decrepit furniture. He waved them to a crumpled sofa and sat in a high-backed rocking chair. Observing them serenely, he began oscillating at an easy clip. His eyes looked grey-green, although it was hard to tell. The room had one light, a ceiling fixture with a single forty-watt bulb, if that. The drapes were almost fully drawn, letting in a thin sliver of morning sun.

Eller started the proceedings. "When was the last time you saw Daniel Fitzgerald?"

"You'd think that's a simple question. But I want to tell you exactly." Heaney rocked rapidly in his chair, then slowed down. "It's been six months and two days. April eighteenth."

"Where were you on the night of October nineteenth?" Eller asked.

"AA meeting, until nine p.m. After that, I went across to the local Dunkin' for a coffee with three buddies. Let's shorten the confab. I had nothing to do with Dan's death. You want me to make a statement? I don't need a lawyer."

"Continue as you are, Mr. Heaney."

"I'm Dan's friend. Haven't seen him for a while, but that's because he sequestered himself on the Vineyard."

*Sequestered*, Bourque thought. An upmarket vocabulary to go with the upgraded accent.

"Why did he isolate himself?" Eller asked.

Heaney rocked at full speed, then eventually stopped. "That's complicated. But the truth is always complicated. I kept telling Dan that. I also told him he was juggling too many balls. One or two were bound to fall and send him down with them. Which seems to have happened. Dan liked to pretend he was a man-of-the-people but he was obviously a blue blood. That could rub people the wrong way." Heaney regarded the opposite wall, apparently considering Fitzgerald's fall.

Eller broke into his reverie. "Do you know anyone he rubbed the wrong way?"

"I wasn't referring to anyone in particular. Not in real life. As for online, I can't tell you."

"What was Mr. Fitzgerald doing online?"

"Social-media campaigns. Getting thousands of people to join him. Hopefully hundreds of thousands."

Eller gestured for Bourque to come in.

"What kind of campaigns?" she asked.

"The aggressive kind." Heaney studied them, apparently weighing the situation. "I might as well talk. He's dead. He can't get into any more trouble. You bombard your e-enemies with hostile messages and posts."

"E-enemies?"

"Corporations, businessmen, politicians, pretenders. Anyone you deem to have evil intentions. Anyone who ridicules you, opposes you, or downgrades your stance. You can't let that happen. You go back at them. It's war. In a manner of speaking. Not my kind of campaign. But I'm an old-timer."

"What was Mr. Fitzgerald's stance?"

"As I alluded to, he had a few avenues. One was cleanup the Appalachian Trail, another was protect right whales, both in the Atlantic and Pacific. Not to mention fight climate change and decapitate Laker online."

"Decapitate the governor?" she said.

"Correct. Decapitate her. Albeit virtually."

Bourque eyed Heaney. The lone light bulb seemed to dim. Or the morning darkened. She wasn't sure which. Most people revealed body language that indicated when they were lying. Not that there were universal tells, just tells for individuals an observant cop could pick up. From what she'd seen of Heaney, he didn't appear to be lying. Or he had no tells. "Did Mr. Fitzgerald run all those campaigns himself?" she asked.

"He had some help off-shore, mostly in India, but he did the majority himself. Don't ask me how, Detective B. For a guy who wasn't a hacker, he knew a lot about networking. He claimed to know how to cover his e-trail. That was his main aim, he said. Internet anonymity, which would foster real-world anonymity. It was why he worked alone. He used hundreds of aliases and avatars but he didn't want me or any friend to get involved. According to him, I might be tracked down in real life, not only in virtual reality. Tracked down and possibly eliminated."

"*Eliminated*? Did he mean killed?"

Heaney nodded.

"What was he doing?"

"I don't know exactly. In his mind, he was conducting full-scale warfare. Trolling, accusing, condemning, blitzing with information. No holds barred. Virtual holds, that is." Heaney shook his head. "When I first met Dan, three years ago, he campaigned in the real world. He went out with me on the water. We confronted ferries, tankers, and container ships. All of Satan's creatures. He was my best crewman. Fearless. Always positioned himself near the bowsprit, like harpooners of old. He'd be crushed if we collided with a big vessel. I have a sixty-five-foot ketch berthed at Old Colony, a Swan SS to be exact, one of the best sailboats on the water. Built like a tank. But no match for a container ship. I don't suppose you know why we confronted ships with a sailboat?"

Bourque had a pretty good idea but let him talk.

"According to the maritime rules of the road, a vessel under sail has right of way over an engine-powered vessel. Hence, ships under power had to give way to us."

In theory, she thought. A container ship couldn't change course on a dime.

"If we spotted a whale that needed protection or safe passage, we'd sail into the path of any ship endangering the whale. Then we'd stay there, making the ship change course. Some days it was like playing chicken with ships hundreds of times bigger than us. Dan lived for that. I'm going to miss him. He wasn't only a brother-in-arms, he was a good man." Heaney began rocking gently, then stopped. "You may not understand this, but we bonded. I'm not afraid to say it: we were two men who bonded. Over a whale. A magnificent creature. A seventy-foot-long northern right whale out in Cape Cod Bay, possibly two-hundred-years old. Dan and I released it from a net. We were close, very close. It looked us in the eye, and not just for a second. I'd say fifteen. What eyes it had. More depth in them than Methuselah's, more wisdom than King Saul's. Christ, I'm sounding like a character in *Moby Dick*."

"Ishmael," Bourque said.

Heaney grinned widely. "Better than Captain Ahab." His chair started slowly oscillating. Paradoxically, despite his rocking, he radiated inner stillness. "Dan and I called the sea the 'whale road.' We got that from Old English, from *Beowulf*. Nowadays, it's a pretty lonely road. Anyhow, when Dan and I were out on the water, I felt light, as if my bones had vanished. He made me feel alive. I know what you're thinking, B."

Bourque shrugged. I'm listening, not thinking.

"You don't know? Then I'll tell you. Some people think I loved him. I did, like a brother. I wish I could eulogize him better but I'm upset." Heaney sighed. "Enough of the maudlin. Dan-Dan wouldn't countenance it."

"Dan-Dan?"

"Our nickname for him, *our* being the crew of my Swan. He was a good man yet, from what just happened, a misguided one. He didn't know when to pull back. *Solitary men make poor warriors.* That's a guerilla warfare maxim. They have no family or people to fight for. Me, I have a wife and a little girl—admittedly, in Alaska. But Dan-Dan had no one. He was too isolated."

Heaney stopped rocking. "He claimed it was temporary. *I'll cut back next week*, he'd say, *next month*. The usual B.S. Like a meth-head—or alcoholic. Believe me, I know. Alcoholics are lost souls. Time disappears after a few drinks. There's no yesterday and no tomorrow. Fortunately, I'm curious. It made me stop drinking. I wanted tomorrow, I wanted hope. Do you know what gives me hope? The world's beauty," Heaney declared. "Coincidentally, right whales have beauty marks on their heads, something called callosities. Each whale has a unique callosity that identifies it. Beauty identifies it."

Bourque didn't comment.

"Dig into Matthew Arnold's 'Culture and Anarchy,'" Heaney went on. "One of my favorites. Dan's too. He used to read in this very chair. Christ, Jesus. And the fuckin' Apostles. Pardon my Southie mouth." Heaney hung his head, then looked up, seemingly composed. "Arnold asserted civilization is nothing without *sweetness and light*, that is, without beauty and intelligence, which he contrasted to radicalism. Too much fanaticism is a death knell."

Heaney shook himself. "Dan-Dan said he had to do it, fight for the oceans, the forests, the trails, for this Blue Beauty of a planet. But now he won't see any of it. That really saddens me. And pisses me off." He raised a mollifying hand. "Don't worry. I'm a father now. I won't go on a tear, not that I have any idea who to wreak havoc on."

"What kind of property did you damage in Alaska?"

"Ran a few ships and docks. Big ships. Did my time, paid the damages. As I'm sure you know. Dan helped me with the damages."

"Are you going back to Alaska?"

"Soon as can be."

Columbo-style, Bourque stood then pretended to change her mind and sat again. "What did you do after Dunkin' on October nineteenth?"

"Came home, called my wife and daughter on Facetime."

"When exactly was that?"

"From about nine-thirty 'til eleven. That's seven in Alaska. We don't let Shania stay up late."

Bourque knew the POI could have been facetiming from anywhere, including Woods Hole. She suspected he was more technically savvy than he let on. Old-timer? Not really. He was forty-three. While the gist of his story wasn't new—Fitzgerald was a political campaigner—many of the details were. Hundreds of aliases and avatars, trolling, accusing, condemning, blitzing. "Thank you, Mr. Heaney."

"I wish I could help you more."

She nodded. Heaney sounded genuine. However, at times, he'd been difficult to read, like Halliday.

Bourque left the house reminding herself to evaluate everything twice. In the event that apparent friends were bullshitters, three times would be better. On the positive side, Heaney was a talker. As an undercover agent, she'd done anything to get people to open up. Talkers were a gift.

# Chapter 8

## Vineyard Sound, Massachusetts

Fifteen minutes from Woods Hole, a nor'easter started building waves that bucked against the *Islander*'s prow. Standing on the forward deck, Bourque could smell rain blowing in from the Atlantic. She'd been wrong about the fine weather. Cape Cod was fickle in the fall. In a matter of hours, the air had shifted from cool to almost cold.

Stepping inside, she suddenly came upon Balan. In Donnelly's eyes, Lurch resembled the love child of a stick man and a stork. The seaman was working on a wall socket. He looked up and stood. "Welcome to ship," he mumbled.

Wonder of wonders, the tar could talk. "Thank you, Mr. Balan. Do you have a minute?"

"I have."

"I understand you were in the Russian merchant marine. Where were you stationed?"

"Black Sea," he faintly replied, his voice as ghostly as his body.

"Did you like your job?"

"Yes," he shyly said. "From Novorossiysk we stop at Constanta in my country, Romania, and then Istanbul in Turkey."

"Did you like Istanbul?"

The tar smiled, revealing a swathe of Soviet dentistry. "Yes. All people meet there. East and west, north and south."

"How's life in the USA?" she gregariously asked.

He grinned. More Soviet dentistry. "Very good."

"Excellent. Let's go back to two nights ago, Mr. Balan. Did you ever see the captain talking to passengers?"

"No. Captain does not leave bridge during crossing."

"Do you talk to passengers?"

He shrugged bashfully. "My English is bad."

"Not true," she said.

He looked away. "I am shy to speak to ladies."

"No need to be." He regarded her nervously. Good, she thought. A nervous POI was often a forthcoming POI. "Was the captain his usual self two nights ago?"

"He is always same. To the point, you say. I spend much time with him. I am his dogsbody, he sometimes calls me." Balan made a face. "I do not like this word, but I like to have work. So I forget. He is fine captain. No problems aboard. All seamen know what he want. All seamen do it."

"What do you do for him?"

"Many little jobs. I bring food, I bring tea, I clean cabin."

"What's your main job?"

"I do electric maintenance."

She thought of the faulty power outlet on the vehicle deck. Had Balan overloaded it?

"In old country," he continued, "I am diesel mechanic, but not here. I do not have correct papers yet. Captain is helping me. He is going to bat for me, he say."

Huh, she thought, Balan owed Macey allegiance. The captain could tighten the screws on him. "Did the captain ever ask you for money?" she abruptly asked.

"No, no," Balan sputtered. "No money."

She leaned closer. Balan appeared to be more shy than uncooperative. However, shifting sands could easily shift again. "You're free here," she told him. "You don't need to fear anyone."

"I do not. Captain is good man."

"When do you do your repairs on the vehicle deck?"

"Never. I do not fix there."

"What about the security cameras? Who fixes them?"

"Security company, not ship. We are not allowed to touch. I would like to say something. In my country, we have saying: *If shoe pinches badly, do not wear it.* Captain Macey is not pinching me. I will stay with this ship."

"I wish you well." But I'm watching you.

□ □ □

Bourque strolled purposefully to the giftshop, pleased to see it had no customers. As hoped, Halliday was in the shop. Bourque switched on her phone's recording device and entered. The shopkeeper looked despondent. Unlike yesterday, she wore dark eyeliner and matching eye shadow. Her sapphire eyes seemed haunted.

"Good day, Ms. Halliday. I have a few more questions."

"More?"

Bourque nodded. "Have a seat. We'll stop talking if any customers come in."

Halliday shrugged. *Please yourself*, her expression said, but she sat on a stool.

Bourque remained standing. "How long did you know Daniel Fitzgerald?"

"A few months. Like I said, I only met him this summer." Her eyes imitated a school of fish, first darting left, then right.

Bourque slowed her pace, thinking *don't just listen to Halliday, look at her*—and let her know you're looking, which often unsettled POIs. She scrutinized Halliday for at least five seconds, seconds that felt like minutes. "How many times did you speak to Mr. Fitzgerald?"

"I told you," Halliday querulously replied, "eight."

Bourque feigned forgetfulness. Irritate the POI, don't indulge them—a Captain Peabody gambit. He claimed it got to the truth faster. "Where do you live?" she asked.

"Like I told the other detectives, my parents' place in Orleans."

Orleans was almost an hour-and-a-half east of Woods Hole. "That's a long drive from the ferry. Did you ever stay in Woods Hole after a passage?"

"Sure. In case you're wondering—" Halliday's look said *I know you are* "—I have friends there. I stayed with them."

"Names?"

"The Reddits, Winnie and her husband Rick. They have three little boys, great kids."

Bourque openly examined Halliday's face. There were numerous theories about how to tell when someone was lying, one being they didn't look you in the eye. Halliday was looking right at her. Bourque moved on to Halliday's lips. Lips were often more revealing than eyes, even quicksilver eyes. People weren't able to manipulate their mouths for long. From the set of Halliday's lips, she wasn't fully at ease. "Did you ever stay in a hotel or motel?"

"No."

"Are you sure you didn't? Say, with Daniel Fitzgerald."

Halliday's eyes narrowed. "I told you, we weren't that kind of friends."

"Did you want to be?"

The POI sighed. "We weren't even friends really."

"Yet you seem distraught today. Why?"

"You wouldn't understand."

"Why not?"

"It's a long story."

Bourque smiled. "It's a long passage."

Halliday sighed again. "I might have misled you a bit last night. I said I didn't expect more from Dan, like I didn't care if anything happened between us. However, I thought things might." She shook her head ruefully. "I should have been more, let's say, *forward*. I went to university for six years and what do I have to show for it? Two pieces of paper. A bachelor's and a master's degree. No husband, no kids. Not even a boyfriend. All the crewmen on the *Islander* wear brown. I hate brown. My mother says I have plenty of time. I'm young. But—"

Halliday pulled a tissue from her jacket sleeve and dabbed her eyes. "Lieutenant," she forlornly disclosed, "I didn't sleep last night. I kept going over Dan's conversations, mainly his politics. I think you should know about them. He mentioned Atlantic right whales a lot."

Right whales again, Bourque thought. Chase Heaney, and now Halliday.

"He said the fight for them was heating up. They're an endangered species," Halliday fervently declared. "There are less than three hundred and fifty left."

"Did that conversation come out of the blue?"

"No. Dan and I were talking about civil disobedience. Henry David Thoreau and all."

"Go on."

"He was speaking about personal principles. How Thoreau believed everyone needs to put their own conscience ahead of bad laws. If a government is unjust, citizens should refuse to follow their laws. That wasn't enough for Dan. He wanted to extend our laws to all mammals." She smiled wistfully. "I challenged him on that. 'Why not all life forms?' I asked. He had no answer. He liked to talk theory. But don't get me wrong, he wasn't a bookworm. He'd been in the trenches."

"Did you see him as someone who'd get in trouble?"

"Unfortunately, yes. He had a fire in his eyes. He wanted to be a real provocateur."

□   □   □

Bourque left the shop wondering about Halliday. She wasn't an obvious femme fatale. She wasn't the type to fall for any male who came along. Who was she then? Simply a smart, attractive young woman? The State Police system didn't have the information Bourque wanted. In the Cape & Islands region, locals knew more about the area than any outside cop ever would. While she refrained from discussing cases with Marty, who was born in Falmouth, she had a go-to local "informant," her neighbor from two houses down. Cal Knowlton was a retired newspaper reporter recognized as an authority by everyone, including himself.

At eighty-three, Cal had lived his whole life on Cape Cod and grown up near Orleans. He claimed to know almost everybody on the Outer Cape, as well as points inland. In truth, he joked, he knew everything and everybody, but was too humble to say so, important things like who cheated at cards, or who had two girlfriends on the go. The shipping news for landlubbers.

On *Islander* crossings, Bourque normally sat on deck but with a nor'easter howling she wouldn't be able to hear Cal talk outside. Knowing the canceled sailings had caused a backlog, she walked past the crowded main passenger lounge to the secondary one. Virtually empty. Finding a quiet corner, she punched Cal's number.

"How's my favorite neighbor?" she said when he answered.

"Bright-eyed and bushy-tailed."

"That's what we ladies want to hear. Got a few questions for you."

"Real questions?"

"Yes."

"Thank God. Old Ellie Trainor keeps asking me what day it is. You hear the wind?"

"And feel it too."

"Ah, yes. A storm's a-coming. Make no mistake."

"I'm with you. I'm sure you know about the murder on the Woods Hole ferry."

"Of course. I watch the news. Do you think I spend all day in bed? Yesterday's belle left at eight p.m. Incidentally, I have a slot today at nine p.m. It's yours."

"I'll likely be occupied."

"I'll give you until ten. My door will be unlocked. You can make it. I know how you drive."

Bourque chuckled.

"Seriously, Lootenant, how can I help you?"

"You can tell me about the Halliday family from Orleans, father Jasper, mother Pamela, two daughters."

"The Hallidays. Well, Jasper's father was Alden, gone now, bless his soul. I went to school with Alden. He was a hard worker. Always dressed in overalls. In winter he'd add full-body long johns." Cal guffawed merrily. "Looked the same, just thicker."

Here we go, Bourque thought.

"Let me tell you, Alden was a character. He used to say the Outer Cape had the worst winters in New England. There was more snow than sand. And that's saying something."

"Can I redirect our conversation?"

"You're starting to sound like a lawyer, young lady."

"*Me*? Do you know Jasper's two daughters?"

"I've met them, but I don't actually know them. However, I do know why you're asking. The eldest, Ruby, works on the *Islander*. Daniel Fitzgerald was killed aboard the ferry, which makes her a suspect."

"I can't confirm or deny that."

"Ah. Well, I can tell you this: the Halliday family is upstanding. They have long roots on the Cape. Jasper's people came over in 1656. It was—"

"Thanks," Bourque cut in, "but you can hold the history for now."

"You police officers, you're too focused."

"Guilty as charged," Bourque admitted. "Is the family wealthy?"

"Prosperous, but not wealthy."

"Have you heard rumors of them owing money?"

"That family? Not a chance. They're not beholden to anyone."

"Appreciate the help, Cal. I have a little something for you in return." She couldn't divulge restricted material but there was no blackout on the case. Fitzgerald's family had been informed. It made sense to involve the locals. Anything she told Cal would soon be public knowledge. "I know you love to share facts," she began.

"Of course I do. They shouldn't be kept secret."

"Most of the time."

"Are you a lawyer or a police officer? Facts are the cat's meow, not the horse's arse."

No argument there. "Daniel Fitzgerald's car was broken into

and swept clean. I don't mind if you, let's say, relay that information."

"Are you using me?"

"No more than usual."

Cal guffawed. "I see. What's good for the gander is good for the goose. I'll let that news slip. I assume you want me to report if I hear of any suspicious articles showing up."

"You bet."

"My pleasure. Any more questions?"

"What day is it?"

"Ask Ellie Trainor."

## Chapter 9

### Martha's Vineyard, Massachusetts

Autumn had reached Martha's Vineyard. The black gums had already turned red. Stands of oak were trending orange and gold. The sky was seemingly boundless, the kind of sky found on islands, a distant blue merging with the sea.

Bourque bought two lobster rolls as she left Vineyard Haven. One for now, one for later. When lobsters were available, she'd eat anything made with them: rolls, bisques, chowders, pasta dishes. Not to mention, tails, claws, or whole crustaceans—boiled at the beach, poached in wine, slow-baked on a bed of seaweed.

At ninety-one square miles, other than Long Island, Martha's Vineyard was the largest island on the U.S. East Coast. Nantucket was roughly half its size—and, according to Vineyard locals, twenty times its inferior. Which island was settled first? The Vineyard. Which had more people? The Vineyard. Old-time Nantucketers had a comeback: Did Melville write about the Vineyard? No, he wrote about Nantucket. *Moby Dick* was the cultural touchstone of New England.

Bourque followed State Road through the interior of the Vineyard. After West Tisbury, the island got sleepier and sleepier. The farm fences looked like they'd been erected centuries ago; the remaining old-growth trees looked pre-Columbian. The fields tumbled and rolled until they were lost at sea.

Approaching Chilmark, she left the road at Lucy Vincent Beach, passing a typical Vineyard marsh, a portrait of muted colors: dusty greens and yellow browns. If the land beyond West Tisbury was off the beaten track, Lucy Vincent Beach was virtually trackless.

Two years ago, she'd cruised past Lucy Vincent on a day sail out of Falmouth with her father. It had been early September, the sun etching a long streak of gold onto the ocean. He'd told her he visited the beach many times when he was younger. It was called Jungle Beach then, full of nude sunbathers and beachcombers. Her father was a liberal man for a police officer. She could see him on nude beaches.

Now, turning into Azalea Lane, she was pleased to find the

area more than she remembered. There were countless places where humans had complete dominion over the land. She wanted parts of the Cape to slip the bonds of progress, to exist beyond the cunning of Dedalus and the cravings of Icarus.

At 5 Azalea Lane, she spotted a State Police cruiser. Pulling next to it, she noticed the trooper was dozing. She would be too, she thought. She stepped out of her car, watching the trooper shake himself. When he powered down his window, she smiled. "Lieutenant Bourque, Cape and Islands."

"Been expecting you," he heartily said. "Trooper Darby. Welcome to our little paradise."

The constable was about five years younger than her, an outdoorsy guy with a sincere look, the kind of look that made women feel good about themselves. No doubt some would want to befriend him, and likely more. "Any signs of a break-in?" she asked.

"Nothing from the outside. I didn't go in. HQ's orders."

She nodded. Troopers were trained not to contaminate potential crime scenes.

"Doesn't mean someone didn't use a key," Darby added. "I'd normally look for one under rocks or flowerpots—the usual places—but don't worry. I didn't this time."

"Any unusual activity today?"

"None. Sorry, hold it." He grinned. "I thought a crow flew out of a tree, but it was a raven. That's unusual over here."

"You can tell the difference?"

"Ravens have long, pointy tails and crows have shorter rounded ones. Pointed versus curved."

"I always forget that." She gestured with her chin in the direction of the cottage. "Looks pretty quiet."

"Most folks here are weekenders or summer people. Some have already closed up for the winter."

"Ever have any problems with Daniel Fitzgerald?" she asked.

"None. No rowdy parties out here. A single fellow with his looks, he should have been having fun. Shame really. You're only young once."

"Shame. I'll probably be awhile, a few hours at least. Why don't you take a break?"

"This is a break."

"Head out. Grab some lunch."

Bourque drove up a long track completely cleared on both sides, denuding it of cover. At the end, the track abutted a thick hedge of Cape cedars, not tapered and elegant but squat and square. Exiting her car, she noticed the property provided a good sightline back to Azalea Lane. It'd be difficult for someone to sneak in from there.

The cottage was hunkered behind the hedge, its roof barely visible. Leaving Fitzgerald's living quarters for later, she walked down a narrow path toward the shore, eighty yards away. She heard no voices, motors, or music. She saw no birds. The wind carried an unseasonable chill, the kind that originated far north of New England, bringing heavy snow and ice. There was a deeper note, one that spoke of the Cape wanting to hibernate and rejuvenate itself, of its desire to drive away the excesses of summer.

As she paced shoreward, she spotted a web camera in a scrub oak. Continuing past the tree, she stopped and looked back. The camera wasn't visible from the shoreside. She scanned the passing trees. By the time she'd reached the shore, she'd seen six cameras, two pointing toward the water; two toward each side of the lot, which was about 150 yards wide. Add in the sightline from the front of the cottage and it appeared Fitzgerald wouldn't be having any surprise visitors. If he wanted security, he'd chosen his spot well.

When she reached the beach, she surveyed it to the east, and then the west. Other than shifting sand cliffs, it seemed as though time had stood still. The ocean, however, was a chaos of roiling greys. Dark clouds were marshalling on the eastern horizon, like a fleet of black corsairs. As Cal had said, a storm was brewing, one that presaged winter. The weather stations were talking about two to three inches of snow tomorrow morning. Her sailing nose told her it would arrive before that.

She walked back inland, the wind biting through her fall jacket and Dockers. Gusts whipped her hair around her face. Leaves flew past her head.

To the southwest of the cottage, she found a protected garden, reminiscent of her father's garden in Boston: six raised beds in two rows of three. The adjacent grass was speckled with white violas. Dozens of tomatoes hung on the vine, embraced by a proliferation of herbs: basil, dill, chives, parsley. As with her father's garden, the sight gladdened her. In her youth, they'd eaten countless tomatoes straight off the vine. He'd always carried a small vial of sea-salt which he flourished like an ampoule of saffron.

The one-story cottage was low and squat, fashioned of heavy timbers, with a steeply-pitched cedar shake roof and small windows, reminding her of Pilgrim homes. The overall effect was utilitarian. Walking the perimeter, she found no signs of a break-and-enter. She stopped at the front door, drew out a clean-suit, gloves, and shoe covers from her crime scene bag, and donned them. Using a set of picks, she unlocked the door and stepped inside. No indication of a cleanout, nor any indication of New England royalty: no valuable antiques, paintings, or expensive electronics. The interior was about 600 square feet: dark-paneled walls, one main room with a kitchen running along the backwall, two doors to one side, one door to the other.

She opened the nearest door and discovered a standard cottage bathroom: a moldy smell, pale blue fixtures about thirty years old, fashionable when a fast PC had two megs of RAM. She checked the shower, sink, and medicine cabinet. Male toiletries only, standard brands, nothing upscale, which fitted Fitzgerald's persona to date.

Opening the other doors, she found two bedrooms, the larger one with a queen bed; the smaller, a bunkbed. She entered the larger room. The queen bed had been slept in recently. She examined the pillow cases. A few walnut brown hairs, probably Fitzgerald's. She tweezered them into an evidence container and kept searching. At the far edge of the bed's second pillow, she spotted two long red hairs. Ruby Halliday immediately came to mind. She claimed she'd hadn't met Fitzgerald in a hotel or motel in Woods Hole, but what about a cottage near Lucy Vincent Beach?

Bourque bent closer to study the red hairs. Both had follicles, meaning they could be linked to one owner. Follicles held nuclear DNA, which yielded individualization. She tweezered the hairs into a container, telling herself to reserve judgement. The Northeast had no shortage of redheads.

She returned to the bathroom but found no more red hairs, not even in the shower drain. It seemed the redhead was a short-term guest, the kind who might have to get back to work—say, on a departing ferry. Hold it, Bourque told herself. The *Islander* made quick turn-arounds, rarely staying in port for more than an hour. It would take fifty minutes for Halliday to drive from Vineyard Haven to Lucy Vincent Beach and back. That didn't leave much time for a tryst. Bourque's mind kept spinning. What about a tryst on a day off? She filed that thought away.

Moving on, she searched the closet and found the same type of menswear she'd seen on Fitzgerald's body—hiker's clothes, she thought of them. A Gore-Tex jacket, two fleece liners, twenty or so shirts and pants, the only difference between them being the shade of khaki. She sifted through a chest of drawers. The usual male accoutrements: socks, underwear, T-shirts, shorts. A box of condoms, almost empty. It appeared Fitzgerald hadn't been all that solitary.

Next, she examined the smaller bedroom. It seemed no one had used it. Finding nothing of interest, she started on the main room, which was dominated by a huge oak table and four heavy chairs. The table was strewn with magazines and newspapers. She flipped through them. Mostly local. On an old desk, she found an article about right whales, then a dozen more. Pulling out an evidence sack, she dropped them in it. The team had a possible lead—still embryonic—but possible.

Under the articles, she discovered a sheet of paper with a name at the top—*Ruby*—and a list of hand-written entries. Halliday, Bourque reflected, again. Of course, it could be another Ruby. Bourque scanned the list. Eight books by Henry David Thoreau, including *On the Duty of Civil Disobedience;* books by and about George Washington, Thomas Paine, Benjamin Franklin, and John Quincy Adams, followed by Paul Watson of Greenpeace. Position papers by Greenpeace USA, the Green Party of the United States, and Defenders of Wildlife. The list ended with websites and documentary films about environmental issues.

Bourque searched for more lists, hoping to find further references to "Ruby." No success. She reminded herself that most Cape Cod murders had a link to the past. The cottage was central to Fitzgerald's recent past. She resumed her search, trying to get a lead on his possible enemies. She found nothing. Changing tack, she looked for PCs, laptops, Wi-Fi modems, etc. There were none.

The kitchen was well-used, stocked with expensive tinned and bottled goods—French wines, extra-virgin olive oil, truffles, caviar, foie gras—plus upscale pots, pans, and gadgets, the only semblance of wealth she'd seen in the place. She opened the fridge. Coffee cream, an array of expensive cheeses, free-range eggs, sprouted wheat bread, tropical fruit, kale, a thick grass-fed beefsteak—best-before-date two days hence. Fitzgerald wasn't expecting to be away for long.

Homes vacated by death often felt empty. In this case, the opposite was true. It felt like Fitzgerald was still in the cottage. Backing away from the fridge, Bourque leaned against the sink, considering the whole interior. A gourmand on site. Evidence of a guest. No computer hardware. Nothing damaged or tossed helter-skelter. So much for her and Eller's theory that Fitzgerald's place would be ransacked. His clunker might have been cleaned out, but the cottage wasn't.

Eyeing the main room, she wondered if someone had "visited" Fitzgerald to dissuade him from *waging his war*, as Heaney put it. In that case, there could be some indication of a dress-down: signs of a scuffle, damaged furniture, a dent on the wall. Victims' homes often provided the best way of knowing them. While family and friends might not intentionally mislead you, they tended to speak out of the corners of their mouths. Conversely, most homes spoke directly. Unfortunately, Fitzgerald's had nothing to say. There was no indication of a dress-down.

Bourque walked outside. Fighting the strengthening wind, she proceeded to a fenced-off area near the kitchen, twenty or so square yards enclosed by a high wooden barricade. A small web camera was perched above the enclosure's door. She picked the lock and opened the door.

What was this? She hadn't seen anything like it. She was facing a mob of satellite dishes: spindly bodies and big heads, chins tilted skyward. She counted sixteen, all with HughesNet decals. She pulled out her phone and checked for available Wi-Fi connections. A slew of them, all password protected. Although she hadn't found any modems in the cottage, there had to be some nearby.

Examining the closest sat dish, she saw a cable at the base of the pedestal going into the ground. The cable was wrapped in a protective sleeve. Using a nearby stick, she carefully dug about a foot down into packed sand, deep enough to see the sleeve turning parallel to the ground and heading north. She scrutinized the other sat dishes. Same story.

Leaving the enclosure, she paced north, soon coming to a garden shed she'd noted before. No sign of a web camera, suggesting the shed was of secondary importance. There was no power line to it, unless the line was buried underground. However, there were four solar panels on the roof, the standard residential variety, about fifteen square feet. Wires led from the panels to the back of the shed and then inside, which told her the panels could be an electricity source for modems.

She picked the padlock on the shed door. Inside, she moved a collection of yard tools, looking for sheathed satellite cables coming into the shed. None. Maybe the cables kept going past the shed? She almost left but stood still, hearing her father's voice: *Open your eyes wider. Dispel the darkness.* She let her eyes retravel the interior. Bingo. The shed's width was shorter than it appeared to be on the outside, suggesting the backwall was fake.

Shifting the tools again, she discovered a swing-door cleverly camouflaged as a wall panel. She opened it. There they were! Two shelves of modems above a bank of solar power batteries, eight of the modems winking little green lights, eight dormant. The fake room was about a yard deep. The batteries were augmented by a generator. She nodded to herself. Fitzgerald was operating his network off-the-grid. He might not be running all sixteen modems at once, but his network connectivity would never be down. If Heaney was right about the social media campaigns, they wouldn't be down either.

She stood back. Why was Fitzgerald concealing his network? Were his social media campaigns that dangerous? On the other hand, he could have been running some kind of internet venture: bitcoin mining or scams with tentacles to the dark web. High power consumption often went hand-in-hand with virtual businesses. She'd check his electricity bills. He'd need more than four solar panels and a generator to run a large e-business. There was yet another angle. Where were the PCs needed to do the actual business? Had they been in his car? Or were they hidden somewhere on the property, perhaps in a concealed cellar or the attic. She returned to the cottage.

An hour later, Bourque had exhausted her latest search. The attic was empty. She hadn't found a cellar. She'd seen no computing gear. That seemed to point in one direction: Fitzgerald had taken his computing devices with him, either intending to keep them in his car, in which case they'd been stolen, or dropping them somewhere for safe keeping, perhaps on Martha's Vineyard— unless, she told herself, he'd left them on the *Islander*. Her first thought was the redhaired shopkeeper. Again.

Bourque stood gazing out the kitchen window, watching waves

roar ashore. A lone seagull sailed the wind. What went along with taking inventory? Moving things around. It would be a good time to create a hiding spot for computing devices. Halliday said Fitzgerald had visited her six times at the shop, which gave her ample opportunity to offer assistance. Would such assistance be genuine or underhanded? If underhanded, Halliday could be part of a plot to befriend and then kill Fitzgerald.

Bourque turned away from the window. The team had Halliday's DNA from her first interview, which would enable them to establish if she'd been in the cottage's queen bed—or, as a lawyer might argue, someone had planted her hairs there. Bourque's mind was in overdrive, seeing conspiracies everywhere. That was detective work. At this juncture, nothing could be discounted, regardless of how far-fetched it looked.

She walked out of the cottage and locked the door. Although police tape wouldn't deter anyone determined to destroy or remove evidence, she put tape around the cottage, sat dish enclosure, and garden shed. In addition to the local trooper guard, she'd get the whitecoats to post surveillance cameras.

As she sat in her car updating case notes, she heard Darby's cruiser zipping along the track. Upon arrival, he lowered his driver-side window and pointed at the police tape. "Evidence?"

She nodded. "Advise your captain to watch the place twenty-four-seven."

"Roger."

Smart perps—which, increasingly, the case pointed to—would know the property would be fully processed in a matter of days. If they intended to break in, they'd do it soon. Driving away, she decided to stop at Chilmark's only convenience store. Inside, she ordered a takeout coffee and assessed the woman at the till. Late thirties. Fake raven hair and a fake smile to go with it.

"Detective Bourque," she said, showing her badge. "Cape and Islands."

The woman's eyes narrowed. Her ersatz smile disappeared.

Bourque wasn't surprised. Occasionally, Islanders were leery of her—as it transpired, often ones with island interests to protect, the most insular kind. She showed Raven Hair a photo. "Do you know this man who lived at Lucy Vincent?"

"That's the Fitzgerald guy. Not that I know him. He's only been in a few times." She harrumphed. "Doesn't shop locally. *Didn't,* I should say. I know he's dead."

"When was the last time you saw him?"

"A week ago."

"What did he buy?"

"A newspaper."

"Anything else?"

Raven Hair harrumphed again. "Nothing."

"Was he alone?"

"Yes."

Bourque wasn't sure about Raven Hair. Had she been a redhead recently? Bourque handed Raven her card. "Call me if you think of anything."

Raven Hair didn't reply.

Leaving Chilmark, Bourque detoured to Edgartown on the way to the ferry, thinking Fitzgerald might have bought supplies in the island's largest town, which had a few gourmet purveyors. An hour later, she'd found no evidence of it. She left town deeming Fitzgerald had stocked up on the mainland, like many half-islanders did.

Taking the road to the ferry terminal, she put her foot down and opened all her windows, hoping it would clear her mind. The cold wind pummeled her face and blew her hair back. She tried to focus on motive. Why was Fitzgerald killed? Money underpinned most murders. She suspected a different root with Fitzgerald. Social media campaigns? Was that it? Perhaps he'd been posting inflammatory information online or, more likely, disinformation. Disinformation made bigger enemies. Though the sat dishes and modems told a story, she figured it was barely a first chapter.

## Chapter 10

**Woods Hole, Massachusetts**

The predicted storm arrived early. Its advance front swept in from the North Atlantic, dropping the temperature on Martha's Vineyard to thirty-one degrees. In Massachusetts, autumn blizzards blew in routinely. People raised on Cape Cod didn't deceive themselves. Life was good, but not easy. *Entitlement* was a foreign word. You accepted that your home was a sandbar sticking out into the Atlantic, a place that never claimed to be paradise.

Despite the weather, the *Islander*'s departure wasn't delayed. It had been a rough crossing over from Woods Hole at noon, with the ship battling a headwind all the way. Now the ocean was rougher. Standing on the aft deck, Bourque watched the island recede. The channel buoys were bent horizontal by the wind. As her grandfather would put it, a herd of white horses was galloping on the sea. The ship rolled and yawed, riding stern waves driven by near-gale-force winds, gusting to thirty knots, carrying heavy wet snow.

Bourque had no intention of dropping by the ferry's giftshop. Halliday would remain on the shelf until more intel came in. Instead, she sat in the secondary lounge, not minding the rolling. She'd experienced worse on small sailboats. Looking back toward the Vineyard, her mind returned to Fitzgerald. All those sat dishes didn't come cheaply, whether he'd bought them outright or rented them. She did a little research on her phone. On the Vineyard, rented satellite packages ran about $150 per month. As for Fitzgerald's solar panels, they'd cost around $1000 each. Then there was the gas generator. It was a large model, the kind that ran over $3000. For a guy who drove a clunker, he'd spent a lot of money for internet connectivity. She did a quick estimate of his monthly costs. Add in generator gas for rainy days, which the Vineyard was no stranger to, and Fitzgerald could be burning through upwards of $3,000 a month. She sat back. Not an excessive amount. She'd soon know his full fiscal profile. M&M, Central's Money-n-Murder unit, part of its financial forensic wing, would be reporting on Fitzgerald that evening.

Leaving the money angle aside, she switched to Ruby Halliday. At first glance, she was beautiful and apparently kind-hearted. Despite Cal's approval of her family, there was something unsettling about her, particularly her eyes and lips. Then again, that was body language, not uncontested facts. Bourque kept thinking. Maybe it was the young woman's education. Having an MA in psychology, she knew how the human mind worked—and, presumably, how to influence and trick it. She could be playing Bourque. More to the point, she could have been playing Fitzgerald, using her charms to set him up. *Could have.* Pure speculation.

Back on land in Woods Hole, Bourque glanced at her watch. The ferry had only docked ten minutes late. A tailwind could be a good thing, even in roiling seas—if a captain knew how to handle his ship. Macey did. The old seadog. He'd made the right course adjustments to counter the wind and waves.

After leaving the terminal, she dropped the brown and red hairs at the Mobile Unit and walked to a nearby Italian restaurant. The air was dense and cold, like seawater changing to ice. The wind howled in her ears and pelted her with wet snow. She could tell it would soon become sleet, what Marty called a mudding of snow.

Sitting at a table overlooking the harbor, she ordered grilled octopus Brindisi style, drizzled with garlic-infused olive oil, followed by garlic lobster orecchiette. She'd be ingesting enough garlic for a week, but she wouldn't be seeing Marty that night.

Outside, the snow had already turned to sleet. It tattooed the windows with increasing zeal. The sky was a murky grey yet the strange autumn moon pierced the gloom, its silver-white rays impervious to the clouds, its potency still making her mind race. Two inches of slush coated the roads—not much, but she knew it was treacherous. Being October, she hadn't yet put snow tires on her car. No one had. For an hour or two, local traffic would be sluggish, mimicking a barely snow-dusted highway in Georgia.

She called Eller. "Can your big Ford handle Cape Cod slush?"

"Oh yeah."

"Come to Luigi's Trattoria. I'll buy you a drink."

"I'm dry these days."

"A zero beer."

"Coke will do. Give me an hour."

Waiting for Eller, she settled in near the restaurant fireplace, pulled out her laptop, and began digging into Right Whales First. Fitzgerald was one of its founding members and its current president. RWF wanted state and federal governments to ban fishing nets in right whale feeding grounds and restrict ship movements in them everywhere in the North Atlantic, but primarily off Massachusetts and Rhode Island.

The RWF protests had begun three years ago on Martha's Vineyard. No coincidence, Bourque deemed. Fitzgerald started summering on the island three years ago. The first protests occurred in Edgartown, once the Vineyard's main whaling port. Ships had set out from it for decades; captains had returned to it to build grand mansions. There was plenty of old whaling money on the Vineyard. Bourque wondered what all that wealth thought of Fitzgerald. No doubt some families had sailed into the twenty-first century, but others remained entrenched in the nineteenth.

She called Donnelly, who still kept his eyes on the Vineyard.

"Good evening," she said when he answered. "It's Macduff."

"Hope you're warm, Lieutenant Mac. Old Man Winter escaped. I'm calling the cops."

She chuckled. "Listen, I have a few questions about your time on the Vineyard. Were you ever called to whale rights protests?"

"Sure was. Used to be mainly retirees and younger Green Party types, normally from Cape Cod. They were respectful. There are more hotheads now, often from Boston and NYC."

"Do you know a Trooper Darby?"

"Yep."

Donnelly's reply was uncharacteristically brief. "What can you tell me about him?"

"He has a bit of a reputation."

"Go on."

"They call him a Ladies Man."

"Yes?"

"I don't like to speak ill of others, but he's under investigation." Donnelly paused. "He was seeing a young widow, a single mother who has a fifteen-year-old daughter. He got too friendly with the daughter. You know where I'm going?"

"Yes."

"Not for the first time," Donnelly added.

"Thanks. You inside for the night?"

"Yep. Cozier than the captain of a cop shop."

"Any shop in particular?"

"My lips are sealed."

Bourque laughed. She'd known something for a while, something she'd never examined, and didn't need to: Donnelly was like a brother. Same sense of humor, same commitment to his job and the larger world beyond it. The fact she was an only child seemed to multiply the fraternal bond.

After signing off, Bourque did more research. There'd been hundreds of whale mortalities off both U.S. coasts due to human activity, and there'd be more. Scientists and activists had strong opinions on how to proceed, from monitoring shipping lanes to banning fishing nets to a full moratorium on shipping in certain regions. Their opponents ridiculed them, saying the oceans were free. Freighter captains, fishers, ferry captains, and container ship owners claimed catering to whales impacted their livelihood. Being the unusual amalgam she was—an ocean-loving, eco-friendly cop, one who loved sailing and swimming—Bourque leaned toward the whales. However, she wasn't a marine biologist. She didn't know all the science; hence she didn't know which way to go. Yet Fitzgerald, a non-scientist, had apparently sorted it out.

Returning to the RWF site, she discovered Fitzgerald had led eight protests over the summer, in NYC, Boston, and Providence, Rhode Island. She viewed a video of his work. There he was with a loudspeaker, chanting slogans, leading a large contingent along Boston's waterfront. Fiery eyes, madly waving arms. He appeared to be in his element. So much for the Vineyard's quiet recluse.

☐ ☐ ☐

"How was the Vineyard?" Eller asked as he sipped a Coke.

"Some possibilities," Bourque replied, "mostly virtual."

He looked at her quizzically.

"Fitzgerald had quite a network: sixteen satellite dishes and sixteen modems, all hidden and off-the-grid, running off his own power supply. I understand that. If you want uninterrupted power up-island, you take care of it yourself. But I wonder about all those connections." She raised her hands palms-up. "I didn't find any computing devices. We need Central to get an IT team to inspect the network, to look into how much bandwidth he was using, what IP addresses he communicated with, what domain names he owned, etc. The team can work with the ISP."

"You're losing me."

"Internet Service Provider," she explained. "Fitzgerald was using HughesNet." Eller wasn't a Luddite. He liked email. He'd decided cellphones were okay.

"Keep going," he said.

"The ninjas should sweep the property. I'm not sure I found everything. The best way to uncover Fitzgerald's full e-trail is to get his computers."

"Switching to low-tech, I got the goods on the clothes you took from Macey, Balan, and Carson. No blood on them, no DNA connected to Fitzgerald. We questioned all of the crew members. According to the first and second mates, Macey didn't leave the fore bridge once during the entire passage, not even to go to the washroom."

"Where was Balan?"

"He was in the engine room for the last fifteen minutes of the passage. As the *Islander* approaches land, the chief engineer lets Balan watch so he can get familiar with the ship's engines. By the way, Peabody ordered us to cut to the chase. Landon and I took formal depositions. Not courtroom testimonies, but binding."

She nodded. Peabody's latest gambit. He liked to "get legal" from the beginning. A deposition was done under oath, which served two purposes: to impress upon a POI that they better tell the truth, and to preserve their statement for later use, often at trial.

"Back to Macey," Eller continued. "He left the bridge roughly half an hour after docking, when he went to inspect the blood, as he told you. It appears he had no opportunity to attack the vic."

"Are you sure about the depos?" she asked. In her experience, you could ask ten people to describe something they'd all witnessed, and you'd get ten different accounts.

"I hear you, Bourque. Some details are slightly different, but very slightly."

"Are we missing something?"

"Like what?" he said in a reasonable tone.

"I don't know." Bourque rubbed her eyes. It seemed the depos cleared the captain, crew, and staff of murder, although one or more of them could be accessories.

"So," Eller concluded, "we need to move on. The ninjas arrived five hours ago."

She nodded. The ninjas, forensic officers Dan Munro and John Wolf from Central, were two of the best whitecoats in Massachusetts.

"They started with Fitzgerald's car. Found no DNA or prints on it except his own. The vid-camera overlooking it wasn't functioning. It had shorted out. Either someone overloaded the power outlet on purpose or it failed."

Being skeptical, Bourque opted for overloaded.

"They couldn't retrieve anything from the vehicle deck," Eller continued. "It was washed after arrival, which occurs every night after the last passage. Incidentally, I got access to the two vid-cameras on the bridge and checked the footage. Where one door closes, another often opens." Eller smiled. "Macey didn't leave the bridge until well after docking."

"There's still Balan," Bourque noted. "He does electrical maintenance on the ship. Consider the vid-camera that failed, the one near Fitzgerald's car that shorted out. Maybe he tripped that wire on purpose?"

"Maybe. Or maybe it was normal wear and tear."

"Could be, but I'm not convinced."

"I didn't think you'd be. If Balan is a bee in your bonnet, keep at him."

"Sometimes you have no choice."

"Is he one of your intuitions?"

"Call it a stubborn impression." To her, impressions were surface perceptions. Intuitions were deeper, things that only arose when her subconscious had time to work. Her job had led her to seek wisdom over knowledge, to favor deep understanding over surface assessments. She didn't know where her intuitions came from, but knew they developed for days, sometimes weeks. Then a series of synapses fired in her brain and suddenly she knew. It was like going from zero to a hundred in a second. However, she realized her intuitions were just part of the puzzle. She didn't downgrade facts. Her right brain acknowledged her left brain.

"By the way," she added, "when Fitzgerald and Halliday met, they talked a lot about politics. I found a reading list at his cottage with 'Ruby' at the top. It's potential evidence of a political bond between them. Of course, the list could be for another Ruby. If it was for the lovely Ms. Halliday, perhaps he was trying to recruit her to RWF."

Eller held his fire.

"Or," Bourque said, "it could just be personal. I found two red hairs in what I took to be Fitzgerald's bed and dropped them off at the MU. If Halliday was at his cottage, and if she was in his bed, she lied to us about the romance angle—just for starters."

"Are you suggesting a romance gone bad? As in she killed him?"

"She works on the ferry. She had potential opportunity."

"None of the crew reported seeing her outside the giftshop on that trip. Apparently, Fitzgerald was alone for days at a time. He had to talk to someone. She'd be a top choice for most men. But I see where you're going on politics," Eller conceded. "Let's keep that door open. The farther the political pendulum swings to the left, the more irate the right gets, and vice versa. Maybe he wasn't recruiting her. Maybe *she* was baiting *him*. Perhaps she was a right-wing plant? Someone inserted to infiltrate the RWF movement."

"I thought the same thing." Bourque shrugged. "Then I thought again." As she sat back, Eller's phone blared.

"Eller here … Yes? … Yes." He sucked his teeth as he listened. The back of Bourque's neck tingled. She felt a foreshadowing. Her father called it a *gut instinct*, which, to him, didn't mean that it had no grounding in fact. It was just that the fact had yet to reveal itself.

Eventually Eller turned to her. "We have a dead body."

"Ruby Halliday?"

He nodded.

"Where?"

"Orleans."

## Chapter 11

### Orleans, Cape Cod, Massachusetts

Like her favorite poet, Ruby Halliday was raging against the dying light. Her heart had stopped, her blood had ceased to carry sustenance to her body. She was physically dead, she could admit that, but she wasn't going gently into that good night.

From outside her body—from mere yards away, or was it a million miles—she watched her killer as he left her room. Although he'd drugged her, she'd regained consciousness to find herself gagged. Her arms and legs had been free, yet too inert to fight back. He hadn't said a word but his averted gaze told her he wasn't completely willing to attack her. Then his arm rose and fell swiftly, repeatedly, the knife blade flashing in the semi-darkness. The pain was ferocious. But she felt his pain too. He was sobbing at the end, his head down, his chest convulsing as he turned away and softly closed her door.

## Chapter 12

**Orleans**

Ruby Halliday lay on her back, her long frame limp, clad in a white nightgown. Bourque knelt next to the victim's bed and placed a gloved finger on her wrist. The skin was warm, signaling Halliday hadn't been dead long. Her bowels had loosened. Bourque shut out the stench. As a homicide detective, when you came across the corpse of a beautiful woman, chances were her beauty would be gone. Halliday's was. She'd been stabbed in the eyes, nose, mouth, and throat; rivulets of blood had dripped from her face onto her nightgown. The pillows were more red than white. The blood flow denoted injuries sustained before death, before the heart had stopped.

The victim's mouth was gagged, although it was difficult to tell at first. Her face was unrecognizable. It bore no resemblance to the face Bourque had seen that afternoon. Legally speaking, the term manslaughter—killing without intent—signified an act less heinous than murder, but Bourque wasn't thinking about the law. She was looking at woman-slaughter.

Bourque examined the rest of Halliday's body. From what she could determine, the victim hadn't been sexually assaulted. There were no other knife gashes. Her gaze returned to Halliday's head, scrutinizing the wounds. All of the entry vectors came from the right side of the head, from roughly the same angle, which suggested one perp. The vectors also suggested a frontal attack, with implied a left-handed perp. The wounds were already bruising around the edges, turning burgundy-red. The human body, she knew, was composed of countless organic compounds, none more important than blood. In death, blood returned to the Earth. Eller stood after studying the weapon imprints. "Looks like a wide knife," he said, "like with Fitzgerald. The same general MO," he went on. "The same killer?"

"Could be," she replied.

He pointed at his phone. "Peabody wants us in Barnstable. Landon will stay behind to handle the med ex and whitecoats."

Bourque made a final inventory of the scene. No bloody boot-

or fingerprints. Halliday's head emitted a whiff of ether or possibly chloroform. Bourque surmised the victim had been sedated and then knifed. According to her parents, it was their elder daughter's day off. She'd arrived home about seven p.m. and gone right to her room, saying she'd eaten supper in Falmouth. Their younger daughter was at a sleepover. The parents hadn't heard anything: no screaming, scuffling, or struggling.

Bourque found that believable. The house was large, over 3,000 square feet; Halliday's room was isolated in a separate wing. There was no blood anywhere in the house with the exception of her room. Landon had made an initial sweep of the premises. He detected no evidence of a break-in. Halliday's father said he'd locked all the house doors before bed at nine p.m., as usual, yet the backdoor was open.

It appeared Ruby Halliday had let her killer in, or the killer had a key. Her father had called 9-1-1 at ten-sixteen p.m., apparently minutes after his wife found Ruby's body. On their way out, Bourque and Eller stopped in the kitchen to re-interview the parents. With any murder or abduction, the family was at the top of the suspects list. No ifs, ands, or buts.

Eller directed Mr. and Mrs. Halliday—Jasper and Pamela—to a Formica table. Ruby's father looked the part of a fisherman: mid-length curly hair, just going grey; ruddy face; weathered hands. Her mother was a pale, wintry blonde, tall, striking, and dignified. The daughter had taken after her mother. Though the house was comfortably warm, both parents wore thick robes. Bourque wondered if they were chilled by events, or hiding blood traces under the robes. Or something else. She'd direct Landon to impound their clothes.

When the Hallidays were settled, Bourque nodded at Eller. She usually let him lead interviews. It allowed her to focus on a POI's body language.

"Let me express our condolences again," he began. "Mr. Halliday, can you tell me exactly when you locked all the house doors?"

"I was in bed by nine p.m., so five minutes before that."

"That's early."

"I get up at five."

"Did you take your youngest daughter to her sleepover?"

"No, Pam did."

"When?" Eller asked Mrs. Halliday.

"Just after four p.m.," she responded. "She was eating supper there too."

"When's she due home?"

"Tomorrow after school, but we'll get her now."

"Are you going fishing tomorrow?" Eller asked her husband. He huffed.

Bourque knew Eller's tack. He was trying to irritate the father, to see if he revealed any cracks.

"No fishing tomorrow?" Eller prodded.

"What do you think?"

"I don't assume things," Eller mildly said.

"I'm not fishing tomorrow."

"What about the next day?"

Mr. Halliday looked at his wife. *You talk to him.*

"Lieutenant," she evenly said, "Jasper runs a charter business. He won't be taking anyone fishing until Ruby's killer is found."

"That could be a while."

"It could be. He'll be looking for the killer too. He's a very dogged man."

Not good, Bourque deemed. Bereaved parents often threw spanners in the works. Bereaved perps—perps who were both killers and outwardly bereft—often threw jackhammers.

Eller turned to Mr. Halliday. "Don't be too vigilant."

Bourque scrutinized the fisherman's face. He'd picked up Eller's innuendo. Smalltown New England wasn't immune to vigilantism. Centuries after the witch hunts of Salem, self-policing still lurked below the surface. If the law didn't do your bidding, sometimes you did it yourself.

"I've seen a lot of dead bodies," Halliday replied, "mostly drowned fishermen." He held Eller's eye. "When Pam found Ruby's body, did I go off the deep end? No, I called you immediately. You do your job, and I'll do mine."

Bourque stepped in. "Mrs. Halliday, what time did you go to bed?"

"About ten after nine."

"Why did you get up approximately an hour later?"

"I wanted to talk to Ruby. We usually talked at night. She was never home in the daytime."

"Did she ever speak of a young man named Daniel Fitzgerald?"

"She told me she knew him. That was yesterday, when his

murder was announced."

"And before that?"

"She hadn't mentioned him."

"What did she say about him?" Bourque asked.

"Not much. You know how young women are. I gathered she liked him but knew he was in another league."

Shades of what Ruby herself had said. "Was Ruby interested in whales?"

Mrs. Halliday revealed a sad smile. "She loved whales."

"Does your husband love whales?"

"Ask him."

"Mr. Halliday, what do you think of whales?"

"Coddled nuisances. Lards of the Sea."

"Have you heard of Right Whales First?"

He nodded. "Misguided do-gooders."

"Did you ever meet Dan Fitzgerald?"

"No."

"Do you know of him?"

"By hearsay."

"Then you know he was a whale rights advocate."

"Something like that." Halliday grunted. "Whales need advocates now? They're fish—all right, mammals. They're certainly not humans. I'm not a fan of coddling, whether it be animals or humans. When governments coddle people, they get lazy."

"Did Ruby agree with that?"

He didn't answer.

"Did she agree?"

"Do any youngsters?"

Bourque studied Mr. Halliday, remaining silent. She wanted to unsettle him, to see what he'd say next. But he simply stared back at her. "Did you ever argue with Ruby?" she asked.

"Of course. She was willful."

"Did you fight?"

He shook his head rigorously. "I never struck my daughter."

"What about when she was younger?"

"Never. I tried to teach her right and wrong. Sometimes she agreed with me, sometimes she didn't."

"Did you go in her room when you heard she was dead?"

"No."

"Why not?"

"When I went to her door, I could see she was dead. What could I do? I called nine-one-one."

Bourque addressed Mrs. Halliday. "Did you fight with Ruby?"

"No. Like Jasper said, we didn't use corporal punishment. We argued with Ruby now and then, but all parents argue with their children."

"Did you ever meet Dan Fitzgerald?"

"No."

"What's your opinion of him?"

"I can't say. I haven't formed one."

"Do you think Ruby would have been interested in his whale rights movement?"

"Yes. I'm sure of that."

"Would she have joined it?"

"Probably."

"Thank you, Mrs. Halliday."

Bourque walked to the front door assessing Ruby's mother. Forthright, even-keeled. Bourque couldn't get a read on the father. Broadly speaking, there were two possibilities. He could simply be a grieving parent, a man determined to bring his daughter's killer or killers to justice. Alternatively, he could be implicated in both recent killings. He might even be the killer.

Outside, the wind had swung around to the southwest. As she strode to Eller's vehicle, she could feel its effect. The air was already warmer; the cloud cover, dispersed. The ground was bare. A nearby pond held no vestiges of ice. The storm had passed.

Sitting in the Explorer's passenger seat, she watched Orleans roll by, a standard New England seaside town: orderly streets, common-sense buildings, everything scrubbed clean by salt air. No inkling of a town visited by murder. She counted six churches as they drove, two no longer in use. Such was the Outer Cape. Every town was teeming with churches, yet many were shuttered. The region had been experiencing a slow arc of decline. Few visitors saw it but locals knew it. Hundreds of jobs had disappeared. While the area had a low crime rate, many residents were taciturn and crafty. A grin on the Outer Cape wasn't necessarily a smile.

The detectives sped south to find the moon hanging over Baker Pond, spilling silver onto the water's surface. Jupiter traveled below the moon, bright in its own right, but a clear second fiddle to its celestial cousin, now two days past full. Bourque tried to forget Halliday's face but couldn't. It was burned into her mind. In death, Halliday's beauty had been eradicated. Bourque wondered if it was a message: *Don't ally yourself with Daniel Fitzgerald.*

She opened her laptop and navigated to the case database. M&M had completed Fitzgerald's fiscal profile. He owned the cottage near Chilmark and had an annual stipend of $100,000. His network and cottage upkeep cost about $3,000 a month. His other major expenditures were travel, food, and his D.C. apartment, which totaled another $3,500 per month. She called M&M for a quick scan of Halliday's finances. The response came back in minutes. Halliday had no loans or debts. Her monthly income was just over $2,900.

Bourque turned to Eller. "What do you think of the father?" she asked.

"Lots of anger. If he ended up in front of a jury, he could have a problem. *Lards of the Sea?* Comments like that might get him a few chuckles but you don't want to alienate even one juror."

"Exactly. Okay, here's the kicker. Is Halliday's death connected to Fitzgerald's?"

"I'd bet on it," Eller replied. "The question is how. Maybe she was an accessory who's expendable now. Or she knows who killed him and had to be silenced. Like I said earlier, she could be a right-wing plant. Her father holds a right-wing position. Take that stuff about 'coddling.' You know what Joe McCarthy used to say about communists? That we were coddling them."

"That was a long time ago."

"It's not a common word. There could have been a partisan link between the father and daughter, one that went bad."

"Bad enough to kill her?"

Eller shrugged. "Possibly. Maybe something set him off."

"If he murdered her, he'd have to dupe his wife and younger daughter, not to mention the whole town."

"It's been done," Eller said.

Bourque nodded. "Okay, back to the Fitzgerald connection. If Ruby Halliday killed him, what's her motive? Not likely money, as in an unpaid loan. I checked her fiscal with M and M. She didn't have any money to loan him."

"Which leaves your romance angle," Eller noted. "Maybe she was a spurned lover."

Bourque sighed heavily. "We're circling drains. Let's switch to

Fitzgerald's computers. They might be on his property or might have been stolen from his vehicle. But there's a third possibility, a longshot: he was hiding them. He could have been hiding them with Halliday aboard the *Islander*."

"The ferry?"

"I did say longshot."

"Longshots never work if you don't take them."

"Right. Potentially, he hid them in the giftshop. Being a retail environment, there's a vid-camera there."

"Did you requisition the footage?"

Bourque winked. "Let me see if it arrived." She revisited the case database. "Bingo. I'll fast-forward it to Fitzgerald's last ferry trip."

A few minutes later, she watched Fitzgerald enter the shop carrying a backpack. "He has a pack," she relayed to Eller, "which supports the drop-off hypothesis. Plenty of room in it for computing devices."

She watched the footage to the end. As Halliday had reported, Fitzgerald had come into the shop once that night, the two had spoken very briefly, and he'd left. From what Bourque could see, he hadn't dropped anything off.

She turned to Eller. "He's tech-savvy. He'd know there was a vid-camera in the shop. He'd know how to avoid it. It's possible he hid something off-camera. Something small, like a USB drive, which he passed to Halliday or secreted himself."

"Let's head over there," Eller said.

"What about Peabody?"

"The chump can wait."

"No need for you to come aboard," she suggested. "With the wind, the ferry will be rolling."

"I'm getting used to it."

□ □ □

The detectives parked near the Mobile Unit and walked to the ferry. Mars had reached its zenith and begun its descent. The midnight constellations were gathering size and shape. Although the moon was waning, it still ruled the sky, its intensity tugging at Bourque, drawing her eagerly ahead. She rushed across the gangway. A private security guard checked their IDs and waved them aboard. They climbed the dingy metal stairwell to the giftshop. The twenty-by-twelve-foot space seemed smaller than on Bourque's earlier visits. Half a dozen open cardboard boxes littered the floor.

Two hours later, the detectives left the ship. They hadn't found anything. No USBs or computing devices. No reading lists or notes. Nothing but gifts: mostly glassware, knick-knacks, and stuffed animals, whales being the number one attraction.

## Chapter 13

**DAY THREE: Barnstable, Massachusetts. October 22nd**

The Barnstable Detective Unit was housed in a former courthouse with high windows and fine wooden trim. It was after 0200 when Bourque and Eller followed Peabody into his office, a room devoid of a woman's touch. The furnishings were angular and cheerless. The decor seemed teleported from the 1920s— maroon walls, a gold chandelier, sapphire drapes—creating an effect gaudier than Peabody's neckties. The olfactory aura was as uninviting as the visual one. Cheap aftershave, burnt coffee, musty armpits.

Arthur Peabody, a thin man with a pinched nose, resembled a bureaucrat rather than a cop. He routinely wore wide suspenders. When he had his suit jacket off, as he did that night, the suspenders made him look even thinner. Conversely, his eyes were large and deep blue.

He addressed the two detectives. "What do we have in Orleans?"

"Murder," Eller bluntly replied. "Could be the same killer as in the Fitzgerald case. Looks like the same knife width."

"And you, Bourque," he asked in his strident voice, "what do you think?"

"Could be. Pending the autopsy."

"You're saying we have a double murder on our hands?"

"Pending."

"I read your recent notes. Fitzgerald and Halliday were friends, maybe more than friends. Let's assume they both had to be silenced. Presumably for the same reason."

"Presumably." Another one-word reply. That wouldn't help matters. It was time to widen their perspective. "Let's consider a bigger question. Are we dealing with murders, or assassinations?"

Peabody pursed his lips. At first, Bourque saw a kissing codfish. Seconds later, his face morphed into a pondering sage. Still, he didn't speak.

She weighed in. "It might be a moot point, but murder has a more personal angle. All murder is personal. So are some assassinations, but they're also political."

Peabody nodded.

"Did you read my notes about Fitzgerald's secret network?" she asked.

"Yes."

"I think it says politics, not e-commerce. I doubt he was running any kind of business, not with his fiscal record. I also checked his electricity bill on the island. Very low consumption. Even with the off-the-grid setup, it's not consistent with an e-business."

"Okay," Peabody said. "Looks like you detectives have two main angles: murder *and* assassination." He leaned back in his chair. "Why is solving homicides like playing chess? Your mind has to be focused yet free—free to see all angles. Don't pursue one at the expense of others. Now Bourque, how does the assassination gambit help us?"

"I have no idea."

"No idea? Well, you better commune with some better angels, not to mention some facts."

"Give us a few days."

"Do I have any choice? Put the two of you together and you end up going in ten directions."

"Blame her," Eller said, pointing at Bourque.

"Blame him," she said and laughed.

"All right," Peabody wearily replied. "We can't do much more with Halliday until we build her timeline."

Good, Bourque thought. In Boston, her last boss had been too focused on victims. He believed you had to bond with the dead, bring them back to life so you could build their complete life history. Peabody didn't. Method sleuthing, he scoffed. Bourque went with him on that one. She didn't study victims to know their entire pasts, but to uncover their potential killers.

"Meantime," Peabody went on, "let's review the Fitzgerald crime scene. Could you summarize the case for us, Eller?"

Eller eyed the ceiling, making Peabody wait. "It's self-evident," he finally stated. Bourque knew he was taking a shot at Peabody. *Summarize it yourself.* "Single man, thirty-three years old, stabbed on the *Islander* and thrown overboard. Died in the water, not on the ferry."

Peabody gestured impatiently. *Go on.*

"His killer or killers—or assassins—got away. It was the last run of the day, making it easier to escape detection. The ferry wasn't unloading, then reloading, and sailing for the Vineyard. Hence the perps could wait onboard until the ferry was quiet—if they thought that far ahead. I suspect they did." He winked at Bourque. "Maybe they were chess players."

The skin around Peabody's eyes tightened.

"They took time to wipe blood and prints off the aft deck," Eller blithely continued. "Although they left a trail, they didn't leave any DNA traces. They were smart. They knew the ferry's layout and routines. Two of the first passengers interviewed reported seeing Fitzgerald on the aft deck about twenty minutes from Woods Hole, when they left to go to the snack bar. We checked the snack bar vid-camera; it corroborates that part of their statement. From what we've reconstructed, the perps killed their victim in a public place that was no longer busy. It was vacated by the disembarkation announcement." Eller signaled he was done.

Peabody turned to Bourque. "What do you see?"

"Well, from the forensic reports we have, Fitzgerald's assailant knifed him twice, but that didn't kill him. Why didn't the perp finish him? I'd say the perp didn't have time and instead tossed him overboard. The ferry was getting too close to port. That is, too close to potential witnesses. The unfinished job also implies there was only one perp. Two would probably have finished the job."

"You're speculating a lot, Bourque."

"I am."

"Let's return to Halliday. What do you think of the timing of her death?"

"Suspicious," Bourque answered. "That isn't pure speculation. It's half speculation. Halliday was likely killed roughly the same time as Fitzgerald. Of course, in her case, we have to wait for the official PMI number. But let me continue. Make a complete fool of myself. Both murders are connected to the *Islander*. Perhaps we have the same perp: a ferry employee." Bourque held up a stop-sign hand. "I know, their shift finishes around twenty-two-thirty, so how could they be in Orleans at twenty-two hundred? They could if they were off that night."

"*Perhaps. Could.* My wife speculates less than you do." Peabody shook his head. "You're the Queen of Speculation."

"Where's my throne?"

"I'll put in a requisition."

"Promises, promises." Bourque smiled. "Okay, I'll shift to more neutral ground. Why was Halliday murdered? The normal first questions are useless: *Who'll benefit from her death? Did she have any debts?* I got a report on her finances. She doesn't have much money or owe any money."

"What about her family?" Peabody asked.

"Pending. As for Fitzgerald, he has a monthly stipend of just over eight-G."

"Since we're on finances," Eller said, "consider this: Captain Macey owns stock in the corporation that runs the *Islander*. Twenty-four percent. That's a healthy chunk, one worth millions."

Peabody regarded Eller dubiously. "Are you suggesting he'd benefit from Fitzgerald's death?"

"Maybe. Fitzgerald's pro-whale stance is anti-shipping, which could impact ferry profits."

"Enough to get him murdered?"

"Show me a shipping company that supports whale rights or eco-politics of any kind. I can see assassination," Eller went on, "especially for Fitzgerald. I'm not sure about Halliday. She could be collateral damage—to an assassination."

"Don't jump to conclusions," Peabody warned. "Keep an open mind on Macey."

Eller looked offended. "I don't railroad people. Period. Back to the victims. Why are vics usually murdered? Money: greed, bribery, blackmail. But these vics appear to be far removed from money. Both of them drove clunkers, Fitzgerald an old Ford; Halliday, a beat-up Suzuki Aerio. At this point, neither vic shows any debts or any savings. Of course, Fitzgerald's family has money and he had one or two well-heeled habits, like gourmet food. Now, look at the political slant. His whole life has been politics, from the time he was born. Political grandparents and parents. Political work in Boston and D.C. The presidency of RWF, which is fundamentally a lobbying group."

"You disappoint me, Eller. Politics gets you killed? Voted out of office, yes. Jailed for misappropriation of funds. But killed?"

Eller held his fire.

"Politics is a blood sport, I'll give you that, but not the kind of blood we're seeing. Not real blood. That's where the truth lies. Don't get hung up on whales. Fitzgerald was a do-gooder, but did he ram any ships on the high seas? Did he kill anyone? Injure anyone? No to all three." Peabody pursed his lips. "Why would someone murder a young man trying to protect whales?"

"I have no idea," Eller said. "There we go again."

Blue Eyes flashed a grin.

It was an olive branch. Eller accepted it with a smile.

In Bourque's view, Peabody had made some valid points. Promoting whale rights wasn't enough to get people killed. Usually.

"What's the status on the ferry passengers?" Eller asked.

Peabody loosened his tie. "Central has interviewed almost half of them," he responded. "I sent the forensic duo from Central to D.C. I believe you call them the ninjas. Whatever, they're fast workers. They're going to process Fitzgerald's apartment, a one-bedroom near Georgetown University. Bourque, you'll examine the contents when they're done. Okay, let's wrap this up. At the moment, it doesn't make any difference if we're dealing with murders or assassinations, although it might later. We have two dead bodies. Keep looking into the political angle, but just call the deaths murders. I don't want any talk of assassinations. If word of that gets to Boston or D.C., it'll rub some bigshots the wrong way. Scare the hell out of them."

The detectives agreed.

"First thing in the morning," Peabody concluded, "you're both off to Groton, where Fitzgerald's mother is waiting for you. From what I hear, not patiently."

## Chapter 14

### Groton, Massachusetts

Five miles from the New Hampshire border, Eller followed a long driveway to an imposing stone house with a wraparound porch, the residence of Fitzgerald's mother. Bourque had looked her up. Candace Fitzgerald née Hogan was recently widowed. Her husband had died of a heart attack. She was the daughter of a Boston banker descended from prominent Irish-Americans.

Beyond the house, Bourque observed a spacious barn and numerous fenced-in paddocks, one containing a trio of magnificent horses. Unlike on the Cape, the adjacent lots were thickly forested. Old-growth trees ranged in all directions. There was no sign of last night's storm, which had stalled on the coast. Exiting Eller's car, she walked to the horses. The trio wore heavy blankets, the kind normally reserved for winter days. Some people might consider the day a bit cool, but it was autumn chilly, not winter chilly.

In Bourque's eyes, the excessive blankets said over-protective owner. Ergo, possibly an over-protective mother. She peeled off and trailed Eller to the house. Looking past him, she saw an athletic woman standing on the porch outside, irritably holding the door open, as if she'd been expecting them for hours. Her long flowing hair was silver; her nose, as sharp as a ship's prow. She wore a quilted amber-hued jacket and taupe jodhpurs. To Bourque, she fit the mold of female New England aristocracy: horsey yet refined.

"Good afternoon, officers," she said and shook hands superficially. "I'm Candace Fitzgerald, Daniel's mother, but I'm sure you deduced that."

The detectives recited their credentials. "Our heartfelt condolences," Eller offered. "We appreciate you speaking with us."

Mrs. Fitzgerald nodded. "Come in." In contrast to the simple cut of her clothes, she wore huge diamond rings on both hands, as though satisfying a need to display her wealth. "Terribly cold today," she said, then turned away and spoke as she walked. "But I am prone to chilblains. Follow me. We'll sit in the library. There's a fire on the hearth."

Once seated, Eller began. "I believe Captain Peabody talked to you yesterday."

"Yes. My son was murdered."

"We'll do everything in our power to bring the killer or killers to justice."

She didn't respond.

"I'll be very direct, so as to spare you a lengthy interview."

"Good."

"When was the last time you saw your son and where?"

"Here. He came for a visit about a month ago."

"How long did he stay?"

"The usual: two nights. I hardly saw that boy. He came, holed up in his suite, and left."

"Where's his suite?" Eller asked.

"Over the garage. It's exactly as he left it. No one goes in there— ever—his *orders*."

Bourque made a mental note to visit the suite afterward.

"Where did he go when he left?" Eller asked.

Mrs. Fitzgerald waved a hand irritably. "Back to that island of his. As if he were Prospero."

"Prospero?" Eller asked.

Bourque stepped in. "A Shakespearean magician, banned to a deserted island."

Mrs. Fitzgerald sniffed with relief. *Thank God one of you reads.* "Like Prospero, Daniel seemed to think he could control every spirit and element in his world—absolutely everything. One never can. I'll be honest," she continued, "I didn't really know him. I never did, not even when he was younger. Unlike Rory—his sister— he had no set center, no focus." She fervently shook her head. "He wanted to be all things to all people. When he became a right-winger, I just couldn't speak to him. Imagine, a Republican in our family, and, horror of horrors, a Laker crony."

"He didn't last long as a Republican," Bourque noted.

"He didn't?" Mrs. Fitzgerald huffed. "A day would be far too long."

"Let's bury the political hatchet." Eller smiled accommodatingly. "As they say, religion and politics are personal matters."

"Not in this family."

"Be that as it may," Eller said in a mollifying tone, "we'll return to the recent past. Do you know what he was doing on Martha's Vineyard?"

She threw up her diamond rings, the picture of affronted vigor. "How would I? That boy rarely spoke to me—except to ask for money. Scads of it. He was profligate."

Profligate? Bourque thought. Other than a gourmet flair and sixteen sat dishes, she'd seen little evidence of Dan Fitzgerald spending money. The words s*poiled* and *idle* were often used to describe the progeny of old money. They didn't seem relevant in his case.

"Who might know?" Eller asked.

"You can ask his sister. I'll call her in now."

"Not yet," Eller said, maintaining control of the interview. "Did he mention anyone on Martha's Vineyard?"

"No, but he spoke glowingly of a young lady named Ruby Halliday from Orleans. He seemed to be quite taken by her."

"She's dead," Eller flatly stated.

"Dead?"

"Yes. She was murdered last night."

"Murdered? What does that have to do with Daniel?"

Eller let the question hang.

"I take it you think the two are connected?"

He nodded. "Where were you last night?"

Mrs. Fitzgerald's chin went up. "Are you asking me what I think you are?"

"I am."

"That's absurd!"

"I understand your indignation, Mrs. Fitzgerald, yet we have to probe every detail." Eller paused. "You might not want to speak of certain details, but you'll have to. If you lie to us, you'll be prosecuted. I'll repeat my question," Eller firmly said. "Where were you last night between seven and eleven p.m.?"

"I was here."

"Can someone corroborate that?"

"Yes. My daughter Rory."

"Did Ruby Halliday ever come here?" Eller asked.

"Not that I know of."

"Were she and your son a couple?"

Mrs. Fitzgerald threw up her rings again. "I have no idea."

"Who owns the cottage in Chilmark?"

"Daniel did. An uncle bequeathed it to him three years ago."

"Who will own it now?"

Mrs. Fitzgerald raised her shoulders. "Daniel didn't make a will. That boy thought he would live forever. You'll have to talk to our family lawyer, Cullen O'Brien."

"Where were you on October nineteenth between four p.m. and midnight?"

Mrs. Fitzgerald's chin went up again. "I'm his mother!"

"Yes, you are. Family, madam. I'm sure you know how often they're involved in murders."

"I do not."

"In the vast majority of cases," Eller asserted. "I repeat, where were you on October nineteenth between four p.m. and midnight?"

"I was here. Rory can confirm that."

"Anyone else?"

"No. Now it's my turn to ask a question. Why would I kill my son, my only son? Why? We may have little in common, but he was my son."

Eller didn't respond.

"I know what you think. You think I'm heartless. I have to be that way," she insisted and regarded both detectives stoically. "Political families have to maintain a resolute front. That's my job, officers. If your husband dies, if your son is murdered, you have to grieve like a man. Just ask Jackie O'Neal. When her husband was assassinated, she kept her mouth shut about his peccadillos and her head down. I knew her well, Lieutenant. She was kind and gracious."

Eller nodded. "Please call your daughter."

□ □ □

Bourque had looked up Rory Fitzgerald's particulars. She was an unmarried academic who lived with her mother. No sheet, almost no internet presence. At thirty-five, she was two years older than Daniel, her only sibling.

As Rory Fitzgerald entered the library, her mother abruptly left. Bourque evaluated their faces but saw no hints of animosity between the two. The daughter was a stately, buxom brunette, taller than her mother. With her swept-back bouffant and serene demeanor, she appeared to be over forty. Her attire underscored the serenity. She wore an ivory white dress, flowing and floor-length. It rustled gently as she sat.

Eller started the daughter off with his patent introduction. "Detective Lieutenant Eller," he gravely intoned, "State Police Homicide."

Bourque followed suite.

"Our deepest condolences," Eller began. "I'm going to assume you're like your mother: a direct person."

Fitzgerald smiled sagely. "I'm not at all like my mother." Her voice matched her appearance. It was soft and stately. "However, you can speak to me directly."

"Were you close to your brother?"

"Yes. Unlike my mother, I got along well with Dan."

*Dan*, Bourque noted. Mrs. Fitzgerald had called him *Daniel* or *that boy*.

"You don't seem saddened or disturbed by your brother's death," Eller said.

"How can you say that?"

"Just an observation. You can prove me wrong."

"I will. I am sad," she simply said. "Death affects everyone differently, as I'm sure you know, being a homicide policeman."

"Detective," Eller corrected.

"Well, Detective, you know death is not to be denied. We're here at the whim of the gods. I'm a classics scholar, a person with a long view. Death is not a time for hand-wringing. I'd feel the same way about anyone's end, my own included."

Eller changed gears. "Where were you last night between seven and eleven p.m.?"

"I was here, with my mother."

"Just the two of you?"

She nodded.

"Where were you on October nineteenth between four p.m. and midnight?"

"Here, with my mother. And Raphael too. He's my boyfriend."

"Your mother didn't mention him."

"She wouldn't. She never knows when he's here."

"When did he arrive?"

"Two days ago. October nineteenth, about three p.m."

"When did he leave?"

"Yesterday."

"What's his full name and address?"

"Raphael William Fulbright. Ten Berkley Place, Cambridge. He's a grandson of J. W. Fulbright. He's involved in his grandfather's legacy. The European commissions."

More American royalty, Bourque thought. J.W. was the founder of the Fulbright Program, which fostered international relations. Eller made a note in his pad, then signaled for Bourque to take over.

"Did your brother mention someone named Ruby Halliday?" she asked.

"Quite a few times. He said she was both kind and intelligent. He was very impressed by her."

"How long did they know each other?"

"I'm not sure. I gathered it was a few months."

"Did you ever meet her?" Bourque asked.

"No."

"Were Raphael and your brother friends?"

"Yes, with a caveat. They liked each other but didn't share the same interests. Raphael is a classicist like me, a person steeped in the past. Dan studied history yet he favored the future. He was always hoping for better things, be it next year or next decade."

"Did you share any of your brother's interests?" Bourque asked.

"Some. His love of philosophy and literature."

"What about politics?"

"I never understood his politics. I supported some of his crusades but I didn't share them. Don't misunderstand me. I admired Dan. He was a private person, yet he was outgoing as well. He had an Odysseus streak: thoughtful and intense, yet adventurous. To be concise, people liked him."

"Don't worry about concision. Why did people like him?"

"He was easy to talk to. He seemed to have no artifice, which was of course his own kind of artifice."

*Keep going,* Bourque gestured.

"Well, when he got on a roll, he pressed his case, convincing you to join him. On the surface, he was like a quiet pool. Underneath, he was a whirlpool." Fitzgerald shook her head. "He had so many sides, I didn't really know him."

"Your mother said the same thing."

Fitzgerald nodded. "I don't know anyone who really knew him. He didn't let them. I don't think it was a conscious thing. It was just his way. Although he liked people, he usually cared more about influencing them. It was obvious."

"Did it get him in trouble?"

"Yes. He made enemies, although he never mentioned them. He didn't want to acknowledge them. He was braver than he knew."

"Why do you say that?"

"He never shied away from a fight. Although quiet, he was bold." Fitzgerald sighed and closed her eyes. "On the flip side," she said when she opened them, "he was too trusting. He thought everyone would agree with him. I used to try to shield him—my little brother—but I stopped years ago. I couldn't be his guardian angel. No one could. My brave brother, my only brother. So full of promise. You know what I told him the last time I saw him?" Her voice caught. She looked away, then started again. "I said it's time you thought about yourself. You're not good at it, but you have to."

Bourque changed tack. "Why did he go over to the Republicans?"

"Rebellion. To spite our parents. Fact is, Dan didn't agree with much on the GOP side. He could pen a fine right-wing speech but he never liked Laker. He thought she was a buffoon. He came to see Laker's Massachusetts as the epitome of degeneration."

"Do you know anyone we should talk to?"

Fitzgerald answered immediately. "Chase Heaney. He lives in South Boston, although I don't know where."

Bourque pretended they hadn't talked to Heaney. "What can you tell us about him?"

"I never met him but apparently he was a fighter, a man who'd battled his demons and won. Oh, here's another name. Try Dan's ex-girlfriend, Karen Symon, in Cambridge."

"Thank you."

"One last thing. Some of the whale lovers won't really care that Dan's gone, but he didn't expect them to. Although my mother thinks he wanted to live forever, she's wrong. Dan looked upon himself as a passing conduit. He wanted people to push themselves." Her voice took on a tenor of disappointment. "To many of them, he was simply a mirror they used to reflect their own interests."

"And to you?"

"He was a window, not a mirror. Always looking further afield. When he saw some of his Harvard friends succeeding in D.C., he followed them. As it happened, they were all driven to the periphery. It didn't surprise me. Like Dan, they felt a responsibility to better the country, not their wallets. We're in a selfish period, Detectives, but we don't see it. Just as people can deceive themselves, so can countries." She sighed. "Forgive me, it's my scholarly side talking. All nations have times of altruism and times of narcissism, times of progress and decline. Dan didn't want to accept that."

Bourque stood. "Can you take us to his suite?"

□ □ □

Dan Fitzgerald's suite proved to be the opposite of his Lucy Vincent cottage: sparse and modern as opposed to crowded and dated. The walls were white; the furniture, Scandinavian: glass, metal, and wood.

When Eller left to inspect the main house, Bourque meticulously examined the suite. Hours later, she'd found no evidence of a redhaired guest, or any guest. There were no computing devices, whale rights material, or reading lists. On the other hand, there were three floor-to-ceiling shelves holding hundreds of films in digital format. Fitzgerald had a penchant for travelogues, epics, and old westerns.

Bourque systematically pulled each film down and looked for notes within the case, then searched the shelves themselves, probing and sounding. Nothing. She walked away from the suite wondering who Fitzgerald was. Did he have a true self, or was he a Proteus, a shapeshifter? He seemed to be a man of many colors: recluse, political activist; Republican, Democrat; pragmatic rebel, idealistic dreamer. She couldn't criticize that. She knew the compulsion to play all sides or, if not to play them, to comprehend them. She'd rather laugh with people than harass them, rather listen to them than condemn them outright. At the same time, when she was on the job, her cop side came first. In her view, Fitzgerald's protean nature was a potential clue. She needed to determine if, and how, it had led to his murder.

# Chapter 15

Eller sped out of Groton in Indy 500 mode. Like Bourque, he didn't heed speed limits when he was on a case. She sat quietly in the passenger seat, mulling over Fitzgerald's suite. Just as the interior was the opposite of his cottage, so was the exterior. She'd found no web cameras or security measures outside. Perhaps he felt his enemies wouldn't come for him in Groton. In her view, the surrounding forest said otherwise: thick cover, countless ingress points. It would be a good place to stalk anyone.

She turned to Eller. "You wondered why Fitzgerald wasn't killed on the ferry. I wonder why he wasn't killed in Groton. Unlike his cottage, there's no surveillance equipment there."

"Dogs," Eller said.

"I didn't hear any."

"Mrs. F kept them outback. Three German shepherds and a pair of belligerent Dobermans. One raised finger from her and they didn't say boo."

"Forbidding. I mean Mrs. F."

He grinned. "Understatement of the day."

Passing through Westford a few miles later, the detectives stopped at a general store, which reminded Bourque of stores her father had taken her to, old New England establishments which sold everything from zippers to jam, where perishables were refrigerated with lake ice, where the floors were spread with cedar sawdust to absorb the melting ice.

It was another ideal October afternoon: the air, crisp; the sun's heat, mellow. Behind it, though, Bourque could feel autumn intensifying. She and Eller bought shaved ham sandwiches and ate them at a picnic table under a massive linden tree, followed by coffees and generous slices of apple pie. The afternoon trended toward evening. They lingered in the belly of the tree's shadow, drawn by the quiet air, a quality autumn always seemed to confer. The tree rained leaves on them, a cascade of hunter-green sprinkled with yellow-gold. She sipped her coffee, thinking of Fitzgerald. In her experience, there was often something "contrary" with a victim. Most weren't angels. They'd alienated someone. She conjectured

Fitzgerald had. He was wealthy and outspoken. In her mind's eye, she saw him attracting animosity—envy, hate, rage—like a magnet drawing steel knives. By the time the detectives left, the table was covered in leaves.

## Cambridge, Massachusetts

Bourque and Eller reached Boston to find the streetlamps coming on. These days, she didn't get to the city often. To some, Boston was open-minded, even radical; to others, past its best-before date. A lot of people disliked the new Boston. To her, it was the city she'd grown up in. Its urban landscape displayed layer upon layer of New England's past, with tendrils reaching back to the Industrial Revolution and beyond, to the previous Ice Age.

When the detectives exited Eller's car in Cambridge, the moon hung low in the sky, three days past full, still big but no longer blazing. Night could already be felt in the shadows. They were half an hour late for a meeting with Karen Symon, who'd agreed to see them on short notice.

Fitzgerald's ex owned a tall narrow duplex within walking distance of Harvard University, where she was already a tenured Economics professor, a significant accomplishment for someone under thirty-five. While her brick duplex was virtually yardless, it was elegant and well-maintained. The bricks were painted white; the trim, cobalt blue. All told, the antithesis of Chase Heaney's house.

Symon lived in the top unit. When the detectives rang her bell, she buzzed them up and met them at the door. Her height and frank gaze reminded Bourque of Fitzgerald's sister. However, she wasn't dressed like Rory Fitzgerald. The POI wore an azure power suit and a lowcut top which showed her cleavage. While Rory Fitzgerald was stately, Symon was sensual. Another knockout, Bourque reflected. Halliday, Fitzgerald, Symon. Daniel Fitzgerald had been surrounded by tall beauties. In addition to Symon's natural height, she was wearing two-inch heels, which seemed to say *Boys, you've met your match.* They made her taller than most men and well over Bourque's five-foot-seven.

"I think you officers could use a coffee," Symon said.

"I wouldn't refuse," Eller replied. "Milk please, no sugar."

Symon glanced at Bourque.

"Thank you. The same."

Symon ushered the detectives to a plush chesterfield and glided to the kitchen.

Coffee served, Eller began. "Our condolences, Ms. Symon. It must be a shock. I understand you were Daniel Fitzgerald's girlfriend."

She nodded. "We were engaged but we called it off last year."

"Why?"

"It was a mutual decision. We'd been in limbo for years. Dan couldn't settle." She shrugged. "Some men never can."

Too true, Bourque thought.

"Did Mr. Fitzgerald harbor any grudges when you broke up?" Eller asked.

"No."

He studied her intently. "Did you?"

"None at all."

"Did you get along with his family?"

"His sister Rory is a jewel. His parents?" Symon paused. "His parents?" she repeated. "We didn't get along. What can I say about them? What can anyone? His mother's an Ice Queen. His father was too driven. I was at a party in Groton one night where he was greeting guests at the door, kissing all the women full on the lips. Why? Because he could get away with it. That was the Fitzgerald motto: "*Get away with everything.*" Symon shrugged. "To give Dan his due, he tried to move past that. At the same time, although he didn't want to follow in his father's footsteps—you know, ride the family name, embrace traditional politics—he was very political."

"When was the last time you saw him?"

"Christmas, almost a year ago now."

"Did you call or email each other?" Eller asked.

"Not often. Every few months."

Eller signaled for Bourque to take over.

"Was Mr. Fitzgerald seeing new people?" she asked Symon.

"Not that I know of. But Dan didn't talk about that." Symon's facial expression seemed to say he should have.

Bourque followed up on the facial tell. "Did he cheat on you?"

"No. That's what I tell myself." Symon winced. "He was overwhelmed by politics." She smiled sadly. "He lost interest. To be fair, we both did."

"Did he ever mention the name Ruby Halliday?"

Symon shook her head.

"Did he mention any friends on Martha's Vineyard?"

"No."

"Do you know why he was there?"

"No. Another thing he wouldn't talk about. Three summers over there. More of him finding himself, or finding something."

"Did you and Mr. Fitzgerald have a busy social life?"

"The opposite. I admit, I was working hard for tenure then. But he could be a hermit. I'm not exaggerating. He was in D.C. a lot, living in a kind of vacuum. Alone far too much. In the end, he was disappointed by the political classes there. I take that back. He was disgusted by them." Symon raised both hands in frustration. "He had no sense of balance. He claimed they couldn't understand people like him, people with beliefs. Head-in-the-clouds Dan. I tried to tell him government was slow-moving and practical, but he wanted action *now*." Symon shook her head. "I didn't agree with him, yet I can't stop hearing his calls-to-action. There was often such frustration in his voice."

"What attracted you to him?" Bourque asked.

Symon considered her reply. "We seemed to have a lot in common. Nature, travel, adventure."

"What about politics?"

"A sticking point. For lack of a better moniker, I'm a laissez-faire economist. I want governments to keep out of the way. Dan wanted them to regulate and control the economy. But competition is natural. Let species evolve, let market forces evolve. Evolution is the way of the world. As I used to tell Dan, laissez-faire isn't a fad. It's been a leading light for centuries. It's still going strong." Symon paused. "On the other hand, I'm not a purist. Occasionally, governments do need to moderate runaway markets. I admit that. The economy is like a maze. The paths and hedges need to work together. You need both freeways and constraints."

Bourque smiled her *lost-me* smile.

"Okay, enough theory. Dan wasn't a Marxist, but he was well left-of-center, far enough to alienate all of my friends."

"Yet he was also a Republican."

"For a short time. Not long enough, in my opinion. Incidentally, that's when we got along best."

"We're trying to understand all his sides. What can you tell me about him?"

"He was always thinking. Truth is, he did too much thinking. He said this country needed more wise men. He thought he could be one of them. I'm not a liberal arts professor but that's called hubris." Symon sighed. "Most people didn't see his obsessive side. He made personal promises he didn't keep. Yet he always kept his political promises. They came before *everything*. Here's something you need to know to profile him, or whatever you do. Nothing went wrong in his life. Nothing. He decided—he himself—to live a form of sainthood."

Sainthood, Bourque thought. Obviously, Symon didn't know about Halliday and possibly others.

"He wanted to go off-the-grid, be an eco-hero, a Friend of Whales. What about a friend of people?"

"You sound angry."

"I'm not, not anymore."

"Where were you last night between seven and eleven p.m.?"

"Here."

"Can someone corroborate that?"

"Yes, Meryl Verdi. She rents the apartment downstairs. She's at work now. She's a fireman, well, firewoman."

"Did Mr. Fitzgerald know her?"

"No, she just moved in. I'm sure they would have liked each other."

Another alibi to be verified, Bourque thought, and another POI. "Where were you on October nineteenth between four p.m. and midnight?"

"I was with Meryl."

"Again?"

"We're partners."

Definitely another POI to investigate. "When did you meet?" Bourque asked.

"Three months ago."

"What makes you think she and Mr. Fitzgerald would have liked each other?"

"They're two of a kind." Symon smiled ironically. "Dan said what he meant and wanted. So does Meryl. Whether you want to hear it or not. So far, I'm listening."

## Chapter 16

### DAY SIX: Barnstable. October 25th

Bourque entered Barnstable Unit just before 0700. She'd spent the night with Marty and had her usual dawn swim off Bristol Beach. It was almost as if Old Man Winter hadn't made his recent appearance. The water wasn't balmy, but it was swimmable.

Standing on the beach after her swim, she'd closed her eyes and let the ocean come to her, bringing its tang of seaweed and tiny marine life. She'd sensed the constellations following their morning tracks and the earth rotating a fraction of a fraction of a degree longitude. The imperceptible movements calmed her. Physically, she'd felt great. She still did. Mentally, however, the cases were wearing on her. The last two days had been write-offs.

After hoteling in Boston following Karen Symon's interview, she and Eller had divided their workload, to no avail. He'd met with M&M, gone to Ruby Halliday's autopsy in Maynard, and traveled to NYC to interview her university connections, calling on NYPD for help. Bourque had attended Fitzgerald's funeral, joined a slew of meetings at Central, and revisited the Hallidays, questioning neighbors and friends. In Orleans, the victim was known as Ruby Red. It seemed she was a Miss Congeniality type, not an enemy in the world. Bourque took that with a grain. Miss Congenialities always irritated someone. *Why are you so popular? I'm richer than you, funnier, smarter.* Fill in the blank.

The morning after Symon's interview, Bourque dropped in on Fitzgerald's funeral at Boston's Holy Cross Cathedral. Wearing a long black coat and veiled hat, she sat at the back of the church, a commanding building with soaring stained-glass windows and statues depicting the icons of her youth: the Holy Trinity and God's army of ever-present saints. It looked the same as it did when her father took her there years ago. Ensconced in her pew, she surreptitiously watched the ebb and flow of Fitzgerald's mourners, a sparse crowd rendered sparser by the immensity of the church. Given his seclusion and virtual campaigns, the paucity of real-world visitants wasn't unexpected. She counted 101, most of whom appeared to be family. She recognized Candace and Rory

Fitzgerald and a few politicians, including the mayor of Boston. No Governor Laker. After the mass, Bourque overheard a small cluster of people talking about the *curse of the Fitzgeralds*, insisting Daniel's death was foretold. His three politician cousins had all died at sea; the first, when his naval ship was torpedoed in the Pacific; the second, when his sailboat caught fire off Los Angeles; the third, when his car careened off a bridge in Martha's Vineyard and he drowned. And now Daniel Fitzgerald, another famous son of Massachusetts, knifed and drowned in Vineyard Sound. All four, a wizened man insisted, had tried to pull the stars down to earth, to control destiny. *Mark my words,* he opined, *in that family, a terrible desire was born. Not simply for success, but for power.*

Bourque moved on and left the church. Outside, half a dozen paparazzi focused on the grieving mother. *Barely* grieving, Bourque thought as she slipped away. Karen Symon and her beau hadn't appeared, nor had Chase Heaney. No alarm bells. Welcome to life as a detective. Too often, you lurked in the weeds and got nowhere.

At Central later that day, she attended a three-hour IT session. The tech-heads droned on about the throughput of Fitzgerald's network. The data packet destinations and origins were IP addresses all over the world. Nothing to narrow things down. Nothing to substantiate what Fitzgerald was up to. They couldn't pursue that unless they got his computing devices, which Bourque already knew. They'd cracked the encrypted USB recovered from his pants pocket but all it held was reference material: environmental studies, white papers, position papers.

On the plus side, they reported some of Fitzgerald's internet evasion techniques. He falsified his real-world presence, claiming he lived in Uruguay, Israel, South Korea, Hawaii, California, anywhere but Massachusetts. He spoofed his outgoing IP addresses and also cycled through the sixteen different modems, camouflaging his location using dynamic IP addresses. While that didn't preclude the ability to trace him, it made it more onerous. As for Fitzgerald being an IT whiz, he hadn't needed to be one. He'd followed a standard template available on numerous Dark Web sites. Its mantra was one word: *Overwhelm.* Keep attacking your opponent. Don't stop the e-barrage.

Now, sitting at her desk in Barnstable, she booted up her laptop and caught up on the case's forensic reports. The initial DNA returns—blood, hair, skin, body fluids—from the Halliday case weren't promising. Ruby's DNA was found in her room as well as the DNA of her sister and mother, but there was no other DNA, including none from her father.

Bourque forged ahead, this time finding a glimmer of useful news. The knife wounds on both bodies exhibited the same incision characteristics, that of a blade 1.22 inches wide at the top and four inches long, with a curved notch near the top of the sharpened inner side. The pathologist was confident the same knife type was used for both murders, possibly even the same knife. Lastly, she read that the red hairs discovered in Fitzgerald's cottage belonged to Ruby Halliday.

Bourque grabbed her car keys. Ruby Red had been putting on an act.

□ □ □

Bourque sped out of Barnstable Unit to Halliday's friends, Rick and Winnie Reddit. They'd fallen through the interview sieve, which often happened. You started with the victim's family and workmates and then got to the secondary POIs.

The Reddits lived near the center of Woods Hole, where Rick was an insurance salesman. They owned a sprawling old home with a detached stable off the back, now a one-bedroom guesthouse. Assuming Winnie would be at home with young kids, Bourque stopped at Dunkin' and picked up a flat of cookies and two coffees. The second she parked her car in the Reddit's driveway, three small boys ran out of the house, yelling cheerfully. "Miss, Miss, play?"

She laughed and ran after them.

Winnie wasn't thrilled with the cookies. Her look said *they don't need more sugar.* Other than that, she appeared to be glad of the company. Her chestnut-colored beehive and chunky necklace brought to mind a 1950s housewife. On the flip side, her kiwi-green satin housedress said *I'm chic and modern.*

"I'm sorry for your loss," Bourque began at her dining room table. "Just a few questions. How well did you know Ruby Halliday?"

"We were good friends once." The POI's doll-like eyes were large and baby blue; her pretty mouth, painted bright red.

"What happened to your friendship?"

"Along came the Little Rovers. Such is life." She gestured at her boys, who were munching cookies, grinning like goats.

"Did Ruby often stay here overnight?" Bourque asked.

"Yes, many times. The boys loved her."

"How many times this summer?"

"That depends."

"On what?"

"On how you count an overnight visit." Winnie stopped. "I haven't told anyone this. She begged me not to. But, now? You see, one morning a few weeks ago I saw her walk into our back lane around seven a.m. and enter the guesthouse with her overnight bag. We'd given her a key. We kept the place just for her. She did the same thing four days later, arriving around seven, then two days after that. I know she didn't sleep here the last three times." Winnie frowned apologetically. "I wasn't snooping. The boys wanted to go into the guesthouse and I let them. The bed wasn't used. Now she's dead." Her doll-like eyes regarded Bourque uneasily. "So is Dan Fitzgerald. Ruby knew him. Maybe I should have called the police. But Rick said to let it ride."

Bourque didn't comment, wondering if Rick Reddit was in the picture. "Did your husband know Ruby well?"

"No. Ruby and I were friends. He didn't do anything with us."

"Did you call her Ruby Red?"

Winnie nodded.

"Did your husband?"

"No, he's from Plymouth. He didn't know Ruby when she was young."

"How well did Ruby know Mr. Fitzgerald?"

"Pretty well, I'd say. When I confronted her, she conceded she was sleeping with someone. She told me it was Dan Fitzgerald but she couldn't say much yet."

Bourque maintained an even gaze. Inside, her mind was buzzing. That underscored the red hairs at the cottage. It could explain the almost empty condom box. "How often was she seeing him?"

"Two or three nights a week. She begged me not to say anything. Turns out she was staying on Martha's Vineyard with him, taking the small ferry to Woods Hole, which leaves the island at six a.m., and pretending she was staying here. What was she hiding, Lieutenant? Was she in trouble?"

Bourque didn't respond. That can of worms had just been opened. She wasn't surprised that Ruby had lied to her. Plenty of POIs lied to her. It went with the territory: people leading double lives, appearing to be one thing while being something completely different. As Bourque knew, lying was easy. She'd spent years undercover doing it.

"She was spinning other stories too," Winnie said, "but I saw through them. I've known her all my life. Like the one about her car. She said she wasn't driving because it was being repaired. *What's wrong?* I asked. *Brakes*, she said. But the brakes were the only good thing on that car. My brother sold it to her. She eventually admitted she'd left it on the island and walked on and off the ferry. Didn't want anyone to recognize her. I didn't, not at first. She looked like a tourist, one not used to fall weather. She was wearing a long, hooded coat and a bulky winter scarf. Sunglasses too, big owly ones. You couldn't see her hair or much of her face."

"When did she start spinning stories?"

"She always spun stories. This summer, they got dreamier. She was going to be famous soon. Live in a big house, have rich and important friends."

"Nice dreams. Where did they come from?"

Winnie didn't hesitate. "Him. Dan, I mean. She was infatuated with him. She tried to hide it from me but she was gone, girl, gone. Head over heels. Heels behind head. Your call. He was so handsome, so smart, so perfect. I wondered how long would it last." Winnie's face revealed her answer. *It was all fleeting.*

"I'd like to see the guesthouse," Bourque said. "Can you let me in?"

"Sure. I left everything the same."

Perhaps, Bourque thought. She wasn't completely sure of any POIs she'd interviewed. Winnie Reddit was no different. Her timeline and story might check but little things seemed suspicious, for one, her knowledge of Halliday's affair with Fitzgerald. When it came to Halliday's affiliations, Bourque's antenna was up. The shopkeeper's lies clouded an already murky picture. She'd been in Fitzgerald's orbit. Her recent trajectory was close to his. Was she his lover, political partner, or an accomplice to his killer? In any case, it could explain why she was murdered. Ruby Red knew things. She had to be silenced.

In the guesthouse, Bourque headed directly to the fridge. People often hid secrets in freezer compartments. She found nothing in the kitchen. She went to the bathroom to search the toilet flush-tank. Again, nothing. She noticed the guesthouse had forced air heating and unscrewed five grills, searched behind each one, and came away empty-handed.

An hour later, she left the guesthouse. No dark hairs, no potential DNA carriers like toothbrushes, gum, or drink cans. No USBs, computing devices, or clues of any kind. In that respect, the guesthouse was a doppelgänger of Fitzgerald's abodes. Still, she perceived there could be hidden leads. She called in the local whitecoats.

□ □ □

Jasper Halliday's fishing boat swayed gently at a dock off Rock Harbor Road, on the bay side of Orleans, a prime location for chartering. You could fish the calmer waters of Cape Cod Bay or reach the open Atlantic in an hour. The Outer Cape was a resilient land caught between two seas. Bourque had a special affinity for it.

Leaving her car, she took in the morning. The southern sky held a mass of towering clouds. As they shifted and parted, the sun appeared and reappeared, endlessly retinting the bay.

"Permission to come aboard," she called.

Jasper Halliday stuck his head out of the cubby. He ran a refurbished twenty-six-foot Fortier Downeaster fitted with port and starboard trolling outriggers which resembled the wings of a gull. Bourque was familiar with Fortier-26s, seaworthy boats that could easily top twenty knots, the kind of speed that, when needed, got you back to port quickly. "Do you have news?" he asked.

"Yes."

He waved her aboard.

"Fine day," she said. "Going out?"

"Tomorrow."

She studied Halliday. His appearance reflected his profession. Though raised on a winter coast, his face and hands were deeply-tanned. His lithe body carried no spare flesh. He was an intense, hard-looking man. "How long have you been fishing?" she asked.

"Started when I was ten. Switched to chartering five years ago. Listen, from what I hear, you're doing your job. I'm going back to work." He unleashed an infrequent smile. "Got two groups tomorrow, both looking for the offshore experience. Maybe a mess of bonitos or a skipjack tuna."

"That'd be nice."

He nodded. "By the way, I apologize for being touchy a few days ago. Had my back up."

"How many times have you been in Ruby's room recently?"

"I didn't go in there," he quietly said.

"Never?"

"Only when she was young. I used to read to her. We'd talk too, sometimes for hours."

"And recently?"

"Not much. We weren't that kind of father and daughter."

"Did you ever talk about politics?"

"Never. It'd be the last thing we'd talk about. Ruby was aware of my leanings. I'm a conservative, I vote Republican."

"You were political opponents then."

"Opponents? We disagreed, Lieutenant. No big blow-ups from me, no wild tantrums from her. We were two people who agreed to disagree."

"The last time we spoke, you seemed to clash with her over many things."

"I was off-beam that morning. I assure you, we were contrarians, not opponents. As Pam would say, *same fish, different schools*. By the way, she said Ruby and I were both bluefins. We liked to roam, seeking our own ways."

"Do you miss her?"

"More than anyone will know."

"Did you uncover anything on your recent searches?"

He shook his head. "Talked to almost everyone in Orleans. Went up to Wellfleet and down to Chatham too. No one saw anything. No one heard anything."

"Do you think a local killed Ruby?"

"She had no enemies here."

"That seems to be the consensus," Bourque said.

"But not the reality?"

"Can't say yet, Mr. Halliday. Here's my news. It appears Ruby was in a relationship with Daniel Fitzgerald."

"I'm fine with that. Pam told me it might be so. But the relationship itself isn't the news. I can see it in your face."

"You're right. According to recent testimony, Mr. Fitzgerald held some, shall we say, radical views. I'm not saying he was an anarchist but he wanted government to be more hands-on, more protectionist. And we think Ruby was on board with that, although we don't know the extent of her engagement."

"So, she was murdered for going too far to the left?"

"We can't say that. What we can say is that we're looking into it."

Halliday nodded and gestured at the bay. "Want to go fishing?"

She smiled but didn't reply. Many detectives avoided fraternizing with POIs but she didn't pay much attention to that stricture. Having been an undercover op, she knew better. You talked to whoever could help you, didn't matter who they were. Halliday had told her what she wanted to know. In her view, he wasn't off the suspects list, but he was near the bottom of it.

"A quick run," he added. "Striped bass are feeding."

"Thanks Mr. Halliday, but I better get back to the office. The captain's watching. You know captains, always watching."

"Bring him a fish."

She laughed. "He eats the frozen kind."

Halliday grinned. "Then the hell with him."

Exactly.

## Chapter 17

Bourque had barely settled in her desk chair when Peabody stuck his head in her door. "Join me. My office."

She blinked as she entered Peabody's lair. After five years in Barnstable, the chandelier still tormented her eyes. The sapphire drapes didn't help. Eller was standing at the office's double-wide window, sucking his teeth, contemplating the park outside.

With everyone seated, the captain squared his shoulders. "Detectives," he ceremoniously announced, "it's your lucky day. Don't thank me. Thank the ninjas. They returned to Fitzgerald's cottage and found a treasure trove. Blackbeard wouldn't be happier. Bourque, your notes were half-right."

She shrugged.

"Fitzgerald didn't have an underground computer room but he had a small underground storage locker filled with USB drives and computers. Two laptops, to be specific. What's on them, you ask? Patience, mateys. The hardware is en route to Maynard's tech lab as we speak."

"Did they find anything else?" she asked.

"What do you want? Treasure maps?"

"Any smartphones?"

"None," Peabody irritably said.

"Don't think us ungrateful, but phones are as valuable as laptops."

"I know that, Bourque. I was born in September, but it wasn't this September. I also know that if our assumptions are correct, those laptops could blow the case open."

*Our* assumptions, she thought. "Can we switch to Ruby Halliday?"

"Go ahead."

"Halliday was sleeping with Fitzgerald," she related. "We have forensic proof: the red hairs in his bed were her's. We also have a witness statement. When Halliday was supposedly overnighting with a family in Woods Hole, she was actually on Martha's Vineyard with Fitzgerald. She was playing us."

"A liar," Peabody mused. "I've had a lot of experience with liars.

Remember that murder trial two years ago in Hyannis?"

Here we go, Bourque thought. Peabody and his legal stories.

"The defense claimed a person doesn't always know when they're lying. Hogwash, but the lawyers brought in an expert witness from Harvard, a top-tier psychologist. Apparently, if someone concocts a fake story accompanied by vivid imagery and strong emotions, they can convince anyone—themselves and scientists included—that their story is true. There's no foolproof way of distinguishing true from false. Anyone can con a brain scan. Vivid memories produce extensive brain activity whether they're true or not. A story's 'facts' aren't enough." He nodded sagely. "That's why you two need to go beyond statements. I know, I called for depositions in the Fitzgerald case. We need both, depos and DNA."

Eller broke in. "Are you suggesting we can't count on the shipboard depos?"

"We can, to an extent. However, we need more, as in DNA evidence or a confession."

True, Bourque thought.

"All right, back to Ruby Halliday. To paraphrase F. Scott Fitzgerald, *the test of a first-class mind is holding two worlds in your head without giving the game away*. It appears Halliday was doing that—and, from what we now know, was good at it. Of course, she's dead, so no one can examine her memories, but a court case could subpoena her phone calls, journals, or other written material, such as texts. The tech lab has her smartphone. Landon recovered it from her room. I'm hoping for good news." Peabody pursed his lips. "If we find one of the victim's killers, it could lead to the other victim's killer, if not be the other's killer."

Bourque couldn't argue with that.

□ □ □

At the Woods Hole ferry terminal, Bourque and Eller waited in her car for the *Islander* to arrive from the Vineyard. Peabody had dispatched them to depo the crew about Halliday's murder. The afternoon mirrored the morning. The sun wasn't strong. The ocean changed hue with the shifting clouds. Some said the North Atlantic was always grey, but to her it was multihued, a maritime coat of many colors. As she watched, the ferry came into view, its funnel plume streaming to port, signifying a northeast wind.

"I've been revisiting something," Eller pensively said in her ear.

"What's that?"

"That Halliday was a right-wing plant. I don't see it anymore."

"Patience, matey." Bourque grinned.

Eller ignored her. "I went over all of Halliday's interviews. She was a big fan of whales."

"And she was a big liar."

"Remember what her mother said. *Ruby loved whales.* I doubt Ruby would have played her mother. They seemed to be close."

"I don't know which way to go on that."

"Try the simpler way," he said. "It's usually closer to the truth. The right-wing plant is too complicated."

"Maybe. Forgive my skeptical mind. We have two allies, Dan-Dan and Ruby Red?"

Eller nodded.

"Why did she join him?" Bourque asked.

"It has to be for more than the whales. The sex?"

"Of course. Probably both. Seriously, I suspect she knew a lot of what Chase Heaney knows."

Eller agreed. "Meaning she knew what she was getting into. If Fitzgerald's work was as dangerous as Heaney says it was, it looks like she put her life on the line."

"That's a big 'if.'"

"You're hedging today, Bourque. Do you want all the T's crossed?"

She understood Eller's chagrin. To date, they had no flawless leads, yet her organic chemistry training had taught her to seek perfection—to at least seek it, if not find it. In her mind, a murder investigation was like reverse-engineering an organic compound, an idea she hid from everyone, even Marty and Gigi. Organic chemists studied atomic elements that formed compounds. As a detective, she treated murder as a compound and reverse-engineered it, searching for its building blocks, its atomic elements and reactions—i.e., perps and their movements.

□ □ □

Bourque and Eller boarded the ferry and entered Captain Macey's cabin. *Welcome back*, his eyes said.

Bourque was surprised. She'd expected a snarly *you two again.*

"How can I help you, officers?"

"We need to reinterview everyone," Eller replied, "staff and seamen. This time about Ruby Halliday's murder."

"A terrible loss. Do what you have to."

"There'll be no change to your schedule," Eller noted. "We'll interview them as the ferry sails. I understand the giftshop is currently closed. We'll use it. First, Captain, we're going to conduct a formal questioning here, that is, deposition you."

"By all means."

"We'll start by swearing you in as a witness, including recording your full name and address."

After the swearing-in procedure was complete, Eller began. "Lieutenant Victor Eller, Massachusetts State Police. Brock Macey, you are now under oath. How well did you know Ruby Halliday?"

"Not well at all. I hardly ever saw her. She was in the giftshop most of the time."

"Did you ever see or meet her when she was off-duty?"

"No."

"Do you know her parents, Jasper and Pam Halliday?"

He shook his head.

"Please reply verbally."

"No."

"Do you know what she thought of whales?"

"No. I never spoke to her about whales, or anything, really. Just the weather, have a nice day. That kind of thing."

"Brock Macey, according to numerous testimonies, Mr. Daniel Fitzgerald was working to save whales. Does it change your opinion of him?"

"No. Why should it?"

"Please refrain from asking questions. Do you agree with his point of view?"

"Not all of it, but I can understand it. A few days ago, I looked at his website. My grandkids sent me there. Since then, I've been thinking about things from his perspective. I believe we can modify some shipping practices to protect whales."

"How?"

"You sound dubious, Lieutenant."

Eller didn't respond.

Bourque was dubious. Another lying POI? She could see it with Macey, even if he was under oath.

"Slower speeds will help," Macey explained. "Two to three knots out on the Sound can make a difference. It'll give whales and ships time to alter course."

Eller raised an eyebrow. "And that will save whales?"

Macey ignored his skepticism. "Four knots would be better. Right whales don't usually come close to Woods Hole or Vineyard Haven. I think we can help them without impairing people's schedules." He folded his hands. "I've been talking to other coastal zone captains. There are some naysayers, but there's a lot of goodwill. We discussed some of the particulars. It's possible. There's already a NOAA slow-down program."

"NOAA?" Eller asked.

"National Oceanographic and Atmospheric Administration. The program designates speed zones when whale pods are detected in northeast waters. All vessels are asked to slow down to ten knots for fifteen days after a sighting."

"*Asked*," Eller noted. "Then it's voluntary."

"Correct. As for the *Islander*, slowing down might add six or seven minutes to our crossing. Passengers will get used to it. They'll have to." Macey held up a warning finger. "Container ships and supertankers are another matter. It takes them much longer to alter course. As for banning fishing nets in whale feeding grounds, that's an entirely different kettle of fish. Feeding grounds shift with the seasons and migrate every year, sometimes a little, sometimes a lot. It'll be hard to establish net bans."

"Are you going to talk to the Steamship Authority?" Eller asked.

"I already have. If the sea is going to survive, we have to protect it, that includes fish and whales too. In due course, laws have to be updated." Macey held up a finger again. "It'll take a while. I'm not saying everyone will be happy. Some whales will die, they always will. Some environmentalists will get antsy, damage ships and all. I don't abide by that."

Eller stood. "Thank you, Brock Macey. The deposition is now closed."

A few minutes later, the detectives escorted Balan to the giftshop. Open cardboard boxes still littered the floor. Eller shunted them to one side and waved Balan to a stool. He and Bourque remained standing.

"This is a formal questioning," Eller noted. "The law calls it a deposition." Formalities complete, Eller began. "Marius Balan, when did you learn of Ruby Halliday's death?"

"I hear at work three days ago, when I arrive for first departure of day. October two-one."

"What did you hear?"

"Girl in giftshop is dead. She is found at home. Now two murders are connected to ship. That is strange."

"How often did you speak to Ruby Halliday?" Eller continued.

"Never. I am shy to speak to ladies, which I tell some days ago." Balan paused. "All is very strange. Like American people say, is *mystery to me*. Seamen do not like deaths on ship. Is bad luck."

"She wasn't killed on the ship."

"I am meaning death connected to ship. Is not good."

"Did you hear Ruby Halliday speak about whales?"

"No, I do not hear her talk."

"Do you know about Mr. Daniel Fitzgerald's position on whales?"

"I hear things. Some seamen say he has 'newfangled' ideas about law-of-sea. Strange ideas, they explain. *But why kill him*? I wonder. Law-of-sea can be changed. Dead people cannot be made alive again." Balan spoke more fervently. "We can update law. It is why I come to this country. We can compromise. Hard left-wing, hard right-wing, I do not like."

"Where were you on October twenty-first from seven to eleven p.m.?"

"On this ship."

"When did you leave?"

"Ten before midnight."

"Thank you, Marius Balan. The deposition is now closed."

The detectives spent the better part of three crossings deposing the remaining workers. Bourque had to give Eller kudos. Multiple crossings and not a hint of seasickness. However, she couldn't give the two of them any kudos. Their inquiries hadn't uncovered much, only that Sam Carson was off-duty on October 21st. She made a note to drop in on him again.

□ □ □

Back at Barnstable Unit, Bourque brewed a decaf and read Ruby Halliday's autopsy report. Her estimated time of death was 2100. Continuing her reading, Bourque learned Fitzgerald and Halliday appeared to have been murdered with the same knife. The blade reconstructions made from both sets of incisions had exactly the same defect, a long, indented nick starting at 2.28

inches down from the hilt, reaching to 2.55 inches. Both reconstructions had the blade attributes—length, width, thickness, shape—of a folding knife called the Strider SMF, which was created for a Special Ops Marine unit formed in 2003. The Strider had a unique unfolding mechanism, making it very difficult to knock off. Only 300 were initially made, 150 for the unit, 150 for public collectors.

Bourque stopped. All of them had serial numbers which were linked to their owners. Finally, a break in the case. Not huge, but she'd take it. The relatively small number made it possible to track the original owners down. Reading on, she saw Central was already looking into the owners.

She called Peabody. "Got a quick request," she said when he answered.

"Okay, Lieutenant. You can come to my office, you know."

No thanks, she thought. "Just on my way home. You know the Strider knife Central is working on?"

"Yes."

"Get them to check for POIs who are Marines or ex-Marines. Run the October nineteenth ferry passengers as well as any POIs associated with Fitzgerald or Halliday."

□ □ □

At Marty's place, the kitchen table was loaded with Finnish open-faced sandwiches: smoked salmon on crispbread; pickled trout on rye; and silli-kurkku voileipä, being herring and cucumber on rye. Bourque returned for seconds. When food was that delicious, she didn't hold back. After their meal, Marty regarded her with a serious look, one she'd never seen.

"Let's go to the living room," he said.

She followed him.

Once seated, he spoke directly. "I've been offered a job. Editorship at a major publication. Swank office, corporate shares. One problem, a big problem. It's in New York City. I have to be there five days a week. At least."

"What's the publication?" It was all she could think of asking, not when he'd be leaving, not for how long, not would he ever come back to Falmouth.

"Can't tell you. If I do, you'll tell me to take it. They're that big. *Jump on a plane*, you'll say, *and kiss their corporate asses*. I'm not sure I want to." He waited. "Aren't you going to ask me why?"

"Why?"

"You, Ivy. You! I don't want to leave."

"You have to take it. You've been working for this. It's your time."

"What about our time?"

"We'll be fine," she said, although she didn't feel it. Her stomach was roiling. She didn't want to lose him.

"I have to tell them tomorrow," he added.

"You've been sitting on it?"

He nodded.

"Then sleep on it." She kissed his cheek. "Whatever you do, we'll be fine."

A heartbeat later, she grabbed his hand and led him to the bedroom. Before his clothes were off, her phone-ringer was off— something she rarely did with homicides on the boil. If Peabody wanted her, he'd have to drive to Marty's house and knock the door down. Even then, she wouldn't go.

## Chapter 18

**DAY SEVEN: Barnstable. October 26th**

The next morning, Marty leaned against Bourque's car as she pulled out her swimming gear. He had the same look in his eyes as last evening. "I decided," he said.

She felt sick to her stomach again, but smiled. *Tell me.*

"I'm going to refuse the job. How can I leave this?" His eyes swept his property, crossed the road to the beach, then came back and stopped on her. "It's you. I can't leave you. Can I ask you something big?" He smiled. "Don't worry, I won't pop the question."

He knew she didn't want to get married again.

"Can you spend more time here?" he asked.

Could she? "Of course. Lots more."

"Another thing, a small thing. I want us to eat healthier. Can you eat less sweet stuff? Cut out the muffins, that kind of stuff." He saw the look on her face. "I mean, cut *back* on the muffins."

Was she getting fat? "My wetsuit still fits. Doesn't it?"

"It sure does." He grinned. "It's not that. I'm, well, taking the long view. For our future, for our family."

"I'm with you." Wait, *our family.* Was he asking her about getting pregnant? "Are you hinting at something?"

He nodded, serious again.

"Is it what I think it is? *Moi*, the big-bellied lady?"

"If you want, when you want."

"I want. We'll talk when later."

He bounced off the car and kissed and hugged her.

□ □ □

Bourque crossed the road to Bristol Beach, thinking *when?* In a few months? Three? Four? Stop. Could she even get pregnant? She was thirty-nine. Then there was her career. Could she take time off? What would happen to her job? She loved it. She'd have to convince Marty to keep quiet about a baby until she was pregnant. Female cops who took maternity leave often got lost in the shuffle, even after they came back to work—especially after, in some units. She wasn't sure what Peabody's reaction would be.

A cold current had stirred up Vineyard Sound, making it too chilly for a swim. She watched shearwaters skim across the face of the sound, dipping and pivoting, cavorting with the waves. She wanted to keep watching them. They were as free as the wind, not a mating decision to make. But work called. When you had a double murder on your hands—not to mention, a Peabody in your office—gamboling shearwaters took a backseat. Mating decisions too.

□ □ □

Sitting at her desk with an open laptop, Bourque saw the tech team had cracked one of Fitzgerald's computers and uploaded the file folders to the case database, to the tune of 3.2 gigabytes. The techies had identified two folders for her to look into immediately, about fifteen percent of the total data: *Avatars* and *Posts*.

*Avatars* contained twenty-six Excel spreadsheets. By late morning, she'd uncovered the scope of Fitzgerald's social media presence. It numbered 421 accounts. Its structure was Byzantine. One account was linked to multiple secondary accounts, which in turn were linked to others. He'd started by creating email accounts on services like Hotmail that allowed him to add aliases to each email account, which were then used to open social media accounts on sites like X/Twitter, Instagram, Snapchat, etc.

The spreadsheets included account names or, as he labeled them, avatars; passwords; two-step authentication parameters; profile photos and background info; as well as links to posts in Word documents which contained text, images, and video clips. There were also links to profile photos: whales, trees, or birds, but never people.

Moving on, she established *Posts* held hundreds of Word docs with the text of social media posts, the docs categorized by week posted and topic, which included Atlantic Right Whales, Pacific Right Whales, Whales at Large, Appalachian Trail, Climate, and Karri Laker. In three years, Fitzgerald and his avatars had uploaded 148,000 posts. Bourque was astonished. Almost 150,000 social media posts.

An hour later, she discovered he'd used scripts to automate the process of replicating posts, thereby disseminating the same content from 400-plus accounts. The replication scripts had been coded by two software engineers in India. She found Fiver invoices for their services. Despite the automated help, she was still astounded. Fitzgerald had been relentless. Many of his accounts had thousands of followers, some of whom he'd bought. There were invoices for follower-brokers in Asia and Africa. All told, she learned Fitzgerald and his proxies had roughly a quarter-million followers. If 10% of them made just one repost over time, he'd blasted the virtual-verse with almost four billion posts: 25,000 followers times 150,000 posts equaled 3.75 billion. She needed a walk.

Bourque grabbed her jacket and left the unit. The sun was well past its zenith; the sky, autumn blue. She felt like walking for miles, leaving the virtual-verse behind. Instead, she strolled to a nearby Dunkin', grabbed a sandwich, and sat inside thinking about Fitzgerald and his massive e-progeny. A drop in the virtual sea, some might say. Not her. What word would describe Fitzgerald? *Fanatical? Dedicated?* He'd certainly been steadfast.

Back in her office, the numbers told Bourque that Laker was Fitzgerald's leading cause. He and his avatars had uploaded almost 29,000 posts on the governor. Bourque scanned through them.

#Laker is ILLOGICAL, ILLITERATE & INCOMPETENT.
#Republicans Against #KarriLies
Anyone with #Laker is against #Massachusetts

@GOPMassChairwoman @GOPMass
Be advised. You hitched your wagon to an ASS. You're going down in #NovElections.
#Republicans Against #KarriLies. Anyone with #Laker is against #Massachusetts

Here's a fact, #Laker. I'm a lifelong #Republican but I have no confidence in you.
You're a useless idiot. #VoteKarriOut.

Bourque sat back. On and on it went, which brought to mind another thing her father used to say about politics. It was usually boring and always repetitive. She wondered if any of the posts would make an impression, as in turn voters away from Laker in next month's election. The tone was taunting but, to Bourque, it didn't seem overly aggressive. However, she wasn't sure about the legal ramifications.

She decided to call her buddy Gigi. They'd done their detective training together. Gigi, a brainy dynamo, soon went to the big leagues—the FBI—which everyone knew was going to happen. These days, the two only saw each other once or twice a year, when Gigi got home to Boston for a few days off.

"Hi Gee, it's your State Police buddy."

"Borky, great to hear from you!"

"Where are you these days?"

"LA, but that's top secret."

Bourque laughed. "I won't ask where."

"Malibu. Beaches are dens of iniquity."

"That's why I love 'em."

Gigi chuckled. "I think I know what's on your plate. Two murders. Fitzgerald and Halliday."

"Yep." Of course Gigi knew. Wherever she was, she always had an eye on Massachusetts. "How's Love-in-the-Sun?" Bourque asked.

"Met a surfer."

"Nice."

"With the mental capacity of a rock."

"And the physical?"

"Reasonable."

"Gotta pick your brain, Gee. It seems people can post anything online as long as they don't threaten someone. Here's a question for you. Nationally speaking, has anyone committed murder in reaction to hostile posts?"

"Not that I know of, Borky, but the Bureau doesn't prosecute many e-threats. The line between them and venting is hazy. Free speech, the First Amendment."

"Can you look into it and get back to me?"

"Sure."

"Thanks." For months, Gigi had been talking about quitting the FBI and joining the Staties in Massachusetts. "Any closer to leaving the dark side?" Bourque asked.

"Nah. Every time I'm ready to print the resignation letter, the boss gives me a star. That's how they keep you engaged and happy. Just like Kindergarten."

"Ask for champagne instead of stars."

"Good point. A case of champagne."

"Next time you're in Boston, we'll behead a Jeroboam."

"Absolutely!"

Bourque signed off thinking that while she'd definitely behead a Jeroboam, she wouldn't be drinking much of it, not if she were pregnant. She knew she had to keep quiet about her plans with Marty but she'd wanted to tell Gigi *now*. Really wanted to.

Bourque sighed, went back to work and scanned more anti-Laker posts. She encountered a lot of semi-violent ones, talking about sticking Laker's head in a dunny. Others promised to toss her in a pigsty. Bourque figured some lawyers would claim the pig posts had harmful intent. Pigs ate humans. However, she read nothing about explicit bodily harm, nothing about assassinating anyone. From what she'd seen so far, Fitzgerald and his avatars were relatively tame. Then she opened a document with posts from two months ago.

#Laker, you're reprehensible. You deserve to die.
Get out of the #MassStateHouse or Die!

#GovLaker, keep up the stupidity and you'll be eliminated.
SERVE #WeThePeople or DIE. Anyone with #Laker is a #Traitor

I warn you, #Laker, #resign before you're eliminated.
I've had enough of you. #Patriots Against #Laker. Get out of #Massachusetts!

#Laker, allow me to introduce myself. I'm your worst #nightmare. I'm the #Devil.
Here's what's coming for you: #TheEnd.

Bourque shook her head. Now the knives were out, the last one with a Rolling Stones reference, a nod to Lucifer in "Sympathy for the Devil." She stared out her office window. Beyond the building, far to the west, the evening sky ate the sun, swallowing the dying light. She'd seen enough for the day. As she powered off her laptop, her phone crooned "Watching the detectives—"

"Lieutenant Bourque," she answered, "Cape and Islands."

"Eller here. You hungry?"

"What's on deck?"

"Fishcakes at Trident."

□ □ □

The fishcakes were excellent. Bourque ate a huge plate with a side salad in lieu of fries. Goodbye fries. Muffins and croissants were another thing. After downing a fishcake appetizer and a jumbo fishcake main, Eller joked he wanted fishcake pie for dessert. He wiped his mouth with a napkin and eyed her. "I can tell you're still in work mode."

She nodded and leaned forward. "Vic Number One was a social media machine. We're talking a hundred-and-fifty thousand posts."

"Is that a lot?"

"With all his followers and reposts, the number could be four billion. But it's the way he was doing it. He was over-the-top. Heaney said Fitzgerald wanted to eliminate Governor Laker virtually. Well, his posts weren't sticking to the virtual. They talked about actual elimination."

"Did he call for killing in plain English?"

Bourque shrugged.

"I take it we have a grey area. Sticks and stones will hurt my bones, bombs and bullets too. But names will never hurt me." Eller shook his head. "You youngsters—not that you're that much younger than me—you have to take your Net with a scoop of salt, not a grain."

"I'd like to agree with you. But I'm forwarding his posts to Legal."

Eller nodded. "Got an interesting tidbit. Macey's wife owns sixteen percent of the Steamship Authority. His brother happens to own another twelve. Between the three of them, they own fifty-two percent. Controlling interest. Now, we can take a positive view and say that'll make it easier for the company to slow down their ferries, thereby helping whales. On the other hand, we can look at Macey as a bullshitter trying to cover his tracks. If RWF succeeded, Macey's ferries could be severely hampered. The company's value could plummet."

"That's a big *could*," she said. "Are you ordering dessert?"

"Of course." Eller put on a serious face. "I want to ask you something." He gestured at the kitchen. "Do you know what kind of flour they use for their fishcakes?"

Bourque shook her head.

"All-porpoise."

She groaned.

"Just trying to keep up with Donnelly. How about some pumpkin pie?"

"Done." And a two-mile swim first thing in the morning.

## Chapter 19

### DAY EIGHT: Barnstable. October 27th

Bourque didn't have time for a two-mile swim the next morning, let alone a mile. Marty woke her before dawn and kept her in bed until well after sunrise. She reached her office at 0830 to find Peabody sitting in her chair.

"You on holiday, Bourque?"

She smiled accommodatingly.

"Late night?"

She smiled again. She was in a good mood. Peabody, on the other hand, wasn't. There was no leniency in his blue eyes today. He rose and stood next to her desk. His pants were sharply pressed. The creases looked like knife blades. "Did Fitzgerald's files tell you anything?"

"Yes. And I'm just getting started."

"Update me at thirteen-hundred. Where's Eller? I thought he was sharing your office."

"He is," she lied, "but he also works from his hotel room."

Peabody shook his head. "He shouldn't be at a hotel. Damn it, he thinks Central mints money."

"It's a long way to his place in Holyoke."

"When I was a gumshoe, we drove hours to get home. Never stayed in a hotel unless we were working out of state."

She held her tongue. And gas was ten cents a gallon. Well, maybe a buck.

When Peabody left, she made herself a decaf in the staffroom and continued investigating Fitzgerald's file folders. The majority of the data proved to be videos and photos affiliated with his posts. There were a lot of whale pics. She switched to skimming his posts again. The more recent they were, the more inflammatory they were, particularly those from the past month. She found thousands of additional posts with the words *eliminate* and *die* and hundreds with references to the #Devil.

Two hours later, Bourque decided it was time to revisit Heaney. No one seemed to know more about Fitzgerald's virtual "warfare." She shut down her laptop and entered Peabody's lair.

"I need to go to Boston," she told him.

"You'll be back tonight?"

She nodded.

"Any farther ahead with Fitzgerald?"

"Far enough to know I need help."

## Boston

In the wan afternoon light, Heaney's tumbledown house looked more derelict than six days ago. A cold wind snapped at a tattered bedsheet drying on the porch. To Bourque's eye, the sheet appeared in need of another wash. Next to it was the purple hoodie Heaney had been wearing on their first visit. Intending to catch him off guard, she hadn't called beforehand, figuring the best way to get intel from him was to arrive without warning.

He opened the front door wearing the same neon cargo shorts, this time topped by a lumberjack shirt.

"Detective B. To what do I owe?"

"Just in the neighborhood."

"Right."

"No hoodie today?"

"Had to wash it. I feel off. I always wear that hoodie. Can't leave home without it." He smiled. "My wife gave it to me."

"Brought you a coffee. Let's have a chat."

"Am I a suspect in Dan's murder?"

"Of course."

"I should say *still* a suspect." His voice sounded rougher than on her previous visit. It was deep yet muted, like a foghorn coming from miles away. "I knew what you figured when I told you I was facetiming my wife and daughter: I could do that anywhere."

Bourque nodded.

"I take it you requisitioned the video chat file."

"In progress."

"The wheels of justice. Round and round like a wonky top."

She shrugged.

"You'll find the location tag on my end is right here, in Southie."

As he'd done previously, Heaney led Bourque to the living room and sat in a highbacked rocker. Given the wan afternoon and closed drapes, the room was darker than six days ago. She sat on the sofa and watched him gently rock, letting her eyes adjust to the dimness.

"Do you know a woman named Ruby Halliday?" she asked.

"No, but I follow the news. She's dead. Apparently, she was connected to Dan."

Bourque nodded. "Well connected."

Heaney shook his head. "That's not good."

"Do you know about your friend's sat dishes on the Vineyard?"

"Yeah. He had a lot of them."

"Sixteen," she said.

Heaney stopped rocking. "Sixteen?" He whistled. "Last time we talked, he had eight."

"When was that?"

"When I last saw him, April eighteenth."

Bourque studied Heaney's lips. Full and relaxed. He appeared to be telling the truth. "What were the dishes for?"

"The social media campaigns I told you about." Heaney started rocking again.

"Your friend was more incendiary than you suggested. He was running wild on social media." She reached out with a four-page printout.

Heaney leaned forward and took it, putting the brakes on his rocking. After reading the posts, he looked up. "That's the new Dan-Dan, the one who liked to say 'hit them with the heavy artillery.' Nice Stones quote: *Allow me to introduce myself.* He's channeling Lucifer. Did you get that?"

"Yep."

"Makes sense. You have to fight a devil with a devil. Can't send in an angel. From what I read, I'd bet those posts are just the beginning."

"I take it you're not surprised."

"I'm not, but I am." Heaney raised his shoulders. "I realized he was going in hard but I didn't think it was that hard. In a sense, it was inevitable. Dan-Dan saw himself as a pending failure. He wasn't from the great or even the good generation. Sure, he worked for good, but that was in Central America, where his role was pragmatic, not political. He ran water pipes and worked with farmers. He didn't build coalitions. In one sense, he was okay with that. He liked outposts."

Bourque wasn't surprised to hear that. "Did he talk about his family's past?"

"The illustrious Fitzgerald past? Not often. He claimed it wasn't much of a past. Said his family wasn't special. They were all bog Irish five generations ago. Not exactly true, I can tell you, yet they weren't much higher up the social ladder. Rurals emigrants from Wexford and West Ireland, fleeing the potato famine. Like my people. Another thing, perhaps minor but valid. Dan was schooled by Catholics, as I was. Indoctrinated in saintliness."

Saintliness again, she reflected, echoing Symon's view. Saints weren't necessarily paragons of virtue. George Orwell, among others, considered them guilty until proven innocent. Fitzgerald had to have a bad habit or three. "What were his vices?" Bourque asked.

Heaney laughed and kept laughing, a laugh that could swallow the sun. "Vices, B? I believe a Victorian wit put it this way: *What's a vice? A taste you don't share.* Seriously, Dan didn't have any. Unless red wine and meat are vices. In moderation, of course. That was Dan-Dan. Personal moderation. But professional excess. In the Middle Ages, he'd have been a self-flagellating wanderer. In the years I knew him, he never talked about his good deeds, only about his flaws. He was too hard on himself." Heaney shrugged. "On the other hand, self-criticism isn't a bad thing. Think of all those power-crazed fools trying to take over the world. They never look inside themselves. Dan-Dan had plenty of self-restraint. But you're on the right track. Look into his ethics. After his Catholic youth, he was trapped in an obsolete value system, a Yankee gentleman's code, courtesy of Harvard. Keep your nose to the grindstone. Don't look up, don't think of yourself." Heaney paused. "You get the picture. Your work is important, not you. In short, you put others first *all* the time. Which sounds laudable, but you have no balance."

"No center," she said, recalling a remark by Fitzgerald's mother. "Do you think his dedication made him vulnerable?"

"Dedication always does. I've been thinking about things. By putting his work first, he pushed himself to the brink—and over it. That's the way I see it. In essence, he killed himself. I'm not saying by suicide, yet he set out on a path that got him killed."

"Why did he ramp up things recently?"

"Any number of reasons. On the Laker file, I'd say it was now or never. Dan-Dan wanted to influence the upcoming election. On right whales and the environment as a whole, I'd say he was fed up with waiting for government action."

"Any idea who wanted to kill him?"

Heaney didn't reply. He started rocking again. "There could be a few entities," he eventually replied. "Laker's people, pro-whaling groups, rabid anti-ecology types. Who knows? Maybe someone he collaborated with, although he told me he kept his plans private. He rarely talked about his work. Just wondering, was Ruby Halliday a political friend?"

Bourque didn't answer. That remained to be seen.

"For such a secretive man," Heaney mused, "he was strangely trusting. *Beware of infiltrators*, I used to tell him, *remember the Russian Revolution*. The true revolutionary, Trotsky, was ousted by the heartless manipulator, Stalin. The movement's ideals were quashed. The people were abandoned."

"What about Mr. Fitzgerald's allies? People like you, for example. Are you in danger?"

"Me? Not a chance. I'm not even a small potato. I'm a pea. I haven't done anything remotely aggressive recently."

"What about your crew?"

"I have no idea."

Bourque was beginning to dislike those words. They still epitomized the team's position.

"All I know," he added, "is that Dan went ballistic. Bazookas to a fistfight."

"Would fists take Laker's people down?"

"Good point. Nonetheless, if Dan were still listening to me, I'd have told him to tone it down."

"Would he have done it?"

Heaney stopped rocking. "Not likely."

"Thank you for your time, Mr. Heaney."

"Am I off the hook?"

She smiled but said nothing.

## Cambridge

Leaving Southie, Bourque decided to drop in on Karen Symon and arrived in Cambridge shortly after five p.m., supper time in New England. As a girl, many nights she'd eaten fish with potatoes accompanied by her mother's two exotic spices: salt and pepper. Every Saturday, it'd been baked beans and homemade brown bread. And it was good. What the food lacked in oomph, it made up for in freshness and sustenance.

Now, as she climbed the stairs to Symon's upper apartment, Bourque caught the scent of roasting chicken infused with rosemary and garlic.

"Lieutenant," Symon said as she let Bourque in, "you're just in time for dinner."

"Thanks, but I'm in and out. Brevity is my name. You two enjoy your dinner," Bourque gallantly said, channeling Columbo.

Symon was sporting a tank-top and yoga pants with flat heels. A striking woman appeared behind her. The woman's skin glowed, her long blonde hair was tied back in a ponytail. She wore a tight lemon-colored track suit which highlighted her physique. She had the body of a female martial artist: strong but not overdeveloped shoulders; ditto for her arms and thighs.

"Lieutenant," Symon said, "this is Meryl Verdi. Meryl, Lieutenant Bourque. She's on Dan's case."

"A few quick questions," Bourque began, "and I'll be off." She'd looked up Verdi. Late-thirties, born and raised in Boston's North End. Before becoming a firefighter, she'd done four years in the Marines, two in Afghanistan.

"Okay," Symon replied, "we'll sit in the living room. A soda, Lieutenant?"

"No thanks." Bourque had two potential leads on Verdi: her Marines connection and her current job. The POI hadn't been part of Special Ops Detachment One but in 2006 she'd been stationed near Kabul Airport, where Special Ops Det One was based, giving her opportunity to acquire a Strider knife. Additionally, as a firefighter, she was a shift worker. She had multiple days off at a time after completing twenty-four-hour shifts.

Sitting across from Verdi, Bourque scrutinized Symon's partner. There were certain people who seemed doubly present in a room. Verdi was one of them. It was as if there was the eye-catching blonde and another version of her, a quiet, strong woman controlling the room. She had the bearing of a soldier who'd done time in warzones—relaxed yet alert. Bourque addressed her. "Where were you on October nineteenth between four p.m. and midnight?"

"Here. With Karen."

"I told you that," Symon peevishly said.

Continuing her Columbo act, Bourque feigned forgetfulness. She was getting good at it. "Apologies. Mind like a sieve." She turned to Verdi. "How long have you known Ms. Symon?"

"Lieutenant," Symon interrupted, "we went over that."

Bourque held up a hand. "For the record."

"Two months and fourteen days," Verdi replied.

"Oh? Ms. Symon said three months."

Symon exhaled. "Two-and-a-half months, three months. Does it matter? I think you're badgering us."

"It's all right, Karen," Verdi said. "We have nothing to hide. I'll tell her whatever she wants to know. Have at it, Lieutenant."

"How long have you known Ms. Symon?"

"We met three months ago. We got together two weeks after that."

"Can anyone other than Ms. Symon corroborate your whereabouts on the night of October nineteenth?"

"No. We didn't go out," Verdi explained, "which is usual. We're both homebodies. I'll be totally honest about Dan Fitzgerald. He wasn't good for Karen. Everyone who knows her knows that. They weren't friends in the end, that's a fact. But she didn't kill him."

"Did you?" Bourque asked.

Verdi balled her fists. "You're badgering me now."

"You said you'd speak."

"All right. I'll lay it on the line. I'll tell you exactly what I think. He didn't do right by her and yet she loved him. In a way, she still does. She'd never kill him or do him any harm."

Symon nodded and leaned forward to speak.

Verdi waved her back. "He kept her in limbo for years. He only thought of himself and his grand schemes."

"It's true," Symon said. "Ask his own mother. He could be a beast."

"And yet," Bourque said, "the last time we spoke, you claimed you didn't hold any grudges."

"I don't."

"But now he's a beast."

"I didn't want to say anything bad about him last week. He'd just died."

Bourque turned to Verdi. "Do you hold any grudges against him?"

"No. Why would I, Lieutenant? That's all in the past. *La Fine.*

The End."

Maybe, Bourque deemed. Two or three months wasn't far in the past.

## Chapter 20

### DAY NINE: Barnstable, October 28th

Peabody called Eller and Bourque into his office just after 1000. As she sat, she shut out the chandelier and drapes. The maroon walls were impossible to banish. Somehow, she'd come to accept them.

"I have news," Peabody said in his rushed voice. "We have a lead on a POI originally from Orleans. He's a known confidence man. Bilks families of college funds and life insurance. He's used four aliases in the last seven years. Currently goes by the name of John Paul Jones, the so-called father of the American Navy. He often preys on mid-ranking naval officers. The J. P. Jones moniker should warn them off." Peabody shook his head. "Too many gullible people. His real name is Jack Irvine. He's a twenty-eight-year-old nightclub bartender working in Plymouth. He has a long sheet: multiple charges of fraud and robbery, three fines, one jail term. Why is he in our net?"

The detectives remained silent.

"He was on the *Islander* on the night of October nineteenth. His alibi for Fitzgerald's murder checked. He was with two other passengers. However, there's new intel. When Halliday was murdered, Central started reexamining every *Islander* passenger. HQ just posted a rider that Irvine is an ex-boyfriend. But that's not it," Peabody divulged. "After she broke up with him two years ago, the court issued him with a restraining order. That's the appetizer, detectives. Our tip line got a call last night from one of Halliday's acquaintances, a young woman named Carolina Pereira, twenty-seven, also from Orleans. Ms. Pereira is sure Irvine had something to do with Halliday's murder. She's in Interview Room Three."

□   □   □

Eller and Bourque entered Room Three to find Pereira sitting restlessly at the table. She wore Doc Martens, ripped blue jeans, and a skin-tight white T topped by a black leather jacket cropped at the waist. The T showed exactly what was under it. No bra,

Bourque noted. Pereira's hair was darker than the jacket; her irises, sea blue. Bourque looked again. The eyes were likely fake, not that most men would care.

Eller introduced himself and Bourque and started the POI off. "Thank you for coming in, Ms. Pereira. I understand you knew Ruby Halliday."

"I know Jack better."

"Jack Irvine?"

"Yeah."

"That's not what he calls himself now."

"I know. His latest handle is J. P. He's had a few handles."

"Do you know why?"

"I have some idea. But that's not why I'm here. Can I get to that?"

"Sure. Go ahead, Ms. Pereira."

"I saw him a few days ago at his place in North Chatham. Seventy Old Wharf Road," she added. "From what he told me, Ruby had it coming to her. Her murder, I mean."

"*Coming to her*? Are those his exact words?"

"Yeah. They'd had a bad breakup. She ratted him out. He ended up doing time: eighteen months. Not much, but Jack is a free spirit. He was stewing when he got out."

"When was that?"

"Four months ago. I know him. He was scheming the whole time he was in there. He wanted revenge."

"What kind of revenge?"

"Can't you read between the lines?"

"I can, but juries can't or, to be more correct, they don't."

Pereira sniffed. "Okay. He wanted to kill her. Like I said, I know him."

Eller gestured to Bourque.

"Did you ever go out with Mr. Irvine?" she asked Pereira.

"Yeah. A few years ago."

"Were you and Ruby friends?"

"Not really, not recently that is."

"Did you call her Ruby Red?"

"Only in junior high." Pereira spoke as if recalling ancient history. "We had the same friends, same hobbies too. Dancing, roller skating. Boys."

"What can you tell me about her?"

"Ruby had her own mind. Jack tried to boss her around. He was bad for her. He's a first-class manipulator."

"Did he manipulate you?"

Pereira tossed her hair. "No."

"Why are you talking to us?"

"Christ. Because I want to help." She eyed Bourque. "Do you think I'm ratting Jack out for fun? I told you, he might have killed her."

Bourque didn't respond.

"I don't get you. I know cops don't trust me but I'm helping." She huffed. "Maybe you think I still like him, so I was jealous of Ruby? Maybe you think *I* killed her?"

"Where were you on October twenty-first between seven and eleven p.m.?"

Pereira sighed. "Plymouth. I dance at Romeo's on Tuesdays."

Bourque knew the spot, a peeler joint on the south side of Plymouth. "How can you be sure he wanted to kill her?"

"Christ! Cops are supposed to be slow, but—"

"You're right, Ms. Pereira, we are." Bourque smiled. "Help us. What makes you so sure?"

"His temper. Jack seems to be *so* in control, but he's not. I've known him for years. Our family lived near his in Orleans." Pereira hesitated. "If you cross Jack Irvine, he comes for you."

"Did he ever come for you?"

"I didn't cross him. Well, not until now."

◻ ◻ ◻

Eller pulled his Ford off Old Wharf Road in front of Number Seventy. Bourque sat in the passenger seat methodically surveying the area. A prosperous neighborhood, well-manicured lawns, upscale beach houses. Irvine rented an elongated ranch with a wide front deck. No garage. One car in the drive, a dark BMW sedan. She ran the plate. Registered to Irvine.

Peabody had just sent an update on his file. Irvine's DNA wasn't found at the site of either Halliday's or Fitzgerald's murder. On the felon front, he had a reputation for being a good subordinate. He was known to be connected to a long-time gangster named Marcus Aldo who ran financial scams throughout New England. Bourque suspected Irvine could be another accomplished play-acter, like Ruby Halliday.

Eller rolled up to the driveway, blocking off the POI's car. They didn't care about secrecy. On the contrary, they wanted Irvine to see them and wonder what was coming his way. Bourque unhurriedly followed her partner to the front door. While he stood to the side with his handgun drawn, she knocked twice.

A big young man came to the door. At close to six-feet-two and 220 pounds, he was both loose-limbed and muscular. "Are you J. P. Jones?" she asked.

He nodded.

"What about Jack Irvine?"

He shrugged.

"Which do you prefer?"

"Doesn't matter."

"We have a few questions about Ruby Halliday."

In the living room, Irvine sat nonchalantly in a La-Z-Boy chair. His eyes were hazel; his sleek brown hair, short. Despite his physicality, he had the face of a confidence man: attractive and friendly.

"I'm Detective Lieutenant Bourque," she began, "State Police."

"Afternoon, Detective," he pleasantly said.

"Detective Lieutenant Eller," her partner stated, then gruffly added. "Homicide."

Irvine didn't react.

"Let's start with the obvious," Bourque said. "Ruby Halliday was recently murdered. You're an ex-boyfriend, which makes you a suspect. Fill us in, Mr. Irvine. Why were you served with a restraining order?"

"We had differences," he casually replied.

"What kind, Mr. Irvine?"

"The usual. She was good and I was bad."

"I understand people called her Ruby Red. Why?"

"Because of her hair. Well, most of them. Not me. She had a temper. I swear, her eyes would go fire-engine red. Everyone thought she was a Goody-Two-Shoes. But she was always a conniver. She got away with murder. *Murder.* I wouldn't be surprised if she killed that Fitzgerald guy."

"When did you start renting this house?" Bourque asked.

"May."

"Why so close to Ruby Halliday's home?"

"Close? It's twenty miles away. By the way, my restraining

order is for five-hundred feet."

"Did you like to watch her?"

Irvine snorted. "I came here to party with friends. New friends."

"Given the restraining order, I take it you and Ruby had a bad breakup. Why?"

"She set me up."

"Elaborate."

"There's not much to say. I did time for it. But you know that."

"We do, but we don't know why she called the police."

"Neither do I."

Bourque waved Eller in.

"I think you know," he told Irvine.

"You can think what you want. Guess is more like it."

"I don't like to guess. I prefer facts," Eller evenly said. "Let me explain the concept. Facts are verifiable details. For example, details that demonstrate why Ruby called the police."

"You expect me to know her mind? She didn't know her own mind."

"I expect you to answer the question."

"I don't know why she called. All I know is that I ended up in Pondville. Effin Pondville! Miles from the ocean. Smells like a cesspool."

"The official records say you were a model prisoner. But word on the inside says otherwise. When you got out you were steaming. You wanted to pay Ruby back."

"Bullshit."

"Mind the language, Mr. Irvine."

"It's my house."

"You take the wrong step, sir, and you'll end up back in prison." Eller paused to let his point sink in. "Where were you on the night of October twenty-first?"

"Here."

"Who was with you?"

"Four buddies. They came down from Boston."

Eller passed him a notepad. "Write their names."

Irvine's writing complete, Eller moved on. "You work in Plymouth. Why are you renting here?"

"Better beaches."

"Summer's over. I hear you have illegal *interests*, Mr. Irvine, or, I should say, Mr. Jones."

"You're wrong, I'm totally aboveboard. I help folks. I'm a facilitator."

"Oh? What kind?"

"Everyone needs help at times. I'm there for them. I cut through the bullsh—the BS. Friends say I could get the Devil back on track."

"Who's your current gal?"

"Too many to mention. I'm a great lover of humanity. As you know, half the human race is female."

"Then why the fixation with Ruby Halliday?"

"That was then."

"Really? By the way, you're going to enjoy our company until Central checks your alibi. No phones or computers."

"Turn on the TV."

Eller shook his head. "Lieutenant Bourque likes to read. Don't want to disturb her."

An hour-and-a-half later, Eller motioned to Bourque and left the room.

"Central just texted," he said in the kitchen, pointing to his phone. "Irvine's Boston buddies were rounded up and interviewed separately. Each one confirmed Irvine was here during the Halliday murder window."

"Huh."

"All four had the same story: drinking, lobsters, strippers. Same beer brand, same strippers. Their names were Candy and Floss."

"Original."

"Always."

## Chapter 21

### DAY TEN: Barnstable. October 29th

The next morning Bourque forwent her usual swim. It was nearing the end of the outdoor season. The ocean wasn't frigid but it was getting too cold to linger on the beach afterward, a ritual she'd miss for weeks.

As she dressed for work, Marty made decaf. Being a night owl, he was normally still asleep. Last night, they'd talked about living in his Menauhant Road house. His great-great-grandfather had built it in 1882. He and his father and uncles had renovated it six years ago. Unlike her, Marty Dalton had a big family: five siblings and dozens of cousins. She was an only child. Her father had lost touch with his family in Quebec. She didn't see her mother often, nor the one maternal aunt she had left, who lived in New Hampshire. According to Marty, his family was like seagrass in July: thick and profuse, found in every corner of the Cape. To boot, he joked, they were as thick as thieves. They loved to *palaver and plan*, as his mother put it. She wanted to hear the pitter-patter of more little feet. Apparently, what she wanted, she got.

Bourque had gone to a few Sunday dinners at his parents' place, raucous events, twenty-plus people at the table, all holding forth, even the kids. She'd been quiet, which wasn't like her. Lying in bed last night, she'd thought about her remaining family, both of pure Yankee descent. Her mother still stuck her oar in without a moment's hesitation. In her view, children—including grown children like Bourque—were meant to be seen, and not heard. Despite her forward manner, she rarely left home. In a sense, she'd recused herself. In her opinion, New England had enjoyed a long and glorious run, but now its Yankee heritage was being eclipsed. Bourque's aunt felt the same way: Northeast Yankees were in decline.

Bourque didn't agree with that. New England's Yankee ethos was still alive. *Yankee ingenuity* was still a catchphrase for competence, self-reliance, and practicality. Although known for thriftiness, Yankees weren't closeminded. For decades, they'd made trading liaisons all around the globe. And yet, with those fine traits, Yankee was often a derogatory term, conjuring a fork-tongued old fart vainly proud of the Northeast. Bourque had a different spin on a Yankee, courtesy of E. B. White:

To Americans, a Yankee is a Northerner.
To Northerners, a Yankee is an Easterner.
To Easterners, a Yankee is a New Englander.
To New Englanders, a Yankee is a Vermonter.
And in Vermont, a Yankee is somebody who eats pie for breakfast.

Now, standing at Marty's kitchen counter, she watched him fill her coffee cup.

"Got any pie?" she asked half in jest, then winked. "I know, it's off the menu."

"Not always." He smiled. "Despite that, what do you think of living on Menauhant Road?"

"No complaints yet," she kidded. "Seriously, I'll like it here."

"Great. It hasn't changed in years. When I was a kid, we biked everywhere. No one worried about us. Well, not until ten p.m. Pretty late for a kid." He sipped his coffee. "All my memories are here, Ivy. You never forget your favorite childhood haunts."

She nodded. Hers was her father's garden in Boston.

"We didn't leave the Cape in summer," Marty reminisced. "Hell, we hardly left at all. *Why would we*, my father used to say, *best place in America*. But that spiel only worked until I was seventeen, when I ran off to join the Navy. Eventually. Am I talking too much?"

She shook her head.

"The height restriction on buildings preserves things. In Boston you see construction cranes everywhere. Apart from the tourists, there's nothing to complain about. The Cape's a family mecca." He grinned perceptively. "Speaking of which, my family can be a handful."

"They're wonderful." And they were: kind-hearted, funny, inclusive. Perhaps too *inclusive*, as in too smothering.

"They hardly know you," he said.

A familiar refrain, she thought. Dan Fitzgerald's family didn't know him, which wasn't something she wanted to emulate. "That will change," she assured Marty. She'd be herself; she'd speak her mind.

"No rush," he replied. "I can see the look on your face. I'm overwhelming you."

□ □ □

Leaving Marty's place, Bourque arrived in Barnstable just after sunrise. The sky was more black than blue, the color of a deep Maine cove. Inside, she made decaf, sat at her office desk, and opened her laptop. Her email inbox was full. The intel wires were burning.

Starting with *Islander* POIs, she read that Central had done further research on Sam Carson. He was an ex-Marine. Before working as a seaman on container ships, he'd served two years in Afghanistan, having been sent to Kabul in 2004. Kabul again. Like Verdi, he'd been in potential contact with Special Ops Det One.

*Potential*, she told herself. It was probably a dead-end masquerading as a coincidence. On the other hand, as her father used to say, coincidences were a detective's best friend. If they panned out, you looked like a genius. If they didn't, you moved on, no worse off.

She called Eller at his hotel. "Bourque here," she said when he picked up. "We need to see Sam Carson pronto. I know you're wondering why."

"I'm wondering why you're calling so early."

"Not that early. I'll pick you up in ten."

□ □ □

On the way to Carson's house, Bourque filled Eller in on Verdi and the seaman.

"Let me see if I have this right," he said. "They were stationed in Afghanistan near Det One. Hence they might, just *might*, have had the opportunity to acquire a Strider knife."

"True. As you know, Carson was aboard the ferry on October nineteenth. Forensics is sure the same knife was used to attack both vics. Same unique notch."

"I can guess what's next. You're going to say *Forensics doesn't f up*."

"Exactly."

"A hundred-and-fifty civilians also have Strider knives."

"Got it," she said. "The perp could have acquired the Strider from a civilian. If we have to track civilians down, we will. But I suggest we begin with ex-Marines."

"A Marine wouldn't have to be stationed in Afghanistan to get a Strider knife."

"Agreed. But the two on our list were. They're low-hanging fruit. Let's hit Carson, then Verdi." Bourque shrugged. "We don't have anything to lose. There are no other suspects on the horizon. Unless you count Irvine."

"I don't think we can. No DNA, no opportunity. All right, partner, I'm going to follow you."

□ □ □

The detectives arrived at Carson's bungalow just as he was getting in his Ram pickup. Bourque blocked off the truck, then stepped out of her car and motioned for him to power down his window.

"Good morning, Mr. Carson. We have a few questions for you."

"Sure, but I'm due at work."

"I'll call Captain Macey and let him know you'll be a few minutes late." She doubled the good cop routine. "The old man won't mind."

"Okay," Carson said. "Let's go inside."

Bourque and Eller trailed Carson down his long hallway to the kitchen. Through the sliding glass doors, a small forest of sailboat masts rose above the nearby warehouse, most of them minus furled sails, another sign of late October.

Carson sat opposite the detectives at the kitchen table. As before, he was wearing a dirt-brown *Islander* jumpsuit. "Coffee?" he asked.

"No thanks," Bourque answered. "We'll get right to it. How long were you in the Marines?"

"Five years. Left in two thousand and seven."

"Why did you leave?"

"You serve your country, the next man comes along. Or woman," he noted with a smile.

Bourque nodded. There was Carson's obsequious side again. "How often did you interact with Marines from Det One?"

"Det One?" Either Carson didn't remember or he was good at pretending.

"Special Ops Detachment One. Stationed in the Kabul region,

like you were."

"Didn't run into a Det One. It's a big region, Lieutenant."

Bourque signaled for her partner to take over.

"Are you a gambler, Mr. Carson?" Eller asked.

"No more than the next man."

Eller smiled. "No less, either?"

"Sadly true."

"What's your poison?"

"Blackjack."

"Fine game. Did you score any big wins over there?"

"A few. Balanced by losses."

"Win any booty? Medals, knives, rings, that sort of thing."

"No. I played for money."

"Where were you on the night of October twenty-first this year?" Eller asked.

"Emerg. Cape Cod Hospital. Went in for gallbladder stones."

"When did you arrive?"

"About six p.m."

"You live in Falmouth. Why go to Cape Cod Hospital?"

"Doc's orders. They're good with internal medicine."

"Did you have to stay overnight?"

Carson shook his head. "Nah. It wasn't a major attack. Got out just after ten."

"What did you do then?"

"Went right home. Had to get up at six-thirty a.m. Summer and fall are a grind."

"Long days," Eller commiserated. "Do you own any guns or weapons, Mr. Carson?"

"A shotgun. Used to hunt ducks in the fall, but I don't have time these days."

"Is your shotgun locked?"

Carson nodded.

"Show us."

Carson's gun locker was located in the basement next to a metal shelving unit. As he opened the locker, Eller leaned in. "Mind if Lieutenant Bourque looks around?"

"No problem."

While Eller checked the gun locker, Bourque searched the shelving unit and moved on to half a dozen storage bins and two battered trunks, not hiding her thoroughness from Carson. Let the ex-Marine know they were looking. She found nothing suspicious.

A few minutes later, the detectives thanked Carson and left the premises.

"Give me your read," Bourque said as she and Eller drove off.

"I didn't see anything. What's next?"

"Cambridge," she said.

Eller sighed. "Both of us?"

"Unless you're busy. I could use your eyes and mouth."

"What about my brain?"

"That too."

## Cambridge

Just before noon, the detectives called on Verdi at work. The POI was stationed at Cambridge's Division 1 Firehouse on Inman Square, a three-story red and white brick structure built in the early 1900s. Walking from her car, Bourque admired the porticoes, indicative of New England's Renaissance Revival, her father's favorite architectural style: geometric without being jagged, elegant and workmanlike at the same time.

Verdi led the detectives to a small meeting room off the foyer, her rigid back clearly showing her displeasure. *Now you're hassling me at work.*

Suck it up, Bourque thought. It wasn't as if Verdi's nose was hitched to a grindstone. Firefighters were normally in wait mode, anticipating action, not engaged in it. When the detectives sat, Verdi chose to remain standing, arms crossed. Her hair was glossy; her skin, radiant. She wore a body-hugging uniform.

"Do you keep in touch with your old Marine buddies?" Bourque began.

"A few of them."

"Any belong to Det One?"

Verdi looked surprised. "Yes, two of them. Do you know Det One?"

Bourque nodded. In a manner of speaking. "Where are your Det One buddies now?"

"One's in Maine. The other one's in Nevada."

"Names?"

"Maria Del Santos; she's in Vegas. And Wanda Kalb, up in

Bangor. The only two females in Det One."

"Where did you meet them?"

"A bar in Kabul. We're of the same stripe. *Don't ask, don't tell,* they say. You don't have to ask. We can pick each other out a mile away."

"Did you become good friends?"

"Hell yah. Saved my butt knowing them. Figuratively and literally. A few hormone-crazed dudes stopped hustling my ass."

"Did the three of you exchange anything? As in dog tags, insignia, or knives?"

"*Knives.* Now I see where you're going. Dan Fitzgerald was attacked with a knife. You think I attacked him. If I did, why would I get a knife from someone? I have my own. Which, by the way, I don't carry. It's not legal carrying size. But let's get to the point. You think I killed him?"

"I think you need to answer the question," Bourque said. "Did you and Wanda or Maria exchange any mementos or gifts?"

"What? Like high school sweethearts? Listen carefully: we were friends, not lovers. The three of us didn't *exchange* anything. No spit, no STDs, no knives. Nothing but laughs and stories."

"Did you buy or win a knife from Del Santos or Kalb?"

"No. I expect you need a better alibi for me on October nineteenth."

"Go ahead."

"As you know, Karen and I were in that night, but we had food delivered about nine-thirty, a margherita pizza from Panera. DoorDash will have a record of that delivery. I paid the driver with a twenty. He'll remember me. I fished it out of my bra."

"How about a better alibi for the night of October twenty-first?" Bourque asked.

"No delivery, but I picked up Mexican food on my way home. At Olé, a block from the firehouse."

"When?"

"Roughly eight p.m. The exact time will be on the order receipt."

"Ms. Verdi, are you aware that an order receipt is not proof of your whereabouts?"

"It can be if there's video proof. Olé has a security camera covering the order desk. I picked up the order in person."

"You better hope Olé's tape was working and is still available."

"I'll consult a lawyer."

"Let's switch to Ms. Symon. Can anyone other than you prove her whereabouts on the night of October twenty-first?"

"We're getting a lawyer. Talk to them."

"Are you—"

"That's it, we're done."

## South Boston

As if on autopilot, Bourque exited I-93 at Columbia Road, drove past Moakley Park, and knocked on Chase Heaney's door. She knew he was home. Intuition. Then there were facts. The purple Guess hoodie was still on the porch.

"Again?" he said when he opened the door. "I'm beginning to think you like me."

"No bull from you so far."

He pointed to a few porch chairs. "Mind if we sit outside. I'm rearranging inside."

Bourque didn't comment. "We're here because you know Mr. Fitzgerald's acquaintances."

"Some of them."

"Who do you know that might help us?"

"Let me think." Heaney didn't think for long. "Well, a few of my crewmen hung out with him a bit, but they didn't know what he thought. Hardly anyone did, except a guy who talked to him every sailing trip. The guy was really into whales," Heaney added. "Kept his job hush-hush but Dan and I knew what he did. He's a marine biologist in Woods Hole, at the Oceanographic Institution. Didn't tell his bosses he hung out with a bunch of eco renegades. But who would?"

"What's his name?"

"Liam Doyle. He lives aboard a Shannon ketch docked near the institution."

Which was near the ferry terminal, Bourque knew. Definitely worth checking out.

Heaney leaned forward, resting his elbows on his knees. "Dan's death got me thinking. He understood that there are things worth fighting for, and dying for. Most Leftwingers don't understand the Right, especially their war ethic. *Damn the ICBMs. Win at all costs.* Dan was wiser than your normal Leftie. However, being Irish, he thought you won by talking. In his case, more writing than talking."

Heaney shook his head. "You don't win with words. You win with words *and* confronting people when you have to. The pen and the sword." He held up a hand. "Not that I killed anyone. I spilled some men into the sea, but they were rescued." He shrugged. "I know, I have things to answer for. Some of what I did was wrong, and some of what Dan did was wrong. Not evil, but wrong. In my opinion, there's a clear line between evil and wrong. Evil people do what they do because it makes them feel stronger. Dan did what he did to make others stronger."

"And you? What's your driving force?"

"The same as Dan's. Make people stronger. I agreed with his hoped-for future, his new whale road, his America of the True. Let me share something, if I may. The ramblings of someone who's fallen into a few pits. Our actions extend far beyond our horizons. They're an Alpha without an Omega. What we do today impacts tomorrow. Dan realized that. But I didn't agree with everything he did. The guy styled himself as the Dark Knight who'd save the kingdom. There he was, always on the job, everywhere at once. Albeit virtually. Apparently, that's the way you do it these days." Heaney sighed. "Christ, I can't get used to him being gone. It'll take months, no years. Goddamn years."

Bourque motioned for Eller to take a kick at the can.

Her partner took his time, staring out at the street. "Did Mr. Fitzgerald ever hang out with party types?" he eventually asked. "Strippers, clubbers, that sort of thing."

"Not his scene. It wasn't a moral stance. He had too much on the go."

"How about friends from Harvard?"

"There was one, this older guy who'd gone to Harvard, a guy living in D.C. Met him once. We sat on my boat and had a few cold ones."

"Name?"

"R. R. Kane."

"Address?"

"No idea."

Bourque shrugged to herself. Those words again. But this time they could get around them. Police tech.

"What did you three talk about?" Eller asked.

"Politics. The guy gabbed about lobbying. However, from what

I heard, he was no pussycat in his youth. He'd been a hardnose political organizer before he went to Harvard."

"Did he and Mr. Fitzgerald argue?"

Heaney huffed. "You detectives, you're so obvious. Yes, they argued. Dan argued with a lot of people. The two of them lobbed points back and forth as if they were nukes." Heaney snorted. "Sometimes I think it would be better if they were. Things would happen."

# Chapter 22

## Falmouth

"I have a scoop for you."

"Is that my neighbor?" Bourque switched to speakerphone and shut off her bath taps.

"The one and only. Mr. Hieronymus Scoop."

She smiled to herself. "Go on, Cal."

"Do you know what *Hieronymus* means in English?"

"No, but I think someone's going to tell me."

"It means *sacred*. I'm a bringer of light."

"And a font of information?"

"You bet. Got a lead on Ruby Halliday's would-be killer. He's in North Chatham."

"Name?"

"Jack Irvine, aka J. P. Jones."

"Of Seventy Old Wharf Road?" she asked.

"How did you know?"

"Telepathy. We cops know more than you'd think."

"And less."

"Got me on that."

"Local consensus has been building on Irvine. I'm just the messenger."

"Whose consensus?"

"Not my bailiwick. I heard a few rumors, I decided to pursue them."

"Fresh rumors?"

"Fresh or festering, you're asking a lot of questions."

"Nature of the neighbor."

"Okay, I'll tell you exactly what I heard. Succinctly."

"One of my favorite words."

"Thought you'd like that. But my sources shall remain hidden."

"All right for now," she hedged. "What if things go to court? Would you testify?"

"I can't be seen testifying. Only snitches do that."

If court came into the picture, she'd cross the disclosure bridge with Cal then. At this point, it was a long way off. "Understood.

Consider this anonymous."

"Anonymous Hieronymus, that's me. Irvine used to be Halliday's boyfriend. He also used to hit her for no reason. That's just the lead-in. My sources say he's been very jumpy recently. He's getting ready to take off."

"Any proof?"

"For one thing, he's been packing since yesterday. In case you're curious, that's from another unnamed source. There are a lot of them around." Bourque could hear the smile in Cal's voice. "A source who also says Irvine just rented a storage locker."

"When?"

"The lease started today."

"Anything else?" she asked.

"Don't look a gift horse ..."

"Thanks for the call. Appreciate the help."

"Just doing my duty. I hear things. If they're important, you hear them."

"I like that. I hear your neighbor's going to bake some pies soon. What's your favorite?"

"Huckleberry."

Bourque pulled the plug on her bath and checked the time: 2210. After dressing in warm clothes, she called Eller. "Just got a tip from the public, a lead on Jack Irvine. Apparently, he's about to make a run. Let's bring him in. I'll phone Peabody."

"Better you than me."

She disconnected and called Peabody's cell. "Bourque here."

"Yes, Lieutenant?"

He sounded sleepy. Not surprising. It was well after his bedtime. "Got a heads up," she said. "We have a lead on Jack Irvine. Local intel."

"Pereira again?"

"No. A Cape man. Please order Irvine in to Barnstable. He may be fleeing."

## Barnstable

Bourque sped east along Route 28 wondering about Irvine. He had no history of violent crime. He'd always been a swindler, not an enforcer or killer. She tried to focus on the road but her mind drifted. As if following a script, it strayed to the recent past, to

Halliday's last months. Had the shopkeeper been in Irvine's thrall, or had he been in her's? Did it matter? Bourque's mind segued to Fitzgerald. Had *he* been in Halliday's thrall? Pondering their relationship, Bourque pulled into Barnstable Unit and left her car.

It was a cold night, the stars bright and hard above her. The wind had dropped. The crescent moon was waxing but still a thin white sickle. She hurried inside to Interview Room One.

Although the room had top-notch camera and audio equipment, to the unpracticed eye it appeared decrepit. Sickly-green paint, rickety metal table, old wooden chairs—all designed to dupe POIs. The foolish ones tended to let their guard down.

As Bourque sat in a chair, Eller entered the room. He looked wide awake.

"You stop for a double espresso?" she asked.

"Nah, regular coffee."

"The wonders of caffeine. Marty has me on decaf, no deviations, no excuses."

"I feel for you."

Two troopers led Jack Irvine in. The POI was dressed in a slick Dodger blue business suit and ultramarine tie, as if he'd been entertaining "clients." Bourque immediately directed him to the suspect's chair, the Slider, which had a heavily waxed seat. The front legs were half-an-inch shorter than the back ones, making suspects slide inexorably forward, into the face of their interviewer.

"Good evening, Mr. Irvine," she began.

"Evening?"

She ignored him. "We have a few questions for you. If you're clean," she facetiously said, "you'll be home for your beauty sleep."

"Funny. How about we head to a coffee shop. Lose the green walls."

"Next time."

"Next time?"

She glanced at Eller. "Do you hear an echo?"

"An irritating one. But I'll overlook it. For now." Eller scrutinized the POI, his eyes hardening by the second. "It's like this, Mr. Irvine. I tell you what we know. You tell us what you know. Simple enough?"

Irvine didn't respond.

"I heard you're leaving town. The troopers who brought you

here said your place is empty. Where's your furniture?"

"I rent it. I'm getting a new set."

"Convenient, especially if you move a lot. Where are the rest of your possessions?"

"Here and there."

"A storage locker?"

Irvine shrugged. "Okay, I'm moving. Is that illegal?"

"Where are you going?"

"Florida. I like beaches."

Eller gestured for Bourque to come in.

"Mr. Irvine," she relayed, "you won't be leaving the state for a few days. Consider it a new restraining order. We have some questions." She smiled falsely. "Why the glum face? I'm going to do you a favor."

Irvine eyed her warily.

"I'm going to start asking them now," she said. "How long have you known Ms. Halliday's killers?"

"Who?"

"Ms. Halliday's killers."

"I don't know them. I don't know anything about her death."

"We'd like to believe you. Your alibi checked. You were here the night of her murder. That sounds good. But it doesn't mean you had nothing to do with her death. Brings to mind the charge 'accomplice to murder.' Not a trivial charge."

"What did I do?"

Bourque didn't reply, intending to keep him hanging on the hook. He hadn't let his guard down. The team suspected he gave the killers the key to her parents' backdoor.

Irvine plowed ahead immediately. "Let's get something right. I'm clean," he proclaimed in a loud voice. "I had nothing to do with her murder."

"What about Dan Fitzgerald's?"

"I had nothing to do with either murder."

"We know her homicide is connected to Fitzgerald's. We know you're connected to her."

"That's enough. I'm calling my lawyer."

Par for the course, Bourque thought. The farther along a homicide case got, the faster POIs called their lawyers.

## Chapter 23

**DAY ELEVEN: Washington, D.C. October 30th**

Bourque's flight touched down at D.C.'s Dulles Airport at 1010. Outside, she hailed a cab downtown. Being late October, it was well past D.C.'s peak humidity. She unzipped her jacket. The temperature was already sixty-five degrees; it had been forty-six when she left the Cape for Boston's Logan International that morning.

Bourque exited the cab three blocks from Georgetown University to find herself in an area of mom-and-pop eateries and one-off shops, not the kind of neighborhood she associated with D.C. She entered an ivy-covered brick building with a wide hallway. The concierge cheerfully led her to Fitzgerald's apartment. "Are you staying long, Miss?"

*Miss.* She liked him already. "A few hours."

"The fridge is empty, so is the pantry. Can I bring you a coffee?"

"Not today, but thank you." Welcome to D.C. Who knew?

Fitzgerald's top-floor unit faced east. With its faded blinds and piles of books and papers, it brought to mind a grad student's digs. It didn't resemble his Groton suite or Vineyard cottage in the least. Another one of Fitzgerald's protean sides. When the ninjas examined the unit, they found no DNA other than Fitzgerald's, and no computing devices, lists, or other leads.

Bourque tossed her jacket on a chair and scanned his book and film collection. The usual suspects, as seen at his other abodes: history, politics, ecology, adventure. In addition, there were hundreds of books about nineteenth and early-twentieth-century European leaders: Napoleon, Bismarck, Franco, Hitler, Stalin, Churchill. More tyrants than statesmen, she concluded.

She carried a few piles of books to an old oak desk, sat in a tatty office chair, and started flipping through them. While the ninjas hadn't found any evidence of Halliday in the apartment, Bourque thought of her as she searched the books. In Bourque's mind, as each day passed, the two cases were more tightly bound. However, she needed proof, something that would shine a stark light on the Fitzgerald-Halliday relationship. Were they merely lovers? How deeply were they linked? Had his murder led by chance to hers? Or were both planned together, two parts of the same scheme?

Just after 1400, having skimmed hundreds of books, Bourque gave up. She'd found countless academic annotations and notes, which underlined Fitzgerald's studiousness, yet nothing that illuminated the cases. His third abode was a washout. That was life as a detective. You dug, you deliberated, you formed new theories, you dug again—and you got nowhere. Peabody wouldn't be pleased. However, she still had a chance to salvage the trip. Last night, she'd arranged to meet R. R. Kane, originally from Gloucester, Massachusetts.

□ □ □

Like Fitzgerald, R. R. Kane had an apartment near the university. Unlike Fitzgerald, the politico owned his unit, a sprawling two-bedroom condo with wainscoting and cornice moldings, the top floor of a building overlooking the Chesapeake and Ohio Canal. The apartment smelled of fresh-cut flowers.

"Would you like a beverage?" Kane asked Bourque as she sat at his kitchen table.

"Do you have decaf?"

"Your wish is my command."

"Thank you." Kane's manner was a reminder of another time, a time coeval with her grandfather's. The man was eighty-two yet wore the type of clothing Fitzgerald favored: hiking gear. His face was leonine; his eyes, pellucid blue. While his hair was thin, so too was his waist. From his pace as they'd strolled down the hallway, he was capable of out-walking her.

Sipping her coffee, Bourque opened with a feeler. "What's your read on today's politics?"

Kane scrutinized her. His eyes were so light and transparent that he looked almost blind. "I take it you want the unvarnished truth."

She nodded.

"It's getting worse by the month—no, the day." His voice went down in pitch and up in intensity. "*Abandon all hope, ye who enter.*"

"Dante," she said.

"Right, the *Inferno*. From the Circles of Hell, which we're in."

"I haven't abandoned hope."

"The prerogative of youth."

"Semi-youth," she noted. "On the phone last night, you mentioned working with Dan Fitzgerald. When was that?"

"About five years ago, for two years."

"What were you two doing?"

"Lobbying. We were representing a center-right movement, one-hundred-percent American. A voice this country desperately needs."

"What exactly did you do?"

"I can't speak to what Dan did. Myself, I'm a lobbyist-at-large. If I agree with an agenda, I represent it. For a fee, that is. Before you criticize that, that's how our democracy works."

"You haven't said what you did."

"Apologies. I'd need clearance from the movement to relay specifics. As for the gist of it, I was lobbying for less government interference."

"On what?"

"I can't say."

"Were you surprised Mr. Fitzgerald was killed?"

"Yes. At Harvard, they don't teach radicalism. I've been following the Boston news, all that talk about far-reaching whale rights. Dan got too fanatical."

"What did you and Mr. Fitzgerald have in common?" she asked.

"A world view, not exactly the same one, of course, but we could see each other's edges. Like Dan, I prefer the business of politics to the business of business. Always have. I was a bit of a rabblerouser when I was young. I think that's why we got along. Hard to see it now, but I shook some big trees then. And hobnobbed with big cheeses. You like the lingo?" He grinned. "Seriously, Dan and I could talk politics for hours."

"Why did he come to D.C.?"

"To help. He was a hard worker. People liked him, but no one was like him, I can tell you that." Kane shook his head. "No one. There are plenty of political junkies in this town. He was different. When he joined a campaign, he didn't pay lip service to it. He put everything into it."

"Is that why he was killed?"

Kane's translucent eyes blinked. "That's a big question."

"The biggest." Bourque decided to use the "a-word." The hell with the upper echelons. "Was it an assassination?"

"Could be."

"Where were you on the night of October nineteenth?"

The POI seemed ready for the question. "Here. I had a friend around."

"Full name?"

"Maggie Jane Burke."

After jotting the name down, Bourque moved on. "Tell me what you know about Mr. Fitzgerald's politics."

"Dan was stirring some deep waters, Lieutenant. Wise political types stay on the surface. They avoid complexity. If a policy can't be sloganized, it won't be successful. He didn't believe that. He tried to do both, champion complexity and truth."

"Did he succeed?"

"No. You can't do both. You have to focus. Simplicity hooks the voter. Dan didn't get that. Then he left for Massachusetts."

"I hear disappointment."

"We needed him. Youngsters these days, they talk about *running and gunning*. Most of them are much better at running."

"I take it you're not."

"I don't run. I never did. In addition, I'm older now. As in more focused and less idealistic."

"What's your political leaning, if I may ask?"

"You may. Republican. Not today's Republican Party," he added. "It's a simple calculus. I believe American exceptionalism is still valid. Dan and I often debated U.S. exceptionalism. He couldn't see it. That's why he didn't make a good Republican. With my help, he tried to, but he failed. You know what changes the world? Conservatives with liberal ideas," Kane avowed. "Not liberals with radical ideas. In my view, all radicalism does is raise a red flag. Or put a bull's eye on you."

"You're saying radicalism got Mr. Fitzgerald killed."

"Are you putting words in my mouth?"

Bourque nodded.

Kane changed gears and smiled. "It's just my view. What do I know?"

Bourque didn't respond. She sensed the man knew more than he was letting on. On one hand, he looked clean. He seemed to like Fitzgerald. He wasn't likely strong enough to assault him. On the other hand, Kane was the kind of man who could pull a lot of strings.

□ □ □

Bourque entered a coffee shop near the canal and nursed a mineral water, mulling over Fitzgerald's political evolution: the left-right-left swings, the stint in D.C., the social media campaigns. He'd kept forging ahead, leaving himself open to being blindsided. Both his sister and Heaney had said he was too trusting. Did he put too much trust in R. R. Kane? Kane could be a covert enemy. *A bull's eye on you*, Bourque reflected. Did Kane put a bull's eye on Fitzgerald? He said Fitzgerald's whale rights were *fanatical* and *radical*. Coincidentally, Kane was originally from Gloucester, for centuries a center of New England's fishing industry, which would be impacted if stringent whale rights took hold.

Bourque sat quietly, considering the angles. In every homicide, lines of inquiry radiated from the place where the perp killed their prey. Place mattered. It always did. In the Fitzgerald murder, the ferry mattered; in the Halliday murder, the location of Ruby's death: Orleans. Was there a distant locus as well, someone pulling strings from, say, Washington D.C.?

Finishing her water, Bourque decided to call it a day. It was time to phone Gigi Lambert. Last night, they'd arranged to meet for cocktails, maybe dinner if Bourque had time before her 2110 return flight. It was 1625. Dinner might be in the works.

"You in Georgetown?" Gigi asked when she picked up Bourque's call.

"Yep."

"Take a taxi to Annapolis. Pronto. I'm paying."

"I got the taxi, Gee. Annapolis?"

"The sailboat show finished two weeks ago but there are still loads of boats here."

"You buying a sailboat?"

"No, you are. Your man loves sailing, you love sailing."

"Yes?" She and Marty had an old Tartan 30 berthed in Falmouth Inner Harbor.

"Has he presented you with child?"

"No." Should she tell Gigi about planning to get pregnant? It was a good time, wasn't it? Bourque parted her lips. Wait, her conscience told her. You promised.

"Then you need a bigger sailboat, Borky. Compensation." Gigi laughed. "That'll learn him. Come to Dock F-Two, Hanse Yachts.

Got a bead on a nearly-new Hanse Three-four-eight. Excellent price, getting better by the day. And the owner's a hunk. Jurgen, I love that name."

"Marty's a journalist, not a stockbroker."

"I know. That's why I'm giving him a lead, deeply discounted. See you onboard."

Bourque didn't reply. When Gigi was flying, she let her soar. Hanses weren't Bourque or Marty's thing. Too much fiberglass, not enough wood.

□ □ □

Bourque found it easy to slough off the Hanse 348. Jurgen was another matter. She had to pull him aside and give him Gigi's number before he left. He seemed to be a decent guy and was no slouch as a sailor. He'd crewed on two round-the-world races. But she wanted a heart-to-heart with Gigi, not an evening of sitting between two hormone-bombs.

As the sun sank, she and Gigi walked into a fish restaurant with a seaside patio. The air carried a miasma of scents: Chesapeake Bay, fish stock, candle smoke. Gentle waves lapped against the deck-pilings. The setting reminded Bourque of mid-September on the Cape, dining dockside in Hyannis. Her best friend looked great: short shorts, long tanned legs, flowing blonde hair. If not for her metal-grey eyes, she might pass for a ditzy bombshell, probably one easily impressed by a man with money. Her gaze quelched that idea.

"What do you think of Jurgen?" Gigi asked as they drank their first margheritas.

Bourque smiled. "A bit young."

"He's at least forty."

"Subtract five. But who's counting? I gave him your cell number."

"You're the best."

"You may not be thanking me in a week."

"Oh, I will. Did you notice those pecs? And those bedroom eyes. I love how he says, 'Ya, ya.'"

"What about the man bun?"

"It's a samurai topknot."

"Right," Bourque said.

"I can cut that off when he's sleeping."

"What? An upper-body Lorena Bobbitt?"

Gigi giggled, a devious giggle. Followed by a longer one.

A few cocktails later, one more for Bourque, two for Gigi, she and Gigi ordered dinner: two lobsters Newburg accompanied by half a carafe of wine. To Bourque's delight, the crustaceans were excellent. She was already cutting back on alcohol so she poured Gigi most of the wine, saying she was returning to work mode after dinner.

"Dessert," Gigi announced afterward. It wasn't a question. "You're having peach dumplings smothered in whipped cream."

Sipping coffees, Gigi turned serious. "Remember that question you asked me? About how many e-threats get prosecuted. Not many, Borky, although the Bureau is working on it. Of course, I'm not." Gigi threw up her hands. "I've been typecast. I'm an extortion specialist, that's it." Her eyes underscored her resentment. "Sorry, I'm feeling mawkish. Had a few drinks with Jurgen before you got here."

Bourque had no reply. She hated being typecast but figured the last thing Gigi needed was an echo chamber.

"A while back, I was surveilling two people suspected of corporate blackmail. They weren't using the usual tools: letters, photos, loans, etc. No way. That's old school. They were using the threat of anthrax. You didn't hear that, not that it would lead you anywhere."

Bourque nodded.

"People are getting more and more desperate. Like in the Dark Ages, but Crime is their panacea, not Religion. Regardless, both are belief systems with no guarantee of happiness." Gigi looked disgusted with herself. "I shouldn't be talking about cases. I'm going rogue."

"You didn't say anything."

"It's not good. I'm losing respect. I have to leave the Feds."

"Hit the reset button," Bourque counseled. "Your career's just getting started. Give it time."

Gigi shook her head.

"Are you sure you want to quit?"

"No. But I'm going to."

"Don't do it," Bourque said.

"Why the hell not? It's simple. I chase egotistical assholes who never confess. You chase murderers."

"Not every day. Not even every month, not on the Cape."

"Enough for me. I'm going to join the Staties as a detective. When you snag a murderer, in most cases, he or she does time. When I snag an extortionist, half of the time they walk away. It's no contest. You do useful things. You put murderers in their place. Remember our training," Gigi said. "We were always the ones who spoke out, the ones who stood for our convictions. Whatever the price, we used to say, justice must be served. Not much has changed in your case."

"In both our cases," Bourque replied. They were both still idealistic. For cops, that is.

"You know that poem you like," Gigi went on, "the one where John Donne castigates death: *Death Be Not Proud?*"

Bourque nodded. She knew by heart over a hundred poems, mementos of her youth. Useless, many now said, and she understood their point of view. You didn't catch murderers with poetry. However, you might encounter their motives, and that could lead you forward.

"It's my new mantra," Gigi said. "I like the idea of a job that puts death in its place. Detectives give people hope."

"Not every day," Bourque repeated.

"Then there's the damn Feds. Every agent thinks the same. They've been brainwashed by the academy." Gigi waved derisively. "They wear the same clothes. Men and women. C'mon. How can you think critically if you face your doubles all day long? It's doppelgängers with doppelgänger haircuts. Madness."

Bourque remained quiet.

"I don't hate it. I really don't. They do a great job, given their purview. They're straightshooters, they're not beholden to anyone. But I want something more personal."

Bourque understood the sentiment. As a Statie, while she was a cog in a machine, she was also herself—for the most part.

"*Your* job matters," Gigi continued. "You can look yourself in the mirror at night and say, *Good work, kiddo.* I want that."

Bourque raised her glass.

Gigi clicked it with hers. "Goodbye, Washington. Hello Beantown. I don't want to work on the Cape, Borky. Too many beaches." She laughed. "Seriously, too sleepy."

Bourque smiled to herself. In time, Gee would learn.

## Chapter 24

**DAY FIFTEEN: Barnstable. November 3rd**

Bourque arrived in Barnstable feeling like a new woman. She'd had three days off—in a row—her first break since the Fitzgerald murder. To her, get-a-ways didn't have to be long, especially if they were sailing trips. A day on the water was like a week at a beach resort, doubly so if chance presented blue skies and fair winds. Keeping a prudent eye on hurricane reports, she and Marty had circumnavigated Nantucket and Martha's Vineyard on their Tartan 30, sleeping one night anchored in Nantucket Harbor, and the next off Lucy Vincent Beach, where they'd put out fishing lines and caught a fat striped bass. Marty had stuffed it with lemon and tarragon and grilled it whole on the stern-rail BBQ. With the ocean beginning its annual cooldown, it had been chilly that night until they retreated to the V-berth, crawled under a down duvet and danced a happy dance. Everyone she knew had their favorite place for doing a happy dance. Hers was on a sailboat. That night, their boat barely drifted, pulling softly on the anchor line, lulling them to sleep.

Now, sitting in her office, Bourque paid obeisance to her laptop. It was a catch-up morning. After clearing her email backlog, she opened a recent message from the tech team. They'd finally cracked the second of Fitzgerald's computers, and had identified one file folder for her to examine, *Posts*. The folder held a massive number of posts—44,000-plus—but only two topics: Whales at Large and Atlantic Right Whales. Forty-four thousand far exceeded the number of Laker posts. She scanned through them. A lot of strident posts, some inflammatory.

#Killing #whales is #HOMICIDE, #killing #whales is #FRATICIDE.
If you #kill whales, you deserve to #die.

No more #whaling. #Banish the #killerships.
Sink any ship that harms a #whale.

Anyone who harms a #whale is a #criminal.
#Prosecute them.
#Persecute them.

#Whale #killers, you are a disgrace to the human race.
#Stop the #Killers!
#Save the #AtlanticRightWhale

In short order, Bourque saw enough to categorize the folder's message: harm whales and you'll be harmed. She reassessed her position on Fitzgerald's social media campaigns. Given the number of whale posts, maybe Laker wasn't Fitzgerald's leading cause.

Opening a second tech team message, she learned that, over the course of three years, 118 of Fitzgerald's avatars had been shut down by social media platforms for incendiary posts. Fitzgerald quickly got around the shutdowns. He created new avatars to replace the banned ones. His number of active avatars had never been less than 300.

As she was about to break for lunch, Peabody entered her office. "Where's your partner?" the captain asked in his wheezy voice.

"At his hotel." The words got out before she could stop herself. She should have spun a story for Eller.

"Tell him to cancel that hotel suite. I mean immediately. If he doesn't, he'll be hearing from Central. He's wasting resources. You're your brother's keeper, Bourque."

"I'll pass on the message." She'd change her plans and meet Eller for lunch.

□ □ □

The dining room at the Inn on the Sound was full. Eller and Bourque sat at a tiny round-top that had scarcely enough room for two bowls of clam chowder and the salt and pepper shakers. Glasses of water? Not a chance. An errant spoon would knock them off the table.

"You're in trouble," she told Eller after eating. "In Peabody's eyes, you're close to a disciplinary call."

"Let me guess. I forgot to iron my socks."

She laughed. "Not that bad. It's your hotel suite. You're *wasting resources*. His words."

"I'm supposed to drive back to Holyoke every night?"

"Yep."

"Bullshit. If I spend three hours driving every day, that's three hours less work. Which will be on him. I'll sleep in my car."

"How about on his desk?"

Eller nodded sagely, as if giving it consideration. "When he smells my socks in the morning, he'll change his mind."

"Seriously, watch your step."

"Thanks. I'll talk to Central. It's their call as much as his."

"That's not the way he sees it. If Central boots you out, you can stay at my place. I'm usually at Marty's."

"That's good of you, Bourque. Thank you."

"You're welcome anytime."

"I'd kiss you—on the cheek—but Marty might hear about it. He's probably already heard about us sitting this close."

"Let them talk."

"Speaking of which, Irvine talked some more. Went to see him yesterday. Apparently, someone offered him two-hundred-and-fifty-thou to kill Ruby Halliday three days before she was murdered."

"I take it he didn't accept the offer, or so he says."

"Correct. Claimed he'd never do it, not even for five million. He can't handle more time inside."

Bourque shrugged. "Don't tell me he's going straight."

"No danger of that."

"Well, my news pales in comparison. It seems whalers were Fitzgerald's main social media target, not Laker."

Eller faked a yawn.

"No respect," she kidded. "You know, it won't be easy to dig into Laker and company. A group that hates whales? A lot easier to crack. If one exists, I bet we can break it in two months."

"How much?"

"Lunch. Not here. At Luigi's Trattoria."

□ □ □

Back at Barnstable Unit, Peabody summoned Eller and Bourque to his office. Stepping into his lair, she stifled her senses. The captain was wearing a different aftershave. It smelled more like fire-accelerant than aftershave. He ordered the detectives to sit and surveyed them from his chair. "There's fresh intel on one of the *Islander* passengers."

Fresh, Bourque wryly thought. Not in this room.

"Plymouth Police called about a thirty-two-year-old carpet layer named Paul Unger from the Ellisville area."

Plymouth again, she reflected. Irvine was also from Plymouth. A small thing, but she looked for small things.

"He has an alibi for October nineteenth," Peabody noted. "It checked. He was with a workmate. They were doing a reno job on the Vineyard. So why are you here?" He paused to let the question sink in. "Unger confessed to killing Halliday."

Bourque leaned closer. A confession?

"He's in custody in Plymouth," Peabody went on. "An anonymous caller tipped Plymouth Police off. They picked Unger up an hour ago. They're processing his DNA. But don't think we're here for a celebration. Unger may be taking a fall. They suspect he's being sacrificed to get us off the tail of the real killer." Peabody pursed his lips. "Although he has a sheet, he's a low-level gang member, usually a delivery boy. In Plymouth's view, if he didn't take the fall, he'd be at the bottom of Cape Cod Bay. Jail time or pushing up seaweed."

The detectives didn't respond.

"I'd say the real perps, or their handlers, are feeling uncomfortable. If, as Irvine claims, he didn't cooperate, they had to find another hitman. Ergo Unger." Peabody kept going. "Plymouth detectives got some info out of him. He insists he's known Halliday for years. Met her when she was an undergrad at UMass Boston. She used to waitress part-time in Quincy."

Bourque broke in. "How long did she go to UMass?"

"Two semesters. Then she dropped out and went to NYU."

"Were she and Unger a couple?"

"No. He said they were friends with benefits. *Benefits*? Used to be medical benefits. That's all I get." Peabody shook his head.

"They call that the evolution of English. How about the paucity of English. Moving on. Unger maintains he attacked her with seven or eight knife thrusts—he doesn't remember exactly. Conceivable, but, according to the med ex, there were fifteen. Also, Unger's timeline is off. He says he killed her just before twenty-forty-five. However, the parents reported they were awake until roughly fifteen minutes after that. They probably would have heard something." Peabody held up a hand. "But we can't get ahead of ourselves. Unger was videotaped at a gas station in Barnstable at twenty-one-twenty, which means he could have been in Orleans at twenty-forty-five."

Bourque didn't comment. One homicide solved? Or one more muddied?

"I'm sending you two to interview him tomorrow. In the meantime, I'm requisitioning *Islander* video footage for the whole summer. We need to establish when Unger was onboard and who he talked to. By the way, Central sent us a new detective yesterday, name of Roberto Ortiz. Real go-getter. A pleasure to work with." Peabody regarded Eller. "Not that you'd know. I'll say this directly. Get the hell out of that hotel."

Eller didn't bite.

"Use your head. You're a senior detective. The team needs your guidance. Hence, they need you *here*." Peabody turned to Bourque. "Ortiz is taking over your enquiry into Karen Symon and Meryl Verdi."

"I'm getting to it."

"You can't fry all the fish, Lieutenant." Peabody waved them off. "Meeting dismissed."

## Chapter 25

**DAY SIXTEEN: Plymouth, Massachusetts. November 4th**

Dense clouds blew in off the Atlantic. Bourque could barely see four car lengths. She switched on her fog lights. Dusk seemed to have descended in mid-afternoon. Plymouth's skyline was missing-in-action. She exited Pilgrims Highway at Long Pond Road and turned into Plymouth Police HQ.

She and Eller entered the station bearing gifts for Unger: a fresh coffee, cream and sugar on the side, and a bag of chocolate-fudge cookies. A little bribery was useful. Though Eller often started interviews, Bourque would take the lead, playing good cop. He'd come in at the end, flip the script, and dig at Unger to dislodge the truth. She figured Unger would stonewall them at first. If they stuck with it, he might reveal—likely not verbally—if he actually killed Halliday. As for him implicating other parties, aka upstream handlers, that was a longshot. Exposing your handlers got you killed.

The interview room looked like Room One at Barnstable Unit. Same furniture, same vomit-green paint. As she arranged a sham accordion file on the metal table—stuffed with bogus reports—a burly officer shoved Paul Unger into the room. He didn't resemble any carpet layers Bourque knew. Not only was he tall and athletic, he was '80s rockstar handsome: long chestnut hair, high cheekbones, Bon Jovi eyes. She could see why Halliday might have fallen for him.

Driving to Plymouth, she and Eller had received an update on Unger's file. His DNA wasn't found at the site of either Halliday's or Fitzgerald's murder. In addition, his confession looked more doubtful. A sworn witness testimony placed him at a takeout window in downtown Plymouth at 2110 on the night of Halliday's murder, which meant it was unlikely he was in Orleans at 2045 when he said he killed her. He'd have to average over a 100 miles per hour to drive from Orleans to Plymouth in twenty-five minutes.

Bourque decided to play Unger slowly, like a fly fisher with a salmon on the line.

"Good afternoon, Mr. Unger," she began and passed him the

coffee and cookies. "I'm Detective Lieutenant Bourque, State Police. I understand you were brought in on a suspected homicide offense."

He nodded and dug out a cookie.

"I'm from the Cape and Islands Unit. That means I'm working on Ruby Halliday's homicide."

"I'm not proud of what I did." Unger sounded contrite. "But she made me do it."

"Made you do what, Mr. Unger?"

Unger's eyes flickered. He bit into the cookie and chewed.

"Made you do what?" Bourque repeated.

"Kill her."

She pointed to the accordion file. "That's not what the evidence says. It appears we're detaining you for no reason."

"No reason? Like I told you, I killed her."

"We're going to release you. Answer a few questions and we might waive the charge for a false confession."

"False confession? I did it, I tell you! She was a bitch, a lying bitch."

"Your confession is suspect. It doesn't match the evidence. However, I'm sure you can help us. We know that a car registered to a Jack Irvine, also known as John Paul Jones, was in Orleans on October twenty-first, the day of Ruby's murder. Do you know Mr. Irvine?" She gave Unger a friendly smile. "Take your time. Think about it." It was another fishing expedition.

The suspect held her gaze. "I never met him."

"I understand you did a recent renovation job on Martha's Vineyard. Where?"

"Twenty Morse Street, Edgartown."

Correct, Bourque knew. But she was after something else, using one of the axioms of detective work. A good way to test if someone was lying was to ask a question you already knew the answer to. "How many jobs have you done on the Cape this year?"

"Three," he said.

Correct again. "How many days did the last job take you?"

"Two."

Also correct. Enough preliminaries. She now had a decent read on Unger. Eller probably had one too. Whenever Unger told the truth, the corners of his lips curled up a fraction of an inch. It should now be easier to catch him at a lie. "Did you do any work in Orleans recently?"

"No." Unger's lips were curled up at the corners, indicating he was telling the truth.

"Ever go there?"

"No. Not until October twenty-first," he added.

"When you killed Ruby Halliday?"

"Yes."

Bourque scrutinized his lips. No corner upcurl. Completely straight. That suggested a lie. "Were you inside Ruby Halliday's house at eight-thirty p.m.?"

"Yes," he said. However, his straight lips said otherwise.

Bourque eyed him, thinking it would be a good time to start a bad cop routine. He was definitely lying. He had a lot to lose by telling the truth: his life.

As if on cue, Eller stepped into the room. He nodded curtly at Unger. "Detective Lieutenant Eller, State Police."

He sat next to Bourque and tilted his head back. "Mr. Unger, you claim you were inside Ruby Halliday's house on the night of October twenty-first."

Unger nodded.

"Then perhaps you can tell us why your DNA wasn't."

Unger didn't skip a beat. "I wore gloves and a hat," he slickly said.

"What kind of hat?"

"A watch cap. A black one."

"So, you covered your tracks. Like you did with Daniel Fitzgerald."

"I didn't kill him," Unger said. "Like I told you, I killed *her*. Read my confession."

"You're sticking with that?" Eller's look said he could play a waiting game far longer than Unger. "Who has your head in a vice?"

Unger remained silent.

"Let's talk," Eller said. "We can protect you."

"I don't need protecting."

"How much money do you owe?"

"None."

Bourque knew it wouldn't take M&M long to examine Unger's bank records. Given he didn't come across as a fool who'd do anyone's bidding, he probably had debts. She sensed he or his handlers had wiped his financial trail before he'd confessed to murder. In her narc squad days, she'd seen a lot of guys like Unger: underlings willing to pay the price.

"I'll ask you again," Eller said. "How much money do you owe?"

"None." Unger didn't appear to be troubled.

"Did someone threaten your parents? Perhaps your siblings? You can tell us."

No response.

"What kind of knife did you use?" Eller asked.

"A good knife."

"Where did you get it?"

Unger didn't answer.

"From Fitzgerald's killer?"

"Talk to my lawyer."

"I don't like bullshitters," Eller stated and turned to Bourque. "Do you, Lieutenant?"

"No." She shook her head sadly, playing good cop. "We'd like to help, Mr. Unger, but lies torpedo your cause."

"Help? You two? I want my lawyer."

"No problem," she said. "If you want to invoke your rights, we won't ask you anything else. But I'm going to tell you what we know."

"What's that?"

"You didn't kill Ruby Halliday."

Bourque left the room, followed by Eller. While she couldn't prove what she'd just said, instinct told her Unger was a fall guy. As on other cases, she trusted the same compass she'd used her entire career: intuition.

□ □ □

"I have to admit to something," Eller said a few miles from Falmouth.

Bourque took her eyes off the road and glanced at him. Since leaving Plymouth, they'd been traveling silently, each of them wrapped in their own thoughts, passing through the late afternoon like ghosts, cocooned by mist and fog. "Go on," she said.

"Peabody is right."

"You must be delirious," she kidded. "About what?"

"He's right about me working from the office. I should be there. I'm going to cancel my suite at the Inn on the Sound and move to a motel. They have good rates now."

"They're much better after Thanksgiving." Eller was oblivious to prices. He never checked bills in restaurants, never looked at stickers in stores.

"All right. Regardless, I'll cut my bill in half."

Doable, she thought. Good for him. Not that Peabody would be mollified, but why bother bringing up the inevitable. "How about we make a little detour before I drop you off?"

"Sure."

"Sam Carson should be home. It's his day off."

"Him again?"

"Got a new angle."

□ □ □

Fog enveloped Falmouth, blanketing the town with billions of water molecules, turning it into a ghostly apparition of itself. Bourque couldn't see across the Inner Harbor. Ten yards away, Carson's bungalow was barely distinguishable from the warehouse next to it. The moored sailboats were wraith-like in the muffled light, their rigging as ethereal as spider webs.

Carson came to the door on her second knock. "Good evening, Officers."

"Let's have a little talk," she said.

"Any time. Come in."

Carson led the detectives to his kitchen, which was bright and warm. He pointed to the oven. "Just made some baked beans. Doc said to eat less meat. Bad for the gallstones. Would you like some?"

Eller nodded.

"A small plate," Bourque said. "Thanks." Was Carson being obsequious, or was he genuinely friendly?

He turned away and dished out three helpings. "There's bread and molasses on the table. Donna—my wife—she loved molasses on beans."

Like Carson, Bourque dug into her beans with a spoon. She noticed he used his left hand. A few minutes later, he stirred sugar into his coffee with his left hand. It wasn't much, but it was a beginning. Halliday was attacked from her right side, which suggested the perp used their left arm to wield the knife, assuming they were facing the victim.

After eating, taking her plate to the kitchen sink, Bourque saw a few left-handed kitchen gadgets, among them, a can opener.

Marty had the same opener; he was a lefty. If Carson was one, it might be relevant. Another *might*.

Back at the table, she scrutinized the POI. "We're curious about something." She paused to make him wait. "From what you told us," she eventually said, "I'd say you respected Daniel Fitzgerald."

"I did."

"Then why did you let someone kill him?"

"Let someone kill him? What are you saying?"

"You must have seen the whole attack."

Carson's eyes widened, regarding her with disbelief. Slowly, his eyes returned to normal. "Where'd you get that idea? I didn't see anything."

"You were smoking near the stern bridge that night. I stood up there. Great sight line below, to the aft viewing deck."

"Not where I smoke."

"Where's that?"

"The port side. There's a comm tower there. I stand behind it. Besides, I wasn't up there when he was attacked."

"How do you know?"

"I read about the case. He was attacked as we came into Woods Hole."

"Where were you?"

"Main deck. I handle one of the aft dock lines."

"What time was that?"

"About five minutes from port."

"Did you look at your watch?"

"No. The disembarkation horn had just sounded. When you're coming into port, clock time isn't important. You concentrate on your job. The horns tell you what's happening and when."

"Do you think someone else could have seen the attack?"

"Maybe, but the aft viewing deck is generally clear at that time."

Bourque held his gaze. Carson's voice and body language had been clean all the way through. No hesitating, no nervous tics, no suspicious eye or lip movements. She gestured to Eller. *Any questions?*

"Mr. Carson," Eller said, "when did you meet Paul Unger?"

Carson thought a moment. "I don't know anyone named Paul Unger."

"We know you're old friends."

Carson shook his head. "Can't be. I never met him. Never even heard of him."

"When did you first ask Ruby Halliday out?"

"I never asked her out."

"Tell us about the first time. Don't be shy. Any man would be interested in her."

"Not me."

"Why's that?"

"In my mind, Donna and I are still together."

"Do you like Orleans, Mr. Carson?"

"Sure, nice town."

"How long have you known Jack Irvine?"

"Again, I never heard of him."

"How about John Paul Jones?"

"Who?"

"J. P. Jones, bartender in Plymouth."

Carson shook his head. "Don't know him either. I don't drink in Plymouth. In fact, I don't drink much in Falmouth." He smiled. "I'm a working stiff."

"How are things at work? Any problems with Captain Macey?"

"No."

"How about with pro-whale advocates?"

"Don't know any."

"Are you okay if the *Islander* has to slow down for whales?"

"It's not my call, but I'm fine with it."

"You could be affected personally. You'll probably have to work faster at the dock."

Carson nodded. "I'll do what's needed."

Eller glanced at Bourque. *I'm done*, his eyes said.

## Chapter 26

**Woods Hole**

Outside Carson's house, Bourque addressed Eller. "One more visit."

"I know we just had some beans, but don't you eat?"

"Plenty. I'll take you to a chowder house afterward. I want to see Liam Doyle, the marine biologist who knew Fitzgerald."

Fog lights and low beams on, Bourque headed to Woods Hole. She'd looked up Doyle. His ketch was docked ten minutes away, at Pinkys Marina in Eel Pond, barely a hundred yards from the Oceanographic Institution. He'd been living aboard the boat for eight years. Doyle had a clean sheet. He was thirty-seven and single. Originally from Houston, he'd gone to Texas A&M Corpus Christi, where he earned a doctorate specializing in cetaceans—whales. Now he was one of the world's foremost experts on North Atlantic right whale feeding habits and feeding grounds as well as a visiting professor at Northeastern in Boston.

Pinkys, a small marina off Water Street, mirrored Carson's neighborhood that evening: another seaside locale with wraithlike boats and ghostly rigging. The main dock was ungated. Knowing Eller wasn't a boat person, Bourque led him slowly along the dock using her police flashlight. He followed carefully. The fog seemed to be alive, a creature pervading every inch of Cape Cod.

Doyle's home was berthed at the end of the dock. Bourque estimated the ketch was at least a forty-footer. A high tide was flooding into Eel Pond, tugging on the hull's mooring lines. The nearby slips were empty, which was unusual. Marina boats were normally cheek-by-jowl. Doyle had plenty of privacy. She saw a muted light on in the main cabin.

"Permission to come aboard," she called.

"Who's there?" came a mellow voice.

"Detectives Ivy Bourque and Victor Eller, State Police. We have a few questions for you."

"Step aboard. Mind the mizzen boom. You know a mizzen boom?"

"Aye, aye," she replied, then winked at Eller.

The deck barely swayed as she and Eller stepped aboard, a sign of a sturdy sailboat. Doyle opened the companionway hatch, releasing a gust of warm air smelling of diesel, an odor she knew well. The ketch had an Espar cabin heater, common in sailboats outfitted for New England. The main cabin had plenty of headroom, allowing a tall man like Doyle to stand upright.

He waved the detectives to a red-cushioned bench lining the starboard hull and sat opposite them with his legs spread wide. The cabin was darker than Heaney's living room. Nonetheless, Bourque could easily see Doyle's eyes. They were large and inquisitive.

"What can I get you?" he asked. "Tea, coffee? Rum?"

"Nothing, thanks," Bourque answered, echoed by Eller. "We're here to talk about Daniel Fitzgerald," she casually related. "When did you meet him?"

"A question first, if I may. I'm curious, Detective Bourque. How do you know mizzens?"

"I sail. A sloop, that is."

"I see. What's the difference between a ketch and a yawl?"

She felt she was being quizzed by one of her former professors, or Wozniak, the med examiner.

What was it with these scholarly types? She played along. "They're both two-masters, but the mizzen sail on a ketch is larger. More wind can catch it. You have to take more care."

"Indeed. Are you a Yankee?"

"On my mother's side."

"You know what my grandfather said? 'A Yankee is a Texan on a sailing ship.' People think Yankees and Texans are totally different, but they're not. Both love their past."

Enough, she thought. Was Doyle delaying to gain time to make up a story? Or for some other reason? He had the hunch of tall men who carried themselves like a coiled spring, one that could suddenly unwind, a trait that, in Bourque's view, made him unpredictable. "On to Dan Fitzgerald," she tersely stated. "When and where did you meet him?"

"About three years ago," Doyle replied, "near Boston. I went up there to see Chase Heaney. We're sailing friends. He owns a beautiful ketch, a Swan SS. Dan was aboard."

To Bourque, it wouldn't matter if Doyle was the Pope's best friend. On a case, she walked the fine line between treating POIs with respect and treating them like liars. "All that way for a sail?" she said. "You have your own ketch."

"I don't take her out often. The Oceanographic Institution—I work there—wants me to use their boats. Insurance purposes."

"How many times did you sail with Mr. Fitzgerald?"

Doyle reflected a moment before replying. "Quite a few. Nine, ten, maybe more."

"Were you friends?"

"Yes. Not close friends, but we got along well. He loved whales, he loved the ocean. So do I."

The cabin light faded. Doyle stood and lit a hanging kerosene lantern with a match. The glow triggered a dance of shadows, which dissipated as the swinging lantern returned to a state of equilibrium.

"Where were you on the night of October nineteenth?" Bourque asked.

"Here."

"Can someone corroborate that?"

"Yes."

"Name?"

Doyle hesitated. "My girlfriend. It's a private relationship."

It was time to put the POI on the defensive. "And she has an alibi to confirm. What's her name?"

"Carly. Carly Rand." He shook his head. "I shouldn't be seeing her. She's a grad student; I'm her Ph.D. supervisor. First time I've ever done that."

"Be careful how you answer the next question, sir. You're not in court but this is a, let's say, formal talk. You wouldn't want to contradict yourself at a later date." Bourque paused. "When did Carly Rand arrive and when did she leave?"

"She got here just after eight p.m. She left about five the next morning."

Bourque signaled for Eller to take over.

"What's Carly Rand's cell number?" he asked Doyle.

Doyle recited it.

"I'm going to step out to call her, Mr. Doyle. You're going to sit tight."

"Mind the mizzen boom. It's the part that sticks out from the mast, the part landlubbers fall over."

When Eller left, Doyle turned to Bourque. "He your partner?

Work partner, I mean."

"Sometimes."

"He's not a sailor, I know that. Sailors descend hatch ladders backward. He tried to come down face-first." Doyle stifled a chuckle. "I thought he was going to land on his nose. You know what else I know? Dan Fitzgerald had enemies."

"What kind of enemies?"

"Let me put it colloquially. Whale haters. Over the last three years, I've read a lot of papers that referenced Right Whales First, the name of Dan's non-profit. His own name usually came up as well. I also attended numerous conferences, both remotely and in person, where he was mentioned on the podium and in the corridors. He was known internationally as an agitator. In my eyes, a good one. Anti-whale groups considered him a major adversary."

"Can you give me the names of the anti- groups?"

"Do you have email?"

*No, I use smoke signals.* She handed Doyle her card.

"Most of them are my enemies too," he confided. "Not that I've confronted them. I'm not a fighter."

"Chase Heaney's a fighter. Why were you sailing with him?"

"*Was* a fighter," Doyle corrected her. "I was there for the science, to research whales under duress. We can save the North Atlantic right whale." Doyle nodded with conviction. "We just have to change our perception of them, and of whales as a whole. Which," he equally conceded, "isn't a simple thing. Humans have to agree that whales are valuable. That's one of the things I admired about Dan. He worked hard to make that happen. And probably got killed for it."

"How do you know that?"

Doyle raised both hands palms-up. "It's a deduction. If Northeast shipping lanes are reduced by whale rights, maritime traffic will decrease. Maybe by thirty or forty percent. Northeast shipping companies wouldn't take that lightly. They're powerful enemies. Enemies of the sea as well. They don't care about spreading invasive species. They don't care about pollutants. But I don't despair for the ocean, Detective. It'll survive. Granted, it'll be different. I won't get into how. You're not here for that. Will humans be around to see the changes? That's the question."

She didn't respond. Professor D was right, not that she'd tell him. In her view—not that her view mattered—humans might not be around. Carbon to carbon. As for whales, many millennia after their ancestors had migrated from land to sea, they might have to move ashore again. Such was evolution. Endless journeys by endless species.

Doyle looked past her to the hatch. Eller was starting down the ladder the wrong way again. A second later, he turned around.

Bourque grinned to herself. Someday she'd invite him onto her and Marty's boat.

Eller faced Doyle. "Your alibi looks good. By the way, your girlfriend told me to pass something on: *You're done.*"

□ □ □

Bourque dropped Eller off at his car. As he returned to Holyoke, she headed home. She needed a night on her own. She felt listless. She wanted to watch a "girlie" movie and curl up in her pajamas. Despite having a big bowl of New England clam chowder with Eller, she was ravenous. She was going to *mangia, mangia*: eat a huge plate of pasta. A girl couldn't ignore her cravings. Besides, Marty was at his place. See no weakness, know no weakness.

First things first. She had a pile of laundry to do, well, more like a midden. Almost a month's worth. Marty once asked her why she owned so much underwear; she replied with two words: *Dirty laundry.* She hated doing laundry. He didn't. Another reason, very minor in the scheme of things, why she saw herself in his orbit. In Gigi's view, finding a good man in the sack took forever. In Bourque's, finding a good one who did laundry was harder. Not to mention, one who was willing to sacrifice his career and stay in Massachusetts.

Washing machine running, she moseyed to the kitchen, wondering what pasta sauce she'd make. Her fridge would answer that question. She found lean pickings. However, she had eggs, cream, and turkey bacon. Alfredo, it would be, just not a real alfredo. Turkey bacon didn't turn crisp like the real stuff, but so what?

Her ex-husband Nico Rizzi would give her hell. He was a culinary purist, unlike Marty. In Nico's world, chefs were semi-divine, Michelin-starred restaurants were cathedrals. His mother knew better. To Mamma Rizzi, a life-long inhabitant of Brindisi at the heel of Italy's boot, a simple trattoria was holy. Sanctity came from filling an entire plate with food, not the center of it. Not that she'd eat an alfredo sauce. That was for northerners and foreigners. In *mamma's cucina*, the tomato reigned supreme. Her fish stews were cioppino-type marvels chock full of tomatoes, garlic, scorpion fish, squid, mussels, and clams. Bourque still missed them.

She started rendering the turkey bacon with olive oil and looked in her cupboard. No fettucine, just rotini. Again, so what? She could hear Nico groan. Banishing his presence, she diced a big clove of garlic. Mama Rizzi had taught her that it didn't matter if pasta was fresh or dry, homemade or storebought. What mattered was that you finished it in the sauce, so that it soaked up the magic. That always worked.

## Chapter 27

### Ellisville, Massachusetts

Paul Unger knew what people said about him: He had bad habits. So what? Sex, drugs, 'n' rock 'n' roll were the true Holy Trinity. Up in Boston, he'd been a lead guitarist in his twenties, before heroin knocked him down. He'd had more paramours than any man he knew, beauties of all ages and races.

He heard his front door lock clicking. Two seconds later, he was staring at a short, beefy man. Unger placed his takeout chai on the end table. "R. R. send you?"

The intruder nodded. "He told me to get three framed photos with you and him on boats. Where are they?"

Unger pointed to the wall by the door.

The intruder rushed at him and covered his face with an ether-soaked cloth. "I have to do this," the man morosely said.

Unger didn't fight back. His time had come. For months, he'd been feeling it coming. He wasn't afraid to die—not that he was looking forward to it. The world was beautiful. Being a diver, he found the ocean endlessly fascinating. But when Death arrived, beauty was irrelevant. His attacker gagged him. The knife descended again and again.

## Chapter 28

**DAY SEVENTEEN: Barnstable. November 5th**

Bourque was deep into reviewing the Fitzgerald-Halliday case when Peabody requested her presence. The captain preferred it when detectives marched into his office for meetings, which is why she sauntered slowly in. Sitting in his lair, she smelled a decent cologne for a change. Kudos to him. How about some new drapes, *capitaine*? Bid adieu to the sapphire eyesore.

"We have two orders of business this morning," the captain officiously stated. "One, Paul Unger. Two, a possible lead. First, Unger. He's dead. Murdered."

Bourque shook her head sadly. She wasn't surprised. Unger seemed to have been trapped by circumstances. "When?" she asked.

"Plymouth PD released him late yesterday afternoon. He was found dead in his apartment a few hours later, around twenty-one hundred. Roughly the same time as the Fitzgerald and Halliday murders. A possible convergence. He was also knifed," Peabody noted. "The autopsy's a rush order, scheduled in Maynard for thirteen-hundred. You have time to get there. Eller will join you from Holyoke."

"Good."

"Plymouth says it wasn't a break-and-enter. The door was open. It's possible the perp or perps had a key."

Another convergence, she thought.

"According to Plymouth, Unger didn't seem worried when he left the station. Maybe he figured he'd done his best. Not his fault we didn't believe him. Plymouth assumes his handlers wouldn't agree with that view and knocked him off. Sounds reasonable to me. On our end, Central has an APB out for Marcus Aldo, the money scammer. They suspect the hit order came from him. Or, if not from him, from someone upstream he had to please. All right, leave it there for now."

Peabody pursed his lips. "On to the possible lead, an *Islander* passenger on October nineteenth named Enrico Conti. Like Irvine and Unger, he works in Plymouth. Looks like *America's Hometown* is taking center stage."

Bourque nodded. The Plymouth connection appeared to be getting stronger.

"He's fifty-six, divorced, two kids. His *Islander* alibi checked." The captain raised an eyebrow. "Just like they've all checked. I wonder if we missed something there, cleared an alibi that needs to be reexamined. Look into that during your case reviews." Peabody kept rolling. "Conti works as a bookkeeper for a shipping company but he has a side gig. He's assistant secretary for the state longshoremen's *club*. Read *mafioso*." Peabody held up a hand. "I know the story. They don't run all the harbors anymore, but they do control a lot of shipping, including some ferry companies. And they don't like change."

Valid assessment, Bourque knew. They'd be opposed to any pro-whale shipping laws.

"As it happens, Conti purchased scuba gear in North Plymouth on October eighteenth." Peabody read from a list, his high-pitched words scurrying from his mouth. "Hooded diving suit, gloves, boots. Pair of extra-long fins, mask, scuba breathing set, two Sherwood tanks." He regarded Bourque. "There was an attempted larceny of scuba gear in Eastham. Conti's purchases were made two days after the unsuccessful larceny. How's this for speculation? When the theft failed, someone had to buy the gear. Maybe Conti was the buyer? But why the scuba gear? That's where you come in, Bourque."

Why the scuba gear? she asked herself. Her mind spun. A diver could get aboard the *Islander* when it was docked. Was the perp a diver? She stared out Peabody's double-wide window. Had they been considering Fitzgerald's murderer from the wrong point of view, from above Vineyard Sound, instead of under it?

"Bourque, are you with us?"

She refocused on Peabody. "Here's a possibility," she ventured. "The gear could be linked to Fitzgerald's killer. All the *Islander* passengers have alibis. The crew and staff check. But the perp was on the ferry. That's undeniable. How did he or she get aboard?"

*On with it*, Peabody gestured.

"A gut instinct tells me they dove and climbed aboard, perhaps via a dock hawser. Old Navy Seals trick. If I'm wrong, so be it. But I don't think I am. They dove from near one of the ferry terminals, either Woods Hole or Vineyard Haven. I don't know which."

"If you're right," Peabody said, "it doesn't matter."

"It could matter. I'm thinking about collaborators. After killing Fitzgerald, when the ferry docked at Woods Hole, the perp waited until the coast was clear and slipped off the ship. How did they get away wearing diving gear or carrying it?"

"Maybe they didn't. They sank it in Vineyard Sound."

"Possible, but there were a lot of potential witnesses aboard. Someone could have spotted them doing that. The whitecoats swept the ferry. They didn't find any hidden scuba gear. Perhaps a collaborator picked up the perp and the gear and drove off. With a getaway driver, the perp could dive from either port." Bourque held up a hand. "Alternatively, if the perp worked alone, they likely parked their getaway vehicle in Woods Hole and dove from there. In that case, they hid on the ferry until it made the return passage from Vineyard Haven with Fitzgerald aboard, killed him, dove off the ship, and drove away."

Peabody shrugged. "More speculation."

"I'm not done. You know what's missing from the gear list? A knife. They didn't buy a diving knife because they had a knife."

"Are you going to tell me they owned a Strider knife?"

"Not yet." She winked. The ex-Marine angle had died on the vine. A few days ago, Peabody had suggested it was too convoluted. Perhaps it was, she'd thought at the time. Or too hard to prove.

The captain moved on. "Conti is a regular at Romeo's in Plymouth. Strip club, as you know. Again, as you know, Carolina Pereira happens to work there. Incidentally, we just learned her stage name is Candy. She was likely one of the girls at Irvine's party the night Halliday was murdered. Don't want to get ahead of ourselves, but we could be looking at some concurrences. Irvine plus Pereira plus Conti."

"Plus the scuba gear."

"Right. After the autopsy, take Eller with you to Plymouth. Question Conti and Pereira, then examine Unger's place." Peabody stood. "Do me a favor. Make sure Eller overnights at home."

She didn't respond.

### Maynard, Massachusetts State Police Crime Lab

Every time Bourque walked into Central's forensic department, it felt like she was stepping into the future. The section was ultra-high-tech: a realm of whirring machines and stainless steel.

Forensics was law enforcement's not-so-secret sauce. However, being a cop, she knew it wasn't enough. You needed a complete case to convict a felon: motive, opportunity, and evidence.

Bourque pulled her hair into a ponytail and joined Eller in the lab. Nothing was hidden on an autopsy table, a reminder not only of humanity's physicality, but of the physicality of crime. Ashes to ashes, carbon to carbon. The chemistry of crime was unavoidable. When a murder occurred, it always left a trail of molecules—no matter how faint. It was just a matter of finding them.

She nodded hello to the forensic pathologist, Dr. Molly Yi, a dyed-blonde of Korean descent, a few years younger than Bourque. Under her lab coat, Yi wore black leather leggings. Like a few females at Maynard, she'd had an on-again, off-again relationship with Leo Bradley, aka Loverboy Bradley.

"Step right up," Yi jauntily said. "As usual, we're taping this. Stop me if you have any questions."

She led the detectives to the table. Unger was covered by a white sheet from the waist down. The muscles beneath his skin had already started to shrink away from the surface. Like Halliday, he'd been stabbed in the face: the eyes, nose, and mouth. Bourque's first thought was another connected murder. A threepeat: Unger, Halliday, Fitzgerald.

Unger's torso was free of wounds. She noted his powerful shoulders and arms. Despite the morgue's first-rate refrigeration, the corpse had begun decomposing, indicating he'd been dead for hours before reaching Maynard. Her nose detected the first stage of decomposition—autolysis or self-digestion, in which excess carbon dioxide triggered cell membrane ruptures. Being a student of chemistry, she knew the ruptures released enzymes that ate cells from the inside out. The air held numerous chemical compounds: cadaverine and putrescine, the olfactory signature of decaying flesh; traces of methanethiol, akin to rotting cabbage; and the rotten-egg odor of hydrogen sulfide.

Yi hit the recording button and used a pointer to indicate the victim's facial wounds. "Consider the widespread bruising, which is caused by extensive blood flow. It specifies injuries sustained before the victim's heart stopped. The victim was stabbed repeatedly before he died. Three of the orbital stab wounds," Yi said and paused to point them out, "were deep enough to extend past the eyes and reach the dura, which indicates someone powerful enough to plunge a knife that deep. It also suggests a skilled attacker, who knew the orbital region doesn't protect the brain as well as the forehead. Any of those three wounds could have triggered subdural hemorrhaging. We need to take a MRA to determine that." Yi stopped. "I can't be certain how long he lived after those wounds. Hemorrhaging could have caused enough intracranial pressure to trigger brain death. That is, death within minutes."

The two detectives remained silent.

"I suspect the brain incisions were the first wounds. The attacker likely inflicted the other wounds when the victim was near death. One thing is certain," Yi continued, "there is no evidence of defensive wounds, which suggests he didn't fight back. Given his musculature and apparent strength, I find that unusual. Where was the body found?"

"The victim's apartment," Bourque replied. "The door was open."

"Not to trod on your turf." Yi surveyed the detectives. "I'd say the victim was resigned to his fate."

"Why do you say that?" Eller asked.

"A strong man like him and he did nothing? He knew what was coming but didn't fight back? I conjecture he knew it was useless. If the knife attack didn't succeed, another attack would."

Eller didn't comment. However, his eyes said *leave the detecting to us.*

"It's just a supposition," Yi stated.

"Appreciate the thought," Bourque said. She'd known Yi for years and didn't mind when the patho speculated. It meant she cared.

"There are fifteen facial wounds," Yi went on. "All of the strikes came from the right side of the victim, from roughly the same arm angle. That says one attacker. The right side is consistent with Halliday's murder. Not to harp on a theme, but the incision imprints also look familiar. You'll have to give us time to process them. I suspect they could be from the knife used to attack both Halliday and Fitzgerald. There's something else to consider." Yi pulled the sheet off the corpse.

Bourque inhaled sharply. Unger's penis had been cut off.

"Unlike the facial wounds," the patho noted, "the penile severance exhibits little bleeding, indicating it occurred after the heart stopped. The victim was dead when his male organ was detached. As you can see, the perp made a very precise cut. Tells me he or she likely had one hand on the knife, and one on the penis, pulling it tight, making it easier to cut off. The cut itself is another indication of a strong perp. Even with a sharp knife, you have to be strong to cut that cleanly through muscle. The male organ is a wonder of muscle."

Bourque nodded. No argument there. To boot, Yi knew what she was talking about. A few years back, before Marty came along, she and Bourque had done a bit of clubbing in Boston's Theatre District. When they headed home, Yi always had a younger man, or two, in tow.

"I won't surmise why it was severed." Yi regarded Eller, then replaced the sheet. "Too many possible reasons, anything from retribution to trophy-hunting. I'll leave that to you."

Eller said nothing.

"Did they find the penis?" Bourque asked.

Yi shook her head. "That could say *trophy*. But, hey, I know how it is. A pathologist's words aren't supposed to direct your investigation." She glanced at Eller. "Yet they are supposed to make you think. All right, final step."

Yi selected a scalpel and made a quick Y-incision in Unger's chest, then excised the chest plate and extracted the inner organs. Having dissected the heart and lungs and examined them, she looked up at the detectives. "Cause of death: multiple knife wounds. Means: murder. Pending toxicology reports." She paused. "One more thing. It appears Halliday and Unger were attacked face-first. They were knifed from the right side, which implies the perp favored their left arm. We may have a left-handed perp."

Bourque nodded.

Yi pulled off her gloves. "If we have the same perp for all three murders, Fitzgerald was probably attacked from the back. His aortal region was targeted, which is on the left side of the body, which fits with a perp using their left arm."

Leaving the lab, Bourque realized she wouldn't be seeing much of Marty any time soon. In addition to the murder weapon, perp strength and handedness were potential factors. The team would have to process new POIs as well as reconsider original ones. Who was left-handed? It appeared Carson was. Other POIs could be ambidextrous. Who was strong? Heaney, she deemed, and Verdi and Jasper Halliday. Macey too. Perhaps Doyle. A long list.

# Chapter 29

## Plymouth

Bourque and Eller approached Plymouth's harbor with the sun setting behind them. A wall of leaden clouds obscured Cape Cod Bay. The detectives stopped for an early supper at Lobster Hut off Town Wharf. After ordering lobster bisques and rolls, they sat overlooking the harbor and ate in silence. An autopsy often shut down conversation. A few fishing boats puttered lazily into harbor, apparently unfazed by the dark clouds. The ocean looked ominous. It was as leaden as the November sky.

Having dispatched her large bisque and two rolls, Bourque sat back, happily satiated. The meal had been simple but five-star. Who needed waiters in white gloves? She regarded Eller. "You seem quiet," she observed. "Autopsy got your tongue?"

"Nah. Well, a bit. That severed member." He shook his head. "Like Pacino said, *fuhgeddaboudit.*"

"Johnny Depp too."

"He doesn't count."

Eller chuckled. "You got that right. I have a question for you. Not a work question."

"Shoot," she said.

"It's about my two daughters, eleven and fourteen. They cruise social media. I can't stop that, but who can. Anyhow, they saw posts about how Dan Fitzgerald stood up for Atlantic right whales. Now they're asking me about them. *How endangered are they? Are we doing enough to save them?* You're plugged in to the environment, Bourque. What do I say?"

She decided to be totally honest. Eller wasn't only a colleague; he was a friend. "Tell them the truth. That the North Atlantic right whale is almost extinct. It's not just endangered. That's sugarcoating. Tell them why too. A major reason is us—humans, that is: collisions with ships and entanglement in fishing nets. I don't lie to kids."

"You don't have kids."

*Yet,* she wanted to say. "Valid point, but they can take the truth. If we give them the goods, they'll do something. If we don't, nothing will change. In the meantime, scientists are tracking the population, monitoring the number of males, females, and calves. It's a jigsaw," Bourque acknowledged, "but a big piece of the puzzle seems to be global warming. Ocean warming, in particular. Right whales are on the move, following food north to New England as early as March. It's one of their main habitats now, particularly Cape Cod Bay and Nantucket Shoals. Tell your kids we need to protect those areas."

"I'll pass that on. Thanks, partner. You *are* plugged in."

Bourque shrugged. "I don't talk about it much, definitely not at work."

"I hear you. Smart move. We're like jurors. We're supposed to be unbiased. Well, as unbiased as cops can be."

□ □ □

The detectives pulled up to a shipshape double-decker three blocks from the Mayflower's iconic landing rock. Bourque knocked on the first-floor door.

The man who answered elicited one word: *patrician*. "Enrico Conti?" she asked.

He nodded.

"Detective Bourque, State Police." She gestured to her partner.

"Detective Eller," he announced. "Homicide. We want to ask you a few questions."

"Go ahead."

"Can we come in?"

"Kind of you to ask," he snidely said.

"We can question you here."

Conti looked up and down the street. An older lady walking a dog waved at him. He waved back. "All right," he said. "Come in."

The detectives followed Conti to the rear of his apartment. He was tall and well-built, with crew-cut grey hair, a trim beard, and granny glasses. Bourque wouldn't have pegged him as a strip club patron. He resembled a gym-going accountant, not a longshoreman. She'd pass him on the street ten times before she saw any hint of a mafioso. On the other hand, he was definitely strong, the kind of assailant who could cleanly sever a penis or knife a grown man. Conti's kitchen featured open shelves and subway tiles. Sitting at a distressed oak table, Eller started the POI off. "Mr. Conti, what did you do on October eighteenth?"

"What's this about?"

"Daniel Fitzgerald's murder. Which happens to have taken place the next day."

"I already told two detectives what I did on October nineteenth."

"Thank you, but we're asking about October eighteenth. The investigation has evolved."

"Evolved?"

"That's correct, sir. Investigations have a habit of changing course. New *dates*," Eller emphasized, "new lines of inquiry. Which leads to you. What did you do on October eighteenth?"

Conti shook his head. "More visits, more questions. Why are the police still bothering me? What have I done? Nothing."

Bourque rolled her eyes inwardly. A typical denier. One of their favorite tactics was to avoid answering questions. Some, like Conti, insisted on asking them.

Eller calmly repeated his question. "What did you do on October eighteenth?"

"Worked from home, went for a walk in the late afternoon, worked again."

"And shopped for diving gear. Among other items, you purchased a hooded scuba suit and two Sherwood C100 tanks."

Conti shrugged.

"Those are good tanks. Are you a diver?"

"No."

"Then why did you buy the gear?"

"A friend asked me to."

"Who?"

"I don't remember."

Eller turned to Bourque. "He remembers he bought it."

"That's a start," she said, "but not a good one." She eyed the POI. "Who did you buy the gear for?"

He shrugged again.

"Mr. Conti, you don't seem to be cooperating. As in cooperating with a homicide investigation." Time for a few white lies. "We know Daniel Fitzgerald was killed by a diver who boarded the *Islander*. The diver used a Sherwood C100 tank."

"A lot of divers use Sherwood tanks."

"Not filled at Divers Market in North Plymouth, where you bought the gear."

"It's a busy dive store. Everyone uses it, divers from Boston to

Rhode Island."

"For a non-diver, you know a lot about the local scene."

"I'm calling my lawyer."

The usual, Bourque thought. Conti knew the ropes. The team would have to see if any evidence led to him. Even with lawyers involved, real evidence opened closed mouths, especially forensic evidence. No one could deny DNA.

□ □ □

Driving to Carolina Pereira's house, Bourque signaled to Eller that she wanted to crank up her music. It helped her mull things over. When he nodded obligingly, she queued her favorite Bowie number, "Ashes to Ashes."

As the sun sank and the earth turned, Massachusetts rolled eastward into the coming night. Bourque's thoughts segued from scuba gear to a killer who slipped away underwater. Was a diving perp a real possibility? A collaborator could alleviate the main complications. Who'd make a good collaborator? Someone with no sheet, but with criminal connections. Conti came to mind. He could be the onboard assistant or the getaway driver, or both.

Think again, she told herself. Look at the whole picture. The diving angle only pertained to Fitzgerald's murder. Halliday wasn't murdered on a ship. Ditto for Unger. In any case, the team had nothing concrete on Conti. He was merely a potential link—to one murder at that.

Turning into a low-rise complex near Plymouth Airport, she switched her focus to Pereira. The dancer had come to the police, but that didn't connote innocence. Like Halliday, she could be playing them.

Bourque pulled up in front of a townhouse with a dark red door. Dusk had fallen. Thick clouds sucked the remaining light from the sky.

The detectives strode quickly up the walkway. Pereira answered the door wearing an oversize Patriots football jersey. Her bare legs were tanned and toned; her toenails, painted bubblegum blue. Her raven-black hair was darker than the first time they'd seen her. Underneath the football jersey, her breasts stood out. Just opening the door, she radiated sexuality.

"Good evening Ms. Pereira," Eller said. "We have a few questions for you."

"Bad timing."

"It won't take long."

Pereira rolled her eyes. Her irises weren't blue today, they were almost as black as her hair. "I'm leaving for work."

Eller was ready for that story. "We'll question you at work then."

"Do it here." Pereira spun on her heel and sashayed into a small living room crammed with two palatial-sized sofas. She plopped into one. The detectives stood.

"Take a load off." Pereira pointed to the other sofa.

Bourque and Eller remained standing.

"Jesus, cops. Always showing how virtuous they are."

Eller didn't react. "When did you start dancing at Romeo's?" he asked.

"Four years ago."

"Do you know a Paul Unger?"

"Nope."

"Do you know why we're asking?"

"Nope." Pereira regarded him scathingly. "I thought we weren't wasting time."

"He's dead."

"Bless his soul. Next?"

"He was murdered."

"Bless his soul. Next?"

"*You* could be next, Ms. Pereira, as in the next victim. You knew Ruby Halliday. That's a direct connection to at least one murder. You also know Jack Irvine."

Pereira shrugged.

"Do you know Enrico Conti?"

"Yep."

"Ever go out with him?"

"Nope."

"Did you ever dance for him?"

"Yeah. What of it? It's not illegal. I go in there, I do my job, I bring money home." Her eyes traveled to the ceiling. "I have an *avó* upstairs, a grandmother. She's seventy-four. With cancer. I look after her."

Eller didn't comment.

"Are you beginning to get the picture?"

He ignored her. "Does Jack Irvine hang out at Romeo's?"

"Haven't seen him recently. Used to show up a few times a

week."

"Did you ever see Enrico Conti with Jack Irvine?"

"Nope. They, like, play on different teams."

"Explain."

"Jack's a front-room dude. A hustler, everybody's friend. Enrico is a backroom guy. Lowkey, private."

"How do you know?"

"I have eyes."

"Expand on that."

"I can't. I'm not involved in that crap. I dance, I go home. You got that?" She took a deep breath. "Sorry. I told you what I know. I usually keep my mouth shut."

Eller turned to Bourque. *Any questions?* his glance asked.

She shook her head. She knew she'd be seeing Pereira again. However, she didn't know what for.

□ □ □

Bourque parked at Paul Unger's building well past 2000. The evening clouds had parted. A gibbous moon rose in the east, casting a faint white light. The constellations had begun their nocturnal pilgrimages across the sky. In the lobby, the two detectives signed in with Plymouth Police. She listened as Eller conferred with a local detective sergeant. Unger's body was warm when municipal officers arrived. He'd been found by a neighbor, an elderly lady. She was an unlikely suspect.

Eller nodded collegially as the sergeant spoke. Bourque liked that about Eller. He always cooperated with other police agencies. She hated playing the *this-is-my-turf* game. Parochialism was the bane of police work. As Eller started asking questions, she gestured she was heading upstairs.

Bourque ducked under crime scene tape and entered the victim's sixth-floor bachelor unit. Although Unger's body had been removed, it was clear where he'd been killed. The room's only armchair, a blue Ikea number, exhibited multiple blood splatter marks consistent with knife wounds. The nearby wall was flecked with blood.

Studying the splatter, she agreed with Yi's assessment that the attacker had approached Unger from his right side, which indicated a left-hander. The floor had been wiped from the chair to the door, leaving no shoeprints or blood underfoot. She immediately thought of the wiped deck on the *Islander*. There was no blood in the hall outside and no balcony or means of exterior access, suggesting the attacker had changed his or her footwear and left the unit via the door.

Bourque moved on. Other than the blood, the apartment was tidy. The bed was made. She saw no empty bottles or dirty dishes. The freezer was empty save for an ice cube tray. The fridge yielded a small carton of milk; the kitchen cupboards, only instant coffee. Apparently, Unger ate elsewhere.

She shifted her attention to his tiny bathroom. It was clean. Nothing hidden in the toilet tank, nothing incriminating in the medicine cabinet. The standard male toiletries.

She returned to the living area to consolidate her initial read. The room was neat but crowded with possessions: books, DVDs, CDs, LPs, mementos. Four guitars, two amps, various dive gear items, old but in good shape.

Near the entrance door, she noticed an anomaly. A small section of the wall was slightly darker than the rest of it, as if framed art or photos had been removed. She stepped closer. Three nail holes, three darker rectangles. Three hangings, from what she could tell. She turned to the main window, a floor-to-ceiling casement facing south. It would get a lot of sun. She looked up Unger's sheet. He'd been living in the unit five years. Long enough, she decided, for sun to fade the wall paint. She conjectured three hangings had been lifted. What did they display? Who'd taken them?

She needed time to think—a commodity whose passing would blur the trail even more. Something was eluding her, a missing piece that pulled at her thoughts like an ebb tide flowing seaward, dragging the piece ever more distant. She couldn't stop the tide, couldn't harness and examine it, no matter how hard she tried.

## Chapter 30

**DAY TWENTY: Barnstable. November 8th**

Bourque got to her office a few days later knowing she had to retrace her steps. The murder investigations had stalled. The first interviews were almost three weeks old. It looked like the team was in for a long haul. As a detective, you didn't always look for new intel. Instead, you sifted through the intel you already had. The solution was often hidden in it. She had to go back to day one and revisit everything from timelines to depositions to forensic reports. With luck—no small part of cracking cases—something would jog her memory.

Other than Eller, Central had recalled all of their officers. Most of the POIs had fallen to the bottom of the suspect's list: the *Islander* staff; Candace Fitzgerald and her daughter Rory; Heaney; Symon and Verdi; Jasper and Pam Halliday; and Doyle. Kane's alibi had checked. He'd been with Maggie Burke. Only Conti and Irvine remained at the top of the list. Both had been prohibited from leaving Massachusetts.

Just as Bourque started her review, Peabody called her into his lair.

"Have a seat," he said as she entered.

No *hello*, no *good morning*. She remained standing.

He gestured at a chair.

"I'll stand."

"All right, this'll be quick. I'm assigning you to close an open investigation, the attempted larceny of scuba gear I mentioned a few days ago, which could connect to the Fitzgerald homicide. Regardless, I can't hold off on it any longer. It's been in the pipe over three weeks. Marsden."

She sat, understanding the assignment now. Carter Marsden was a junior detective in Barnstable. Hollywood-handsome and he knew it. Not even Peabody could control him. Marsden's father was a superintendent. He'd let everyone know his son was destined for big things. The station had to put up with Sonnyboy until he moved on.

"Eastham is near Orleans." Peabody winked. "While you're out there, you can call on the Hallidays. Not that anyone needs to know."

She nodded.

"Don't say I don't look out for you."

□ □ □

Bourque appreciated many things about working the Cape. The local driving was one of them. As she headed to Eastham along Route 6, the lakes bordering the road mirrored the rising sun. A cavalcade of snow geese flew due south, tracking three long Vs across the sky.

Thirty minutes later, she parked at a weathered dive and surf shop named Atlantis. She'd looked up the larceny case before leaving the office. Marsden hadn't entered much detail. Attempted theft under $2,000 by one male; date and time of said attempt, being October 16th at 2050; business name and contact details. Nothing about the targeted goods, no description of the thief or his means of transportation. Sonnyboy wasn't celebrated for his thoroughness. He'd dropped half the ball, as he often did.

Atlantis looked like it had been parachuted into Eastham in the late-sixties. The building was painted in a blue/pink/yellow tie-dye pattern. The front yard was a mutiny of tall grass and tangled vines. The cedar-shake roof was growing moss. There were windchimes everywhere.

Inside, she pulled a bell cord to announce her arrival. Like many small retail shops, Atlantis was chock-a-block with merchandise, leaving just enough room to traverse the aisles.

A lean young woman walked her way. "How can I help you?"

"Are you Glenda Lowell?"

She nodded.

Bourque immediately pegged Lowell as a surfer. Laidback and lithe, with a grace that spoke of riding big waves. Her face was tanned; her long russet-brown hair tied back in a ponytail.

"I'm Detective Bourque, Cape and Islands. Is this your place?"

"My dad's. He passed it to me."

"I understand you were robbed a few weeks ago."

"Attempted robbery. I ran the guy out. He dropped what he had."

"Anyone get hurt?"

"No, it was after-hours. Luckily, I was in the shop." Lowell pointed behind her. "I refurbish surfboards in the backroom. Do some late nights. Gave my report to a Detective Marsden. I called the number he left me three times. Always went to voicemail. Haven't heard boo from him."

Bourque tried not to show her displeasure. She didn't succeed. "No email or text update?"

Lowell shook her head. "Don't want to cause any trouble, but I need a follow-up for my insurance. The thief jimmied my front door around the lock. Had to get a whole new door."

Bourque hadn't noticed.

"Well, a new old one. They won't process the claim without a police report."

"Did you hear him jimmying the door?"

Lowell shook her head again. "I was running my sander. Looked up and saw a guy in the store. Roared in there yelling like hell."

"Do you have surveillance cameras?"

"Yes, but they're broken."

"What about an alarm system?"

Lowell looked sheepish. "Broken too. Bit expensive to fix."

"Mind showing me the damaged door?"

"Follow me."

Bourque trailed Lowell to the backyard, which was as congested as the interior. One side of the yard seemed to be a surfboard mausoleum, jammed with abandoned boards of all sizes. The rest was stacked with wooden beams, windows, and doors.

"There it is," Lowell said, pointing to a faded oak door. "See that *Atlantis* lettering. My dad painted it. It's the original door."

Bourque studied it. In this case, good enough for her. She snapped a photo with her phone. The doorhandle area had been split open by a crowbar. It was beyond repair. A crowbar again, she thought, reminiscent of the jimmied door on Fitzgerald's car. "The paperwork will be completed today. I'll send you a PDF."

"That's great," Lowell said. "Reports, forms, they never end."

"Never. Best cure for paperwork? A swim in the ocean."

Lowell smiled. "Or a surf."

"You still going out?" Bourque asked.

"Yep. All year round."

"I envy you. I'm done for the winter."

"Get a thicker suit."

"Can't swim far in them. Too restrictive in the shoulders."

Lowell nodded.

"A few more questions. Has Atlantis been robbed before?"

"No. We've been lucky. Knock on wood." Lowell rapped her knuckles on a thick beam.

"What was the thief after?"

"A dry suit and scuba tank. He had a size Medium-Large in one hand and a full tank in the other."

"Did you get a good look at him?"

"No. He was running away. Didn't see his face but he wasn't young, not from the way he ran. Fiftyish, I'd say. Bald, wearing a jumpsuit."

"What color?"

"Dark blue."

For a second, Bourque had thought *Islander*. But the jumpsuit was blue and none of the crewmen were bald. How about Conti in disguise? "Was the guy tall?" she asked Lowell.

"No. Short and dumpy."

"He run to a vehicle?"

"Yeah, a van. White, dirty. I didn't catch the plates. Happened too fast."

"Did you tell Detective Marsden about the van?"

"No. He didn't ask." Lowell shrugged. "Must be a million white vans in Massachusetts."

Bourque kept her counsel. Bent cops rubbed her the wrong way. Lazy ones were a close second. "Did he lift any fingerprints or take any evidence?"

Lowell shook her head.

Bourque wasn't surprised. She wondered why she'd even asked. "Appreciate your time, Ms. Lowell. You'll have the paperwork by dusk."

Bourque walked to her car thinking about Sonnyboy Marsden. He needed a few months directing traffic in Southie with locals giving him the finger. As her father used to say, cops had a place and some had to learn it. They were public servants, not TV stars.

◻ ◻ ◻

Bourque left Atlantis with the sun strengthening by the minute. As she drove south, an iconic Cape Cod view unfolded, leading her eye past Salt Pond Bay on the National Seashore to Nauset Marsh and a maze of blue-green inlets, all the way out to the Atlantic

Ocean. She was tempted to stop for a swim, but a strong sun in November didn't mean warmth. To everything a season.

She turned off Route 6 at Orleans and reached her destination before noon. If no one was home, she'd head to Jasper's boat slip. The Hallidays lived at the end of a tree-lined crescent. The lawn had been raked. A few stray maple leaves whirled across the grass.

Walking the sheltered footpath to the house, she observed late-sprouting thyme, myrtle, and sage. In the path's cosseted zone, she felt a change of climate. Early autumn was still evident. Birds flitted in and out of a juniper border: sparrows, blackbirds, and kinglets, the usual November holdovers.

Bourque knocked on the front door. Pam Halliday opened it wearing a pantsuit the color of dark honey. As on Bourque's previous visits, the POI was striking and dignified. Bourque took in her appearance from the ground up. Umber-brown slip-ons with no heels, no belt, no jewelry. Her face was free of make-up; her long blonde hair, parted in the middle. She appeared to have established her look years ago. It was still chic.

"Detective Bourque," she pleasantly said, "come in." She had the kind of upbeat voice that didn't age. When she was eighty, she'd sound as if she were twenty. "Do you have news?"

"Nothing new. My apologies. Investigations have a timeline of their own."

Halliday's eyes projected acceptance.

"Can I ask a few questions about Ruby?"

"Yes. Tea? Coffee?"

"Nothing, thanks. Just a quick visit."

Bourque sat with the POI at the kitchen table. "How's your husband?"

"He's more resilient than I thought he'd be. He's been a great help."

"And how's Corrine?"

"She misses her big sister. But she knows Ruby's gone. I'm grateful for that. It's the first step."

Bourque nodded. The blinds were open, letting in the autumn sun. Halliday's face was open as well. "I'd like to talk about Ruby's male friends," Bourque said. "The questions might be difficult."

"That's okay."

"As I told your husband, Ruby was seeing Dan Fitzgerald."

"She was seeing a lot of men."

A lot? Bourque thought. She'd pegged Ruby as the demure type. "You didn't mention that the last time we spoke."

"You were with a male detective. I didn't want to talk about it with him."

Landon, Bourque remembered. Not exactly a sympatico face. "Please continue."

"Well, how can I put this? Not many people around here knew it, but Ruby used boys and, later, men. She slept with them to get what she wanted."

"How do you know that?"

"She and I talked about it."

"Please elaborate," Bourque said.

"If I do, I want anonymity. My husband can never find out I told you."

"Agreed."

"He doesn't know how *wanton* his daughter was. That would be his word for it."

"Do you know about her relationship with Jack Irvine?"

Halliday nodded.

"What about with Paul Unger?"

"Yes. Ruby didn't want much from him. Luckily. He couldn't give her much."

"Do you know he was murdered?"

"Yes."

"Do you know anyone who might know why?"

Halliday shook her head. "He's not from around here."

"It appears his murder is connected to Ruby's. When did she last mention him?"

Halliday thought for a few moments. "It was years ago. At least three."

"Would either Irvine or Unger kill her?"

"No. Jack is a schemer, not a killer. Paul was self-absorbed. He lived in his own world. Neither one would kill her."

"How can you be sure, Mrs. Halliday?"

"They wouldn't." The POI's voice was steady. "Ruby was in control of both those relationships, or alliances, as she took to calling them. She pulled the strings."

"We understand that Irvine manipulated her."

"He did, but only when they were younger."

"What kind of men did Ruby like?"

"The tall, handsome kind."

"Can you give me names from this year?"

"There was Dan Fitzgerald, of course, and Jimmy Keane and Lucas Rodriquez, both from Boston. Plus three or four from New York. I'm not sure I remember all of them."

Bourque handed Halliday her notepad. "Please write down whoever you remember."

When Halliday was finished, Bourque moved on. "What do you think Ruby wanted from Dan?"

Halliday hesitated. Her open face clouded over. "I don't know a lot about him."

Bourque sensed otherwise. "Tell me what you know. Anything will help."

Halliday stared out the window for a long time, head held high, eyes distant. Finally, she shook herself and spoke. "I knew all along that Ruby was seeing Dan. The night of her murder I told you otherwise to protect Jasper."

Bourque studied Halliday's face, looking for indications of lying. Like daughter, like mother?

"Ruby reeled Dan in," Halliday went on. "She told me how she did it. She studied poetry as an undergrad. She said it was the story of the Coy Mistress retold. Because Dan was quiet and shy, she pretended to be quiet, shy, and chaste herself, then overcame him one night. Let me rephrase that. She seduced him."

"What did she want from him?"

"More than a lover. She wanted a true friend and, hopefully, an intellectual equal. Someone she could talk to. Someone other than me, that is. I wasn't enough. I don't say that with animosity. Mothers aren't meant to be their daughter's best friends. I wish she'd never told me about her *alliances*. I wish we'd talked about marriage and babies, like other mothers and daughters." Halliday stopped abruptly and leaned on the table, holding her head in her hands. A cascade of blonde hair covered her face. When she sat back up, her eyes looked resolute. "Beauty makes promises that beauty can't keep. Ruby once told me her greatest fear was that she'd never live up to her beauty. She was sure she wasn't beautiful inside. I've seen it before. My mother was a beauty and a liar."

Bourque waited.

"I don't know what Ruby saw in any of them except Dan. But parents can't interfere," she insisted. "You have to let children make their own mistakes. In Ruby's case, I was sure she'd learn in time. Then along came Dan. I thought she was finally on track. Dan was a real possibility."

"What did she say about his politics?"

"Very little. She said he was secretive about it."

"Did she know much about it?"

"I think so. From what I gathered, he told her a lot. But she didn't talk about it. He didn't want her to. That's one thing that made me realize she really liked him. She respected his wishes. I know my daughter had a problem with facts, I know she was manipulative. But she could change."

"Why didn't you tell us about her proclivity for lying?"

Halliday looked away, then returned Bourque's gaze. "I wanted to protect her memory. And I didn't want Jasper to know. Or anyone else. The whole town will know soon." Halliday sighed. "Secrets always come out on the Cape. They're like bones buried in the sand. Sooner or later, the wind and waves uncover them."

She nodded with acceptance. "Ruby was easily bored. Jasper used to think she was needy, but she wasn't. She was just bored. I suspect that's why she hopped from man to man, from hoped-for lover to lover. Part of love is being surprised by the person you love, even after many years. Wonder keeps love alive. Ruby didn't know how to extend the wonder."

"It's not easy."

Halliday nodded again. "The night she told me Dan was dead, she was devastated. Then she was dead herself. I wanted people to remember her good side. *Why focus on the bad? What good would it do to tell you about that?* That's what I thought then. I was wrong. I should have told you everything the night she was killed."

Bourque didn't comment. If Pam Halliday had spoken earlier, it might have helped the team. Regardless, they couldn't change her timeline. POIs often took weeks to tell their story. Whether Halliday's current story was the complete story was another matter.

## Chapter 31

**DAY TWENTY-ONE: Barnstable. November 9th**

The next morning, Bourque ran half a dozen overdue errands and arrived at her office at 1100. Settling in, she resumed her case reviews. Halfway through the Day Seven material, she sat straight up. She'd just listened to her interview with Winnie Reddit and realized she'd dropped the ball. She hadn't questioned her husband, Rick Reddit.

Bourque wanted to call on him with a sidekick. Knowing Eller was in catchup mode, she phoned Donnelly. "Lieutenant Mac here," she said when he answered. "Are you free to ride shotgun?"

"Sure. Where are you headed?"

"Downtown Woods Hole."

"Dangerous," he kidded. "You afraid someone's going to steal your car?"

"Hey, I had it washed."

◻ ◻ ◻

Donnelly whistled as he opened her passenger door. "Waxed too. Must be worth two million now."

"Oh yeah. We're going to see a POI named Rick Reddit. Insurance salesman."

"Can't trust them. Bring your torture kit."

She laughed. "You'll find a few date squares in my lunch box. Have one."

"Homemade?" Donnelly asked after a bite.

"Yep."

"How do you find the time?"

"Got myself an assistant."

"You talking Marty?"

She winked.

Bourque took Route 28 to Woods Hole. It was a typical November day on the Cape: dank and chilly. She'd looked up Reddit before leaving her office. Forty-nine, twenty-two years older than his wife. No sheet. First cousin to Winston Reddit, who ran Reddit Underwriters, a well-known maritime insurer that had been underwriting shipping for three centuries, having started in the whaling industry before expanding to clipper ships, then fishing fleets, ferries, tankers, and container ships. Rick Reddit was a managing partner. Reddit Underwriters operated out of a three-story brick building fronted by a pair of leafless oaks. The entrance foyer was bare but for two varnished wooden benches reminiscent of church pews.

One sidewall was empty; the other, hung with brass-rimmed clocks set to various time zones: Boston, Reykjavík, Greenwich, Muscat, Mumbai, Shanghai, Los Angeles. The far end of the foyer hosted a fat-bellied wood stove with no chimney funnel, the lone piece of décor *sans* function.

Bourque and Donnelly were directed to the middle floor, where the POI occupied a large, opulent office, the opposite of the entrance foyer. Bourque almost did a doubletake. Reddit was a ringer for William Shatner at fifty. The same disarming smile and twinkly eyes. The same short, thick body. He wore an open-neck white shirt and three-piece navy suit.

After introducing herself and Donnelly, she watched the POI surreptitiously, wanting to see how he reacted to the trooper's six-foot-five presence. Reddit didn't seem intimidated in the least. He waved the officers to a pair of leather armchairs. "Coffee?"

"No thanks," Bourque said. The mischief in Reddit's eyes put her on alert. She sized him up right away, thanks to twenty-plus years of men trying to get into her pants. Still in the game, or thought he was. "We won't take much of your time. We're here to talk about Ruby Halliday."

"How can I help?" he asked in a seemingly earnest voice.

"How well did you know her?"

"Barely," he replied. "I met her through Winnie, my wife. She told me she spoke with you a few weeks ago. Was she able to help?"

"Yes. Did you spend much time with Ruby Red?"

"Who?"

"Ruby Halliday."

"Oh, Ruby. A little."

"What did you talk about?"

"The three boys, the weather, the tourists. She stayed a lot during the summer," he added.

"How many times?"

"I'm not sure. Maybe six or seven."

Bourque glanced at Donnelly. She could tell he wasn't sure about Reddit. Considering the POI's shortness, she wondered if Ruby Halliday had been interested in him. Then again, while his height might be unfavorable, his presence wasn't. *I have power and prestige*, it said. Bourque could see Halliday being interested in that.

"Let's go over what your wife told me," Bourque continued. "She said Ruby lied about using your guesthouse in October. Ruby wasn't actually there. She was on Martha's Vineyard with Daniel Fitzgerald. Would you agree with Winnie's statement?"

"Yes."

"She said you told her not to call the police about it. Why?"

"I didn't tell her that."

"That's not what she said." Winnie's interview was fresh in Bourque's mind. "Her exact words were *Rick said to let it ride*."

"Did she say that?"

"She did. Why let it ride, Mr. Reddit?"

"If I said that, I don't know why. It was a mistake. We should have called the police. My livelihood is based on not letting things ride." He smiled professionally. "That's one of the principles of insurance. When you act with foresight and full disclosure, you protect your assets."

Reddit's desk phone rang. He indicated he had to take the call.

"Done," he said a minute later, and wrote a few lines on a legal pad.

Bourque noted he used his right hand. He waved her on.

"When did you first meet Ruby?" she asked.

"About four years ago. Winnie invited her to dinner."

Bourque paused. "Ruby Halliday wasn't who she seemed to be. She was lying about a lot of things. Do you think she lied to you?"

"Lied to me?" He shook his head. "Why would she?"

A common evasion tactic, Bourque knew. Answering a question with a question. "Did you mind when she stayed overnight?"

"Never. She was the perfect guest. Enchanted the boys, even babysat them a few times. Left first thing in the morning."

"How do you know that?"

"I'm an early riser."

"Did you breakfast with Ruby?"

"No. She was Winnie's friend." Reddit's eyes were steely now.

His previously genial voice had hardened.

Bourque deployed a Columbo maneuver: play affable cop, let the POI think he had nothing to worry about. "Forgive all the questions. Standard procedure."

Reddit's face relaxed.

She surveyed him quickly. His forehead might be smooth, but his eyes were still steely. "Thank you for your time. We appreciate the help."

"Glad to be of service."

Bourque and Donnelly walked to her Mazda 3 without a word. A chilly wind blew in off the Sound, reminding Woods Hole citizens of two things. It bordered the North Atlantic. Winter wasn't far off.

Donnelly spoke as they reached her car. "He's hiding things. When are you seeing him again?"

"I'll let him cure for a day or two. Soften his shell."

"Exactly, Lieutenant Mac. Make him easier to open."

"Like a steamed clam. Are you free for another visit?"

"Sure."

"We'll keep walking."

"Did you hear the one about the Saints in Heaven?" he asked.

She shook her head.

"Well, most of the Saints live along Archangel Avenue, at the south end where it curves along All Souls Bay. A nice neighborhood: no police, but no crime. That's no miracle, Mac." He grinned at her as they walked. "We're talking about heaven. No crooks. So, anyhow, up in heaven the Saints sit on their balconies with their saint-may-care attitudes. Nice easy religious life. A little boring though. So, one day this Saint dropped down to Boston, saw a society lady walking her blue-rinse poodle and decided to play detective, divine-style. 'We know your sins!' he proclaimed in a booming, God-like voice. She stepped back. 'I didn't do it! The idiot fell out of the boat.' 'When?' he forcefully demanded. 'When I pushed him. Ohh, I didn't say that.'" Donnelly laughed. "Just goes to show, the right attitude will crack any perp. Make them feel guilty. We could use some of that with Reddit."

☐ ☐ ☐

As Bourque and Donnelly strolled up the Reddit driveway, three lightning bolts dashed out the door.

"Mister, mister," the Reddit boys called to Donnelly. "Catch us if you can." They squealed as Donnelly ran after them to the backyard.

From the look on Winnie Reddit's face, she didn't mind seeing them go. "I was expecting you," she said when Bourque reached the door.

"Oh?"

"Rick just called. He said he'd had a few visitors."

Bourque nodded. It wasn't unusual for a POI to tell his wife about a police visit. However, it made Bourque more suspicious of him.

Winnie ushered her inside. As on Bourque's previous visit, the POI wore chunky jewelry and an expensive satin housedress. However, her chestnut-colored beehive was off-kilter, suggesting she was rushed that day. Her lips weren't painted.

Seated at the kitchen table, Bourque could hear Donnelly laughing and the boys shrieking. She remained silent, letting Winnie make the first move.

"Let's be straight, Lieutenant. From what Rick said, it sounds like you think he was having an affair with Ruby. He wasn't. In truth, he didn't like her."

"He told me he didn't mind Ruby's visits."

"He didn't, but he didn't like her." Winnie's doll-like eyes narrowed. "She was too flighty for his liking, always talking about making the future better. Green this, green that. Cars, houses, ships."

"I see."

"Too flirty too," Winnie added.

Bourque could see that. She could also see Rick Reddit lying to his wife about Ruby. "So, Ruby liked your husband?"

"She *liked* a lot of men. Temporarily, if you get my drift."

"But he didn't *like* her?"

"No."

"What makes you sure?"

"I know Rick."

A common refrain, Bourque reflected. Wives knew their husbands; husbands knew their wives. Most didn't, not about everything. As she was about to reply, she heard a knock on the backdoor. A boy called out. "Open sesame!"

Winnie rose and let Donnelly and her boys enter. They were

sent to the living room to play.

"This is Trooper Donnelly," Bourque noted as he joined her at the table. "Let's start over, Mrs. Reddit. You were saying your husband didn't like Ruby. How can you be sure?"

"Simple," Winnie replied. "Rick genuinely likes people. That's what makes him a good salesman. He rarely says anything negative about anyone. But he did about Ruby. A few things, in fact. Her green streak, as I mentioned. Her cheapness too. She never offered to pay a night's rent. I explained she was poorer than us, but he said *Just one night, just an offer to pay.*"

"Sounds fair," Bourque said, wanting to project empathy.

"He is. Rick's very fair."

Bourque nodded accord, maintaining a friendly façade.

"My husband's a Quaker. A good-hearted, upstanding Quaker. Some Quakers are charlatans, but not him. He's a churchgoer and wonderful family man."

Bourque nodded again. "One more thing. The first time we talked, you said you and Ruby were once good friends. What made you good friends?"

Winnie waved the question off. "That was years ago, when we were in elementary school."

"Just curious, what made you friends then?"

"Proximity. We were both from Orleans. It was a small town. Still is."

□   □   □

As Bourque and Donnelly returned to her car, she waited for him to speak. She knew he would. While he might not want to be a detective, he liked to weigh in.

"The missus sees no wrong," he said. "Apparently, hubby's an angel."

"Sounds like it."

"*A good-hearted, upstanding Quaker.* The lady doth protest too much."

"Agreed."

"She loves her husband, but she's covering for him."

"Probably. We'll let both of them cure for a few days."

"You know who was a Quaker? Richard Nixon."

"You don't say."

"Scout's Honor. Not that you can trust them these days. But

who can you trust? Back to Tricky-Dicky. Parents were upstanding
Quakers. Young Dick was brought up to abstain from alcohol and
swearing. Dancing too. That's a terrible habit."

"Scandalous," Bourque said.

"Seriously, Quakers can be hypocritical, but all faiths can. The
holiest of the holy are often the biggest crooks."

"I have to agree with you."

"Have to?"

"Yep. I'll say it again. You'd make a—"

He chuckled. "Not me."

"You sure of that?"

"Sure. For the moment," he added.

# Chapter 32

**DAY TWENTY-FIVE: Barnstable. November 13th**

A few mornings later, Bourque left Marty's place and crossed Menauhant Road. It was a fine November dawn, clear and crisp, almost fifty degrees. The sky looked like polished blue steel. Standing on Bristol Beach, she took off her shoes and rolled up her pantlegs. The sand felt good under her feet, a bit cold but not uncomfortable.

Head turned to the surf, she walked the beach barefoot, trying to conjure spring and ocean swims. No luck. Work broke into her thoughts. She, Eller, and two Plymouth detectives had spent the last three days questioning Unger's associates. Their alibis checked. The detectives' enquiries brought the diving angle to the fore. When asked about the missing wall hangings, half a dozen people, including Unger's sister, stated some photos of his diving friends were gone.

Strolling along that day, Bourque was sure the photos hadn't disappeared by chance. She deduced they showed the killer's face, or the face of someone who could lead to the killer. She stopped and stood staring out to sea, recalling the three crime scenes. The killer was proficient. He or she targeted the ideal area on Unger's face to impact his brain: the eyes. They also targeted the optimal area on Fitzgerald's body to puncture his heart: between the fourth and fifth ribs. Halliday and Unger were sedated but that didn't mean the killer was incompetent. Conversely, they'd acted prudently. They'd avoided a struggle which would have alerted someone nearby.

Bourque considered the murder windows, which spanned roughly the same time of day, coalescing around 2100. Coincidentally, the attempted scuba gear theft occurred at 2050, within the windows. It could point to a worker who got off duty near that time, likely someone local to the Cape or Plymouth.

"Watching the detectives—" Bourque fished her phone from her pocket, recognizing the incoming number: Heaney. "What's shaking?" she said.

"*Shaking*? Are you really a cop?"

"Sure as sh … I mean, sure as hell."

Heaney chuckled. "I like you, Detective B. Which means I'm going to pass you on to another contact I know. If he's available, you'll need to follow his directions to the letter."

"All right."

"You'll have to alter your appearance as much as possible."

"Understood." She'd done a lot of decoy work in her days as an undercover cop.

"You'll take a specific route to see him. By the way, don't ask his name. He won't tell you. All you need to know is that he worked with Dan in Boston. He's a former staffer at the Massachusetts State House."

□ □ □

Bourque drove to UMass Boston, parked at a residence hall on University West, then applied a thick layer of rouge to her cheeks and donned a bulky down jacket, a ballcap, and sunglasses. Outside, she followed a track to the Harbor Walk, took a circular path counter-clockwise, and rejoined the Harbor Walk. Strolling briskly, she made her way past the Fitzgerald Library to the Fallon State Pier. She'd been directed to continue fifty paces south of the pier and sit on the first empty park bench she saw. Finding one, she slumped as she sat and rounded her shoulders to diminish her size. The nearby benches were empty. A warm breeze tickled the back of her neck. She unzipped her jacket. The sun was almost overhead, filtering through a large oak tree.

Five minutes after her arrival, a short figure approached and sat beside her. She couldn't tell if the person was male or female. They wore a loose-fitting boxy grey suit, wide wraparound sunglasses, and a unisex sunhat pulled low over their face.

"Are you Lieutenant Bourque?"

Soft male voice, probably fifty-plus. "Yes," she very quietly said, keeping their words private.

"Show me your ID."

Bourque obliged.

"I hear you want to know about Dan Fitzgerald. What do you want to know?"

"Whatever you can tell me."

"I was quite taken by him. Most people at the Mass State House were." The voice was matter-of-fact. "Not because of his family or his looks, although he was very attractive. More than that, he was a decent young man. In a world of political predators, he was the exception. Someone of high ideals, born in the wrong time." The man sighed. "He championed equality when almost everyone else has one goal: to enrich themselves. Speaking of which, we have the governor. The woman pretended to like Dan, but she was envious. People get fooled by Karri Laker. She can be very civilized. However, she loves no one but herself. Look at her cruel mouth. Tells you everything you need to know. For a while she had Dan in her web. That's how she does things. She charms people, uses them, and then deposits them in her web for future use. If people are wise, they wriggle their way free. Dan was wise."

"Did you know him well?"

"No. I didn't have to. I'd seen the movie before. I worked for four governors, Detective. They all used people, of course they did. Part of the role. But Laker is different. She wants to use you until there's nothing left."

"And Mr. Fitzgerald realized that?"

"Yes. Realized and took action. The governor disliked him for that reason alone. Most people are too star-struck or scared to leave the web. Dan went farther. After he left, he began criticizing the governor publicly. That infuriated the woman."

"Why did you leave the State House?"

"No comment."

"Why are you talking to me?"

"Chase asked me to. I want you to know the truth. Things are going to end badly. I'm not talking about Laker being a maverick. That'd be okay, but crazy blows the whole thing up. The governor's vindictive and erratic. She's a wrecking ball. Beyond that, she's a dud on every front: rational, organizational, attitudinal. And that's not elitist or deep state. That's a plain-speaking Bostonian talking."

"Are you campaigning against her?"

"In my way."

"Do you use social media?"

"No. I avoid it. Social media turns political discourse into a food fight. Look at Laker: Exhibit A. Social media posts are defining her term in office. She posts like we breathe: continuously and without thinking. She gets printouts of the damn things and pores over them to see which ones get the most attention, so she can replicate them."

"Social media might be a good way to hit her back."

The unnamed man nodded. "It might."

Bourque pulled out her four-page sheet with Fitzgerald's posts on Laker and handed them to the man, not saying who their author was. "Would these work?"

Five minutes later, the man looked up. "They could, but that's not good news. It's a sad sign of the times. We called Laker the dynamite-behind-the-door. No one knows what will set her off, which makes her a dangerous woman. I'm not suggesting she'd do anything herself. However, her minions might."

"Do you know the names of any, let's call them, *aggressive* minions?"

"I don't think you'd be able to pin anything on any minions, let alone her."

"Why?"

"She may be erratic, but she's not stupid. On the other hand, well, from what I saw, she never let scruples hold her back." The man shook his head. "She's a sack of lies, interested in power, not truth."

Bourque didn't comment. *Unbiased* was her name.

"Here's the frustrating reality: no one can pin anything on her. The Commonwealth of Massachusetts is sinking, yet most people don't see it. They let a madwoman take control. I never thought it would happen here. The light doesn't die overnight, Detective. It's sucked into the void gradually but then the people's dreams turn dark. We haven't hit rock-bottom yet."

Again, Bourque withheld comment. Laker was certainly a blowhard but the Commonwealth wasn't a basket case. In Bourque's view, the system was working. She had faith in it. Then again, what did she know? She wasn't a political animal. "Did the Governor ever threaten Mr. Fitzgerald?" she asked.

"Not that I saw, but I heard two men were sent to 'visit' him at his cottage on Martha's Vineyard."

"Why?" Bourque asked, playing dumb.

"To get him to back off his journalism and social media posts, his attacks on Laker's character. Laker called them a witch hunt. She said it was Salem all over again." The man snorted. "Like she knows anything about history. The Salem 'witches' were scapegoats, not potentates."

"When were the two men sent?"

"Last year, about mid-March."

"Do you have any proof of Laker's complicity?"

"No."

"Do you have any proof thugs actually went to the cottage?"

"No. But I wasn't hearing things. I overheard the same thing twice, on two separate days. From the same people. They didn't know I was in the vicinity."

"Who did you overhear? No need to name names. Just tell me the department at the State House."

"That would be like naming names."

"Your words will be completely anonymous."

"Won't work. Laker's people can get around firewalls, be they physical or electronic. By the way, the phone I used to talk with you is going to the bottom of Boston Harbor. It's a burner."

Bourque moved on. "Did you work directly with Laker's inner circle?"

"Yes, so I know what they're capable of. I value my life."

"Who else knows about the two thugs?"

"Very few people. Basically, Laker's inner circle, who would deny it. And Laker too."

"Thank you. I appreciate your help." Bourque handed the man her card, knowing she'd likely never hear from him. "Call me if you think of anything."

"Wait here ten minutes after I leave. Exit to the west."

☐ ☐ ☐

Bourque hid behind the nearby oak tree and shed her ballcap and sunglasses. Using her compact, she removed the cheek blush and added lipstick. Next, she tied her jacket around her waist, fluffed out her hair, then slipped through a gap in a high juniper hedge and followed the junipers west.

What did she have? An apparent shot across Fitzgerald's bow, the kind of thing that had been done millions of times. Given the lack of proof, the thugs weren't a lead. Using a circuitous route, she returned to her car wondering why the man had talked. He'd put his neck out if he were telling the truth, which seemed possible. According to the rumors, Laker knew plenty of thugs.

☐ ☐ ☐

Bourque arrived at Barnstable Unit realizing she had to move

Karri Laker back up the suspects list. While the team had no evidence to prove the thug visit, they couldn't disprove it. It could explain why Fitzgerald secured the Chilmark property with web cameras and long sightlines. He was expecting another visit. He wasn't messing with small fry. He had big enemies, enemies with the means to avoid prosecution and implicate others—which didn't bode well for the investigation. Then again, as Bourque's father used to say, a homicide investigation was the incremental discovery of what already existed. The facts were out there, as well as the perps.

When Bourque entered her office, Eller was seated at the corner table bent over his laptop. He turned to face her as she sat. "Unger's autopsy report just came in. Maynard confirmed the same weapon was used in all three murders."

Bourque welcomed the news. Unfortunately, it didn't get them much farther ahead. "Anything else?"

Eller regarded her wryly. "What do you want? You got your knife match."

"Not enough." She sat at her desk with a sigh. The cases were linked by forensics but a common motive was missing. While she'd benefited over the years from remarkable technological advances, technology was just a start. What human thread connected the killing of a left-wing activist, a beautiful liar, and a carpet layer? Did everything hinge on the first murder, which triggered the second, which triggered the third? Was it that simple? It usually wasn't.

"Got an update from Plymouth Police," Eller went on. "Conti gave a statement saying he bought the scuba gear for a Marcel Berry, guy up the coast in Duxbury. Plymouth checked Berry out last night. No sheet, no known criminal connections."

"So, it's nothing? Conti buys scuba gear for a *friend*." Bourque exhaled. "Maybe Conti wasn't involved in the last two murders but I have a hunch I can't get rid of. I suspect he helped with Fitzgerald's. He acquired diving gear for the perp. He was aboard the *Islander* the night of the murder so he could have hidden the gear while the perp killed Fitzgerald. He also could have picked the perp up afterward."

Eller shook his head. "You and your hunches. Sometimes they fly, sometimes they nose-dive. This one sounds like a sinker. Let it go."

She lifted her hands, then let them drop. She valued her hunches—even when she knew, deep down, that some were lucky guesses.

"The world's an unjust place," Eller noted. "Look what happened to Peabody."

"What?"

"He noticed I wasn't driving home every evening. He was sure I was staying in a hotel again. Then I told him I'm staying at your place. Ruined his day."

"Probably his week."

"That's what I want to hear." Eller smiled. "I'm off to Plymouth. Got a report that Unger used to be a crack addict. Apparently, he cleaned up his act in the spring but still owed a few dealers. Might have something to do with him ending up as a fall guy."

She nodded.

"Tell you what. I'll question Berry myself after I finish in Plymouth. Then I'm homeward bound."

"You'll be *à la maison* tonight?"

Eller gave her a quizzical look.

"Home with family," she explained.

"Yes. You're part French, aren't you?"

"French-Canadian. Well, my father was."

"Mine was Danish. Not that I speak any Danish. The only vestige left of that past is Christmas dinner. Roast duck with cherry sauce."

"Sounds good."

"I like cherry schnapps better."

"Have one for me."

After Eller left, Bourque opened the Fitzgerald case database, navigated to the data section, and pulled up the *Posts* file from his second laptop. Scanning to the end of the document, she found hundreds of violent posts about right whales, as strident as any she'd previously read.

#Whale-killers are #criminals.
#Persecute them. #Prosecute them.
#Lock-them-up!

#Killing #whales is #cowardly.
If you #kill whales, you're a #shithead.

Got it, shithead? You deserve to #die.

#Whale-killers, your sins will be #broadcast for all to see.
#Stop the #Killers!
#Save the #AtlanticRightWhale

Hours later, Bourque had read enough. Given some of
Fitzgerald's avatars were shut down, she knew many of his pro-
whale posts had been deleted. Regardless, thousands of them had
seen the light of day, and were still seeing it.

# Chapter 33

**DAY TWENTY-SIX: Barnstable. November 14th**

After her morning beach walk, Bourque entered Marty's kitchen inhaling her favorite morning smells: coffee and a bed-warmed man. Marty was standing at the stove. She saw he was naked under his robe. Which gave her ideas. How about a quickie? The sofa was close. So was the kitchen counter. Unfortunately, it was only an idea. She was late for work as it was. They'd talked about the future a few times. He'd agreed with her that they wouldn't say anything until she was pregnant. There was another big question. When would they start living together, not just for days at a stretch but all the time?

Marty had made porridge with dried blueberries, which lent it a sweet, earthy flavor, as did hefty drizzles of Quebec maple syrup. After eating, she decided to break with tradition. She felt a rare urge to run a few things by him. He was far more politically aware than she was.

"I'm trying to connect some dots," she said.

He waved a wooden spoon. *Go on.*

"Well, there's this case. Hypothetical case," she added, "which seems to link two murders and possibly an assassination, as in a politically motivated killing."

"You could be talking about the Dan Fitzgerald case."

"Could be," she hedged.

"I know, this is private."

She nodded. "A prominent left-winger was killed," she began, "not an actual politician. However, the left-winger is a political lightning rod with a national reach. Maybe even an international one. I wonder if the killing was an assassination."

"Huh. Well, there haven't been many of them in the U.S. recently. A half dozen or so in the last twenty years: local officials—judges, mayors, etc. There hasn't been a major national assassination since the nineteen-sixties." He tilted his head. "Do you suspect a certain state governor is in the picture?"

"State governor?" Marty was two steps ahead of her.

"From Massachusetts, perhaps? As for arranging an

assassination, the governor I'm thinking of wouldn't go that far. At heart, she's a coward. If she got nailed, she couldn't do time."

"She has minions," Bourque said.

Marty shrugged.

"So, it's not an assassination?"

"Not likely," he replied. "Maybe this left-winger made state or regional enemies, such as business entities. Follow the money. I know," he stopped and winked, "you always do."

"That's us. Now for something completely different, as my dad would say. Can I get your opinion on a diving matter?"

"Sure."

Being an ex-Navy Seal, Marty was a top-notch diver. "Could a Navy Seal diver get aboard a ferry docked in Woods Hole or Vineyard Haven?"

"Absolutely. Any trained diver could. Neither port is protected. The ships aren't properly guarded."

"Thanks for the help." She stood and kissed him on the cheek. "You're the best."

"Hypothetically."

"No. That porridge was real." She grinned. "Same again tomorrow?"

"Never. It's a half-grapefruit day." He laughed. "You should see your face. Followed by scrambled eggs."

"I'll take it."

Tomorrow's breakfast, that was. Marty's belief about Laker's non-involvement was harder to take. Bourque drove to Barnstable wondering if the cases would ever point in one direction. Was Laker in the mix, or should the team be looking at anti-whalers? Or something else? Bourque couldn't say. However, she could say one thing: at the moment, they were going around in circles, like two people rowing in opposite directions, pulling their oars at odds with each other, making their boat spin on its axis.

□ □ □

When Bourque strode into her office, Eller was already there. He'd been staying at her place. She was at Marty's all the time.

"Beat you in again," he said.

"You must be getting a good night's sleep."

"The best."

"Happy to hear."

"It's almost too quiet."

"You insulting my neighborhood?"

"No way. Never bite the hand that sleeps you."

She chuckled, then booted up her laptop and returned to Fitzgerald's posts, scanning thousands more. They were all painted with the same brush. She assessed the big picture. The latest posts pointed to whales; other intel pointed to Laker. However, Marty's evaluation didn't finger Laker. If Fitzgerald's killing wasn't an assassination, if the motive wasn't political, what was it? There was an obvious answer. His pro-whale posts pointed to an environmental motivation. He was killed to stop his whale campaigns. Unfortunately, in her experience, an obvious answer was often a wrong answer. She needed to look beyond the obvious.

Bourque felt stymied. *Open your eyes wider. Dispel the darkness.* She walked to the local Dunkin' and got another morning coffee. On the way back, she realized she hadn't scrutinized dogs that weren't barking. The scuba angle wasn't barking. It lurked quietly in the background. In addition, it was relevant whether the diver was connected to Laker or whales.

Thinking about the diving scene in Plymouth, she considered asking Marty to dig into it. Bad idea. He could help, but she couldn't involve him in police business. Besides, she had an alternative: Carolina Pereira, just not in person. If Pereira *had eyes*, as she'd said, other people did as well. Bourque didn't want them to know Pereira was talking to cops.

Sitting at her desk, she called the dancer. "Detective Bourque," she said when Pereira answered.

"You." A relatively friendly *you*. "How did you get my number?"

"I'm a cop," Bourque deadpanned.

Pereira laughed, a guffaw as deep as it was unexpected.

"Listen," Bourque said, "we're not going to visit you again."

"All right by me."

"And you're not going to come to us. We don't want anyone seeing you with cops."

"Could be too late for that."

"Ms. Pereira, if you ever want police protection, just say the word."

"Thanks, but forget it. We're good. I didn't reveal anything you couldn't find out yourself."

"Do you know if any scuba divers come to Romeo's?" Bourque

asked.

"Some do."

"Got a favor to ask you."

"Okay. I suppose."

"Find out their names. Off-the-cuff, casually. Get my drift?"

"I'm not a dumbass."

"Nicknames, first names, last names, whatever. You have your ways."

"So do you."

It was Bourque's turn to laugh. "Do you feel comfortable doing that?"

"Yeah. You get guys to a certain point, they'll tell you anything."

"And forget it five minutes later."

"A minute."

"You have a talent," Bourque said.

"Guys in strip clubs, Detective. It doesn't take much. They're not the brightest bulbs."

"Not by a mile."

"You know what my *avó* says. If God exists, and if He created Adam first and Eve later, it shows that Man is simply a prototype. An inferior model. Woman is the flawless version."

"Exactly."

"I'll call you," Pereira said. "This number?"

"Yep."

"Give me a few days."

Bourque didn't reply. A few days felt like a long time, maybe too long.

◻ ◻ ◻

It was after 1330 when Bourque pulled into the parking lot at Brolly's Bar in Chatham. The eastern sky was the color of New Hampshire granite. The afternoon sun gave no heat. The lot was virtually empty. She'd arranged to meet Jack Irvine at a public house, a safe middle ground, ostensibly for a "drink," not that she'd be drinking any alcohol. If Irvine knew what was good for him, he wouldn't be drinking much. She had a highway trooper on speed dial.

Inside, she saw Irvine seated at the bar and waved him to a remote booth. Privacy. The lunch rush was over; the place was almost deserted but she didn't want any eavesdroppers. A waitress instantly trailed Irvine to the booth, seemingly eager to be in his good graces.

Bourque ordered a Virgin Caesar.

Irvine followed suite, then waited until the waitress left. "You didn't drag me here for the party vibe." He looked around. "Don't see any, don't hear any. You have something to tell me."

"Guess, Jack."

"Oh, we're on a first-name basis. What's yours?"

"Lieutenant."

"Okay, Lieutenant. You're going to tell me I can leave for Florida."

"Maybe."

"I don't like the sound of that. How about *absolutely*."

"Not my call." She sipped and smiled. She'd been expecting Irvine's posturing. With guys like him, blustering was as common as mud. She'd use it against him. "But I can put in a good word. Or a bad one. So, tell me about your friends at Mass State House."

"Mass State House?"

"The Governor's people."

"You kiddin' me?"

"You help the big players, Jack, they help you." Pure speculation. "Keep you out of jail in the future."

"Sure," he sarcastically said.

"That's the word on the street."

"Not any street I know. Listen, if I was ever headed that way— *if*, I say—I wouldn't be looking for political help. Politicians? Christ. All they do is talk their way *into* jail. Idiots. I have useful friends, friends in low places. Well, medium."

"*Medium*. Good to know."

"Who will remain unnamed."

"Let's ditch the theoretical and turn to reality, as in Ruby Red and her men friends. She had quite a few, as you know."

"How would I know?"

"Don't *Jack* me around." Bourque smiled. It wasn't a pleasant smile. "Did Ruby know Marcus Aldo?"

"Who?"

"Don't do it, Jack."

"Not that I know."

"Do you know Aldo?"

He shrugged.

"Jack," she warned.

"Okay, yeah. But you're way off track. Aldo had nothing to do with Ruby or Fitzgerald."

"How do you know?"

"That's not Aldo's business, not to mention in his best interests. Hold on. I can see you're ready to pounce. Or his boss's business. Any of his bosses. Aldo's a dead end."

"You would say that. He's your boss."

Irvine shook his head. "Focus on the now, Lieutenant."

She almost rolled her eyes.

He regarded her earnestly. "Let's help each other."

Bourque wasn't sure what he was thinking, but it wasn't something earnest.

"You want some useful info?" he asked.

"I'll be the judge of useful."

"How about I tell you about Ruby's latest man friend? Other than Fitzgerald, that is."

She nodded.

"Here's the straight goods," he said, "I tell you, no bull, no holds barred. You tell your boss I can leave for Florida. Fair?"

"Name?"

"Don't have a name."

"Really?"

"Hang on. Just listen."

"Continue."

"A buddy used to see this guy and Ruby together. They'd meet at a place in Hyannis, a steakhouse. My buddy's a bartender there."

"What's his name?"

"Bob."

"Last name?"

"You get me to Florida, you get his full name."

"No holds barred," she reminded him. "Full name and the name of the steakhouse."

He nodded. "Done."

"When did Bob see them?" she asked.

"This summer. Three or four times. Apparently, the guy's an insurance bigshot. Ate at the steakhouse all the time with clients. Bob said he looked like Shatner."

"William Shatner?"

"Yeah. A younger Shatner. Bob said it was, like, a revenance."

"A revenance?"

"Revenant. Right. A Shatner ghost. Same face, same smile."

Rick Reddit, she thought. "Did you ever see the guy with Ruby?"

"Once." Irvine glanced at her sheepishly. "Just happened to be in the area."

She raised an eyebrow. "Did he look like Shatner to you?"

"Totally."

"Where did you see them?"

"Parking lot at the steakhouse."

"How did Ruby look that day?"

"Gorgeous. She always looked gorgeous. On the other hand— see, this is me telling you the truth—she didn't look happy. She seemed, well, subdued. A bit scared even. The guy was really laying into her. I could hear him. I was in my car but my window was down. She wasn't talking back. That wasn't like her."

"What was he saying?" Bourque asked.

"Didn't hear much. I was too far away. Nothing interesting, as in nothing *incriminating*. Isn't that how you detectives talk?"

"That's prosecutors, Jack. Who you could be seeing soon. Tell me what you heard."

"*Don't get creative, get smart.* That kind of stuff. The rest was in a low voice, as if the guy knew people might be listening in."

"Were you worried about her?"

"Not really, nah. She's a tough cookie. Well, *was* a tough cookie."

"Maybe you should have been worried." Bourque changed tack. "Too bad about Unger."

"Who?"

"Paul Unger."

"Am I supposed to know him?"

"You gave him the key to Ruby's backdoor."

"Bull. For starters, I don't know any Unger. And I never had a key to her place."

"He's dead now. Murdered."

Irvine didn't react.

"Would you give a sworn deposition that you don't know him and never had a key to her place?"

"Absolutely."

"Plus the information about her and this Shatner look-alike."

"Sure."

"I'll talk to my boss."

"So, I'll be in Florida before the big snow flies?"

"You could be."

□ □ □

Bourque walked to her car thinking about Reddit's business: maritime insurance. A hunch told her there was a connection to the case. What was it? As she was about to start her car, it came to her. She recalled the list of anti-whale groups Liam Doyle had sent her. Most were shipping companies or affiliated with shipping. Ships needed insurance.

She booted up her laptop and navigated to the list. Six shipping companies on it. She opened Google, tracked down six head office numbers, and set to work. In one sense, her job would be tricky. She had to use the right tone of voice and say exactly the right things. If she didn't, she could get stonewalled and there was no time for that. In another sense, the job would be simple. One phone number after another, one question after another, a routine progression.

In an hour Bourque determined all of the companies had a common denominator. They bought insurance from Reddit Underwriters, who stood to lose a slew of contracts if whale rights shut down shipping lanes. What had Doyle said? Northeast shipping could decrease by thirty or forty percent. That was a lot of business.

There was another possible box to check. Was Rick Reddit a diver? She could ask his wife. But Winnie might lie. Why not get a warrant to search the Reddit property? Then again, why not take a faster route? Warrants could take forever. Besides, you never knew if a judge would grant one. Bourque googled the phone numbers for local scuba associations and started calling. Bingo! The fifth number on the list checked the box. Reddit belonged to a dive club in Quincy.

At first, the club was hesitant to divulge Reddit's diving background. She told them it was a police matter. When she said she'd be coming by with a warrant, they admitted the information wasn't private. Reddit had been certified in 2013, trained by an ex-Navy Seal. A Seal, she instantly thought. The kind of trainer who could show you how to sneak on and off ships. Perhaps two checks in one box.

# Chapter 34

## Woods Hole

Bourque fishtailed out of Brolly's parking lot and sped to Woods Hole. The hell with Peabody's no-speeding sermons. She had a potential suspect to track down.

Outside Reddit Underwriters, the leafless oaks looked spectral. The building appeared to be closed. There were no lights on in the office windows. However, the front door was open. As on her first visit, the foyer was empty. On her way upstairs, a tall young woman with flinty eyes stopped her.

"Can I help you?"

"I'm here to see Rick Reddit."

"He's not here."

"Where is he?"

"Attending to a family matter," Flinty haughtily replied.

"Where?" Bourque asked.

"I'm not at liberty to say."

"Yes, you are." Bourque showed her badge.

The woman was taken aback. "I don't actually know."

"Why did you say you couldn't tell me?"

The woman shrugged.

Bourque handed Flinty her card. "Call me as soon as you find out." The usual spiel, usually fruitless.

"Of course."

More like of course *not*, Bourque knew, but she'd push it. "I'll expect a call by five p.m. That's today," she added.

On the way to her car, her phone crooned "Watching the detectives."

"Lieutenant Bourque," she answered, "Cape and Islands."

"Hello, it's Carolina Pereira. I have something for you. Four names."

"Thank you, Ms. Pereira."

"People call me Caro."

"That was quick, Caro."

"Your voice told me you needed help fast. All four are originally from the Plymouth area. One lives in Woods Hole now."

"Tell me that name." Bourque was pretty sure she knew it.

"Rick Reddit. Salesman type."

Bingo. The Reddit ducks were lining up. She listened to Pereira recite the other three names. "Thanks. Much obliged. You've done your civic duty."

"Whaddya know. I can tell you're interested in that Reddit guy. I never liked him. He'd sell his mother to get a feel."

"Appreciate the help. Don't ask around anymore. Keep a low profile."

"I'm not a dumbass."

Bourque smiled to herself. "You're certainly not. Thank you, Caro."

□ □ □

Bourque tore up the driveway of Rick Reddit's house. When you wanted to know where somebody was, you didn't always hunt them down. You could call on somebody, somebody with better connections, like Winnie Reddit.

No little boys ran to Bourque when she left her car. She drew her handgun and edged to the front door. To her surprise, Winnie opened it.

"Where's your husband?" Bourque asked, not anticipating a straight answer.

"At the family cottage. We need to talk. Come in."

Gun by her side, Bourque followed Winnie to the kitchen table. "Are the boys there?" she asked.

"No. They're with my mother."

"In Orleans?"

"Yes."

Bourque holstered her weapon and sat at the table with Winnie, evaluating the young woman. No beehive, no makeup. Straggly hair, sallow skin. Although she sounded steady, she looked hollowed out, as if *she'd* seen a revenant and was still seeing it. "Where's the family cottage?"

"On Cuttyhunk Island."

Bourque knew Cuttyhunk. It was the outermost of the Elizabeth Islands, about an hour by boat from Woods Hole. "When did your husband leave?"

"Yesterday afternoon."

"Is he there alone?"

"I don't know. I just don't know," Winnie wailed and abruptly burst into tears.

"Okay," Bourque soothed, "it'll be okay." She wasn't sure she could trust Winnie. The perfect housewife appeared to have been stricken by sudden despair. Her baby-blue eyes were streaming; her nose, blubbering. Her chest heaved. However, she might be putting on an act.

As Bourque made tea, Winnie stopped blubbering, and then started again. Her shoulders rose and fell. She sniveled and blew her nose. Her large eyes seemed to be filled with regret.

A few minutes later, Bourque had Winnie calmed down, sipping chamomile tea. She'd stopped crying. Bourque sat across from her.

"Can you talk?"

Winnie nodded. Her eyes were dry; her chest, still.

"Your husband was seeing Ruby Halliday," Bourque began.

"I know."

"You know?"

"Yes. I was too stupid to see it, but he was. Dammit, he was! The bastard!"

"When did you find out?"

"Yesterday," Winnie haltingly said. "He told me after breakfast. Said it like he was relaying a weather report. *It's a fine day. Ruby and I were lovers.* Bastard! You know what I think, Lieutenant?"

Bourque waited.

"I think he had something to do with Ruby's death. It's the way he's been acting recently. Guilty. About what, I don't know."

"Do you think he killed her?"

"I don't know."

"Do you think he *could* kill her?"

Winnie nodded.

"Does your husband know you suspect him?"

"No."

Bourque took that with a grain. "Is he a diver?"

"Yes."

"Where does he keep his dive gear?"

"In the basement."

Bourque would send a forensic team to process it. She'd observed Reddit writing with his right hand. The knife wounds indicated the killer was likely left-handed. However, if Reddit was ambidextrous, he could have killed Fitzgerald, Halliday, and Unger.

"Is your husband ambidextrous?"

"Yes. How did you know?"

Bourque didn't answer. "A few more questions. Where's the family cottage on Cuttyhunk?"

"Close to the main dock on Cuttyhunk Pond."

Bourque had been to the island numerous times. It was less than a square mile and had fifty or so residents, usually under twenty at this time of year. "How close to the dock?"

Winnie wrinkled her nose. "A hundred yards?" she guessed.

"What's the address?"

"Six Pinehill Road."

"How did your husband get over to Cuttyhunk?"

"I don't know." Winnie shrugged. "He has a boat in Eel Pond."

"Is it still in the water?" Bourque asked. In mid-November, most boats were on the hard.

"I don't know," Winnie cried. She seemed about to lose control again.

"Not a problem," Bourque quickly said. God forbid she distress Baby Blue Eyes. "We're almost done, Mrs. Reddit. Are there any guns in the cottage?"

"No. Oh, a friend keeps a shotgun there for duck hunting."

"Does your husband keep guns here?"

"No. He's not a shooter. Part of his Quaker upbringing."

Quaker or not, Bourque wouldn't be taking any chances. She'd treat Reddit as a firearms expert. "Does your husband work long hours?"

"Yes, he often works until midnight. I hate it. It makes the boys so antsy. They don't get enough time with their father."

Bourque nodded. If Reddit were the killer, they'd be getting much less time. Prison visits and nothing more. "I'm calling a trooper here."

"I don't need anyone."

"You do. I'll stay until he gets here." Bourque wouldn't leave Winnie alone, ostensibly to safeguard her, but actually to watch her, and stop her from contacting her husband. Winnie was more than capable of deceit. She'd spent a lot of time with at least two liars: her husband and Ruby Red. The perfect wife might be collaborating with Rick Reddit or planning a runner.

"For now," Bourque calmly ordered, "give me your phone. For your safety, you can't be answering it." Overstated, but a line that normally worked.

"Oh. Okay."

Standing in the living room with a view of Winnie, Bourque called Donnelly.

"It's Lieutenant Mac," she quietly said when he answered. "I need your help pronto."

"Sure thing."

She walked five yards away but kept an eye on Winnie. Covering her mouth with her phone, she spoke softly. "You remember Winnie Reddit?"

"She who doth protest?"

"Right. Do you remember her address?"

"Yes."

"Come to her house ASAP. She thinks her husband had something to do with Ruby Halliday's murder. She might be in danger herself. On the other hand, she could be scamming me. Either way, she needs watching."

"I'll be there in twenty minutes. Where's her husband?"

"On Cuttyhunk Island. Apparently."

"You going out there?"

"Yes." She had to assume Reddit was on Cuttyhunk. The team couldn't wait for his next move.

Bourque returned to the kitchen and led Winnie to the living room. With the POI installed in a large recliner, Bourque sat in the room's bay window behind a drape, scanning the street. She couldn't set her mind about the young wife. *Always*, she ruefully reflected, *always*. There were two sides to every POI until a case was closed. Assumptions of innocence were as useless as assumptions of guilt. In Rick Reddit's case, however, the guilty shoe could fit. The pieces seemed to dovetail, the big ones like motive and opportunity: the potential loss of millions of dollars; the late hours "at work" which coalesced with the murder windows; the ability to dive; his connection to Ruby Halliday. The small pieces dovetailed too, the hesitations and attempted deflections she'd picked up in her only interview with him. A lot of things fit. Cuttyhunk ho. She was confident he was there—as confident as she could be.

Ten minutes later, she saw two police cruisers parking in the street. Donnelly jumped out of the lead car followed by a man in civvies. The second cruiser divulged a uniformed trooper. She opened the front door.

"Right on time," she said as Donnelly reached her.

He smiled.

After debriefing the uniformed officer, she and Donnelly walked to her car.

"Cuttyhunk," he mused, "good place to hide. I'd say Reddit's in turtle mode. How did he get out there?"

"Not sure. He must still have a boat in the water. There's a ferry from New Bedford Monday and Friday mornings, but Winnie said he left for Cuttyhunk yesterday, a Sunday. I don't think she's lying about that."

"Not telling you anything new, Mac, but the local Marine Unit won't get you out to Cuttyhunk."

Bourque nodded. The unit focused on the Cape itself, not the islands. "Okay by me. I don't want a police launch, or a copter. Too obvious. It would forewarn Reddit. We can requisition a ride from the Oceanographic Institution."

"I'm coming with you," Donnelly announced. "Don't say anything."

She didn't. Eller was in Holyoke, too far away to bring in. Besides, while he was okay with ferry crossings now, an extended small boat ride was another matter. In any case, Donnelly was a better partner for an op. Although big, he could move like a fox.

He pointed at the man in civvies standing next to his cruiser. "Brought a fisherman to join us. Just kidding. He's a trooper from my barracks, Sean Malley. Top marksman, quick thinker. Plus, big plus, he's a boater. Knows the Elizabeths inside out. What do you think?"

Okay by her. If Donnelly recommended Malley, he was in. The "landing party" was taking shape. "Where's your civvies?" she asked Donnelly.

He smiled. "In the trunk."

"I'm calling Peabody. He'll have to get us a boat."

"Right, can't do it ourselves. The big hats have to do the *logistics*." He shook his head. "My brother-in-law's son could get you a boat. He's fourteen."

She grinned and phoned Peabody. "Nice afternoon for a boat ride," she opened when her boss answered.

"If you're an Eskimo."

"I need to get a few officers over to Cuttyhunk Island," she said. "I believe there's a murder suspect there, a Rick Reddit. All I need is a motor launch."

"One suspect?"

"Yes. Possibly armed. He might be our knifer. I don't know if he's a shooter."

"Regardless, you'll have to surround him. I need to get you at least half a dozen SWAT officers."

*Let me handle this*, she almost said. "Too many," she replied. If they came after Reddit with multiple launches or a copter, he could read the tea leaves and slip away. Or he might make a stand. Both bad outcomes. She wanted a small op, carried out by a few officers. However, in Peabody's eyes, that would be renegade policing, Rambo-style. "One launch means seven of us in total," she clarified, "most hiding in a cabin or under a tarp in the bilge. I already have three. Me, Donnelly, and a Trooper Malley. Send a SWAT team of four."

"You need more backup."

"Thanks, but I don't." She hated big policing. Small teams let you think on your feet. For a man who loathed spending money, Peabody didn't hesitate to call in other unit's troopers. It was often a win-win for him. Outside units footed the bill and, if an op blew up, it wasn't only his fault; he could point a finger at others. "Save some money," she added, Peabody's favorite words. "Seven of us can handle it."

"All right," he agreed. "Where's Eller?" he asked.

"Holyoke."

"I thought he was staying at your place."

"He is, but not tonight."

"Not my business, but I thought you had a man friend."

"What's wrong with two or three?" She chuckled to herself, then stopped. Maybe she shouldn't have said that. From now on, she wanted Peabody to see her as a family type. On the other hand, she'd never stop ribbing him. That wasn't in the cards.

"Look," she continued, "can you contact the Woods Hole Oceanographic Institution? Requisition a motor launch, at least a thirty-footer. Forget about a police launch. Statie markings would announce the op. Oceanography markings are okay. A research vessel headed into Cuttyhunk Pond is good cover."

"Will do."

That was easy.

"But I'm going to put the Coast Guard on standby."

Not so easy. "Keep them at bay, not in view of Cuttyhunk. If we spook this guy, he'll run. I want to arrive with one boat, with one man at the helm. I have Malley in mind."

"Why?"

Why? Micromanagement to the fore. "Donnelly and I met with Reddit a few days ago. He might recognize us, even from afar. In addition, Malley is a boater. He can also pass for a research scientist."

"Fine," Peabody said. "One last point. The suspect could have associates. We have to be ready for more than one adversary."

That was true.

"I'm putting two helicopters on standby," he stated.

Christ. What about an aircraft carrier. "*Standby* being the key word."

"Correct, Bourque. They'll stay on the ground until I say so. Keep me in the loop."

"Roger."

She signed off and signaled thumbs up to Donnelly. She liked the team's size. Seven, not too large, not too small. And a lucky number to boot. Her thoughts segued to Reddit. What was he up to? If he was on Cuttyhunk, what would he do next? Dig in? Take his boat to the mainland, or steal a boat? Hitch a water ride with someone, wearing a disguise? She had to think a few moves ahead. Solving murders *was* like playing chess. Peabody had that right.

## Chapter 35

### Cuttyhunk Island, Elizabeth Islands, Massachusetts

Consistent with most places on the Cape, Cuttyhunk's arc of growth was determined by geography. Though remote, its location had been deemed propitious to harvest sassafras in the 1600s, which led to a permanent village, in turn making Cuttyhunk one of two islands in the Elizabeth chain not privately owned by the Forbes family.

Having sailed to the island many times, Bourque knew Cuttyhunk's topography: an amalgamation of glacial rocks, clay, and sand topped by grass, bushes, and the occasional copse of wind-driven trees, bent toward the mainland by nor'easters. The island's highest elevation, Lookout Hill, was 150 feet. Its buildings were hunkered close to the ground.

Bourque's team set out from Woods Hole at 1735, barely an hour after sunset. The oceanography institution had given her a ten-year-old Back Cove 340 with a 320-horse diesel. More than sufficient. As the boat motored southwest, the moon climbed higher, eating the nearby stars. She experienced a sense of déjà vu. She'd seen that moon before. It was strangely metallic, as on the night of Fitzgerald's murder. Although a day or two from full, she felt its influence. She sensed herself being propelled forward, driven headlong to Cuttyhunk Island.

Other than Malley at the helm, the team was crammed into the boat's cabin, dressed as outdoorsmen: watchman caps and all-weather jackets. Bourque's hair was hidden by her cap, pulled low to cover her eyebrows. She wore a thick sweater under a Size-L men's jacket. From a distance, she could pass for a male.

Waiting for Peabody's SWAT quartet to arrive, she'd devised a plan with a little misdirection. When the Back Cove neared Cuttyhunk, it would stay offshore. If Reddit were on the lookout, as he might be, that would likely lower his guard: the boat hadn't approached the main harbor, Cuttyhunk Pond. Malley would continue south for five minutes, then pull into Westend Pond, which wasn't visible from Six Pinehill.

As Cuttyhunk came into view, Bourque's phone vibrated. She'd muted the ringer. Peabody again, she saw.

"Hear me out," he said when she answered. "I realize the suspect might be alone but HQ is readying a marine unit from Bourne, five men."

"They'll crowd the field," she objected. Given her years undercover, when it came to ops, she had more experience than Peabody. In addition, he hadn't been on the ground in decades. "Call them off," she advised.

"No can do. HQ's masters want them there. Do you smell that, Bourque? It's the scent of royalty in the air."

"It stinks," she said.

After disconnecting, she breathed slowly in and out, stilling her mind. She realized it wasn't only Peabody. The brass had to err on the side of caution. Nonetheless, she was going to do things her way: the low-key way. She wasn't going to wait for the Bourne marine unit. There was nothing to gain from storming Reddit's cottage. As her father used to say, don't confront a suspect until you have to. It was common sense, not cowardice.

Heartbeat slower, she checked the time: 1854. The November sky already held the patina of night. She, Donnelly, and the SWAT quartet blackened their faces. The Back Cove slipped into Westend Pond on a flood tide, squeezing through a narrow opening. She smelled the hum of seaweed decaying on the shore, then detected the odor of wood and tar: the pond's old dock. The moon shed enough light for her to pick out two mooring cleats. Malley had seen them as well. He pointed the boat's bow at the lead cleat and cut the engine. The Back Cove glided soundlessly to the dock. While Malley secured the boat, she pulled on her night vision goggles and kept everyone else in the cabin as she surveyed the surrounding land. No lights, no sounds. No one about. She donned a helmet and readied her Smith & Wesson, an M&P 45. Her Kevlar vest was already on. When she signaled *Go*, the officers grabbed their gear, put on their goggles, and disembarked single file.

The team split into two groups and proceeded offroad, Bourque and Malley to advance on Number Six from the front, Donnelly and the SWAT quartet to take up positions around the cottage. Donnelly looked calm, almost disengaged. However, she knew he was on full alert. His head was cocked toward Lookout Hill, resembling a fox in hunting mode. Given Bourque was going to be in the open, she'd partnered with Malley, not Donnelly. It was impossible to camouflage the big trooper's size. Reddit might recognize his bulk. In the event Reddit was monitoring VHF or walkie-talkie channels, the team would communicate by cellphone, ringers muted, screen lights off.

Donnelly led the SWAT men toward Westend Road, hugging a low hedge. Soon they melted into the night, small shadows swallowed by a vaster one. Six Pinehill was approximately a mile from Westend Pond. They'd have the cottage surrounded in half an hour.

Bourque and Malley hiked the track to Lookout Hill. Malley's job was to get the suspect to his front door or, even better, outside it. *Flush the target*, Bourque's father used to say, advice from his partridge hunting trips to Maine. Malley would drop by Reddit's cottage posing as a friendly neighbor, inviting Reddit to go fishing tomorrow. She'd begin the op at 1945, knowing Malley should call on Reddit before 2000. In New England in November, 8:00 p.m. was late for a neighborly drop-by. The team had to keep Reddit as unwary as possible. He could have night goggles, but she didn't think he'd be expecting "visitors." His wife certainly wouldn't be talking to him. Her trooper guard would ensure that. He'd been debriefed not to let Winnie use phones or computers. And yet Bourque felt a sense of anxiety. Reddit appeared to be a logical man, but many killers masked their intent by projecting normalcy.

At the pinnacle of Lookout Hill, Bourque knelt behind a disused WW II bunker and surveyed the tiny hamlet near the main harbor. It was absolutely still. Within minutes, she felt the nocturnal cold sneaking into her body. Number Six wasn't exactly a cottage. It looked to be over 2,500 square feet, with large windows and a wide veranda. There were lights on in the house two doors downhill. What she wanted to see. Boating to Cuttyhunk, she'd used her phone to research Reddit's neighbors on the island. The Conner family owned the property two doors downhill. Malley would pose as "Will" Conner, an infrequent visitor to Cuttyhunk. Assuming the suspect had watched the boat using binocs and seen Malley at the helm, the trooper had changed his coat and removed his watchman cap.

Bourque hunkered down. All she could do was wait. Time never stood still in the field. Situations could warp and mutate, what Gigi called the op uncertainty principle: if you knew what a suspect was going to do, you couldn't be sure when, and vice versa.

The air oozed ocean brine. The ground smelled of wet grass. Bourque scanned the cottage surroundings, internalizing the terrain and angles: Cuttyhunk Pond to the northeast, roughly 250 yards away; a clear sightline to the boats in the Pond, one of which was likely Reddit's; the range of shooting positions from the cottage windows.

She kept her vigil, watching for minutes that felt like hours. The stars winked above her. The night breathed slowly in and out. At 1945, she checked in with Donnelly and company. He'd taken up a position twenty-five yards from Reddit's cottage, ready to tackle the suspect if he ran—which was right up Donnelly's alley. He'd played linebacker for the Patriots. Finding everyone in place, she signaled to Malley. *We head out in five seconds.* She'd take up a position offroad on the uphill-side of Reddit's cottage, behind a stonewall about three yards away. Malley would slink through long grass to the harbor side of the Conner house, join Pinehill Road, and then turn uphill so he'd appear to be coming from the Conner house.

Leaving Lookout Hill, Bourque didn't know how the op would unfold. However, one thing was certain. It wouldn't unfold the way she planned it. Ops never did. With a full moon rising, the night was brighter than she'd hoped for. Most people didn't realize November nights in New England weren't inevitably dark. On a night like this on the Cape, the sky supplied millions of stars, with the swollen moon amplifying all of them.

Hiding behind the stone wall near Number Six, Bourque drew her Smith & Wesson. When Reddit came to the door, she'd order him to surrender. She'd inform him he had no choice. He was surrounded.

The air smelled strongly of scrub pines, as she'd expected. In late autumn, pines worked overtime. Like all trees, they were half water. Now each pine was an organic factory in overdrive, one oozing arboreal compounds as the tree prepared itself for winter, making its membranes more pliable, which allowed water to migrate out of its cells, so as not to freeze within them. The factory also converted starch to sugars, sweetening any remaining liquid, in essence, making antifreeze. The tree's job was to keep living cells from freezing, just as, she reminded herself, her current job was to keep both eyes peeled, one on Reddit's cottage, one on

Malley. She watched as the trooper sauntered uphill, hearing his boots crunch on the gravel road, hearing her heart beat in her ears. Handgun raised, she waited for Malley to knock on Reddit's door.

□ □ □

As Donnelly would later say, everything was aces until it wasn't. Reddit wrenched the door open, bowled Malley over and ran. Bourque jumped up, yelled for the suspect to stop, and fired a warning shot in the air. He kept running, immediately veering down a lane toward Cuttyhunk Pond.

"Suspect running to harbor!" she barked into her phone and tore off to the lane. Reaching it, she saw no sign of Reddit. The lane was about seventy-five yards long with four small buildings on the left side skirting the harbor. To the right was a wide grass border, recently mown. No cover for Reddit there.

She wanted to go after him instantly but had some housekeeping to do. Moreover, she didn't need to rush. The team had a big advantage: night goggles. In addition, Reddit had disappeared quickly, meaning he hadn't gone far. She conjectured he was in one of the buildings.

Keeping the lane under surveillance, Bourque backed away a few yards. As she crouched behind a bush, Donnelly and Malley joined her. She made a team-wide call, speaking softly, telling the SWAT quartet to cordon off Pinehill Road above the lane, confining the suspect to the harbor side of Pinehill. "Suspect not carrying a long gun," she quietly added. "He may have a handgun."

She disconnected and called the Bourne marine unit. "How close are you to Cuttyhunk?"

"Five minutes away."

"Drop two officers at the ferry dock," she said, "and keep three aboard to blockade Cuttyhunk Pond. No one gets in or out until further notice. Tell the dock duo to block land access to Nashawena Island. You can swim to it from Cuttyhunk's eastern spit."

"In November?"

"It's only two-hundred yards."

Bourque signed off and turned to Donnelly and Malley. "Reddit may be heading for a boat. We'll have to hold the harbor exit by land for now."

She regarded Malley. He seemed to have recovered after being shoved off Reddit's porch. She waved him close, gestured for him to remove his night goggles, and studied his eyes. They were clear and attentive. "You okay?" she asked.

"Absolutely."

Given her previous trips to the island, Bourque had transited the exit channel a dozen times. At one point, it was about seventy-five yards across, narrow enough for small arms fire to at least target Reddit. "Hold the harbor exit," she ordered Malley. "There's cover by the ferry dock: an old concrete pillbox." Although Malley had a handgun hidden in an ankle holster, she gave him her spare M&P 45 and extra ammo.

Bourque switched her focus to Reddit. Time to move in on the suspect. With the SWAT noose in effect inland, the job was simple. Keep Reddit moving toward the harbor. As Malley sprinted for the channel, she smiled at Donnelly. "Ready for a little hunt?"

He grinned and nodded.

Bourque rescanned the lane. No hedges or stonewalls. Good sightlines. At the end, a short finger dock extended into the pond. There were no boats tied to it. Two weak dock lamps radiated faint strobes of light. She directed Donnelly to take the lane's right side.

Handguns raised to shoulder height, the officers set off in pursuit mode, sweeping the path ahead with left-right scans along gunsights, soon approaching the first building, a wooden boathouse about thirty-feet long by twenty wide, with a ramp to the water. Bourque eyed it warily. Reddit might be older, and he might be a desk man, but Cuttyhunk was his territory, not theirs. They'd already been surprised.

At the front door, Bourque motioned for Donnelly to cover her, kicked it open, and entered on an oblique angle, minimizing her exposure as a target. No gunfire from Reddit, no sign of him either. She stopped and listened, on full alert. No movements. She knew Reddit was in one of the four buildings. Intuition. Then again, where else could he be? The building smelled of old fish heads. There was one boat, roughly a twenty-six-footer, and a mass of fishing nets on the far wall.

She signaled for Donnelly to straddle the doorway, to cover both the building's interior and the lane. Resuming sweep-mode, she surged forward. Her adrenal glands had kicked in, flooding her heart and muscles with epinephrine. Her mind was racing, and yet the seconds ticked by as she searched. Other than a creaking floorboard, there were no sounds at all. Her heart pounded. She found no one inside the boat or under it. There were no closets or hidden compartments. The mass of nets was nothing but nets. Hunt complete, she left via the water-side ramp door and rapidly circled the building's exterior. No one present. She glanced at her watch. She'd cleared the boathouse in under four minutes.

Continuing along the lane with Donnelly, Bourque breached the second structure, a shed full of nets, which smelled of the sea. The shed was a fifth the size of the boathouse. Its confined area magnified the sea tang. She quickly determined the building was clear. She moved on, pulse racing, epinephrine heightening her senses.

Two buildings left, she told herself. One had to hold Reddit. If not, he'd fled the lane. She'd have to reset, perhaps expand the noose.

Like the second building, the third was a net shed. However, it was triple the size, with triple the sea tang. As Donnelly spanned the doorway, covering her and the lane, she swept the shed. Two minutes later, she left. No Reddit inside, no sign of any human ingress and subsequent egress.

Bourque readied herself as she and Donnelly maneuvered down the lane to the final building, another boathouse. Reaching it, she took three deep breaths, adjusted her goggles, and entered obliquely. Her visual cortex registered one boat and a wall of lobster pots. As she stepped forward, she heard a rumble. To the right, a pile of pots toppled to the floor. A short, wide figure bolted for the water-side door. Reddit, Bourque saw. Bingo. She motioned for Donnelly to pursue Reddit from the outside, then ran after the suspect.

Barreling through the water-side door, she spotted him by the water's edge, jumping from rock to rock. She instantly aimed at the back of his head, not his legs. Her training had taught her to shoot to kill, not to injure. Maiming suspects didn't stop them; in fact, it often prolonged the bloodshed. Reddit was a danger to others, including his wife. He was a fleeing murder suspect. Just as she was ready to shoot, he stumbled and fell.

In a matter of seconds, Donnelly was on him. Bourque raced forward, her handgun trained on the suspect. As she arrested him,

Donnelly applied handcuffs. She directed him to frisk the detainee.

Reddit had no weapons. He had a smartphone, which Donnelly passed to Bourque.

□ □ □

Four SWAT officers escorted Reddit to the main dock. He walked arrogantly, holding his chin high. His eyes were steely grey. Bourque assigned Malley to secure the suspect to a mooring ring. She watched the trooper carefully. Cops could go rogue when they'd lost face. Barely minutes ago, he'd been bested by Reddit. The trooper showed no signs of irritation. He methodically did his job. After ordering the SWAT officers to guard Reddit, she sent Malley and Donnelly to bring the Back Cove to the main dock.

Bourque strode uphill to Number Six, reflecting that overkill was usually a charm unto itself. In most cases, when you were fully prepared nothing happened. Not this time. She might have a thing or two to explain to HQ. Nothing she couldn't handle. Her father had taught her how to talk to the big hats: always tell the truth. Don't apologize unless you've done something wrong.

The smell of pine was thick on the air; the moon, fronted by burgeoning clouds. Upon entering Reddit's cottage, she stood at the bay window. It provided excellent visibility north and east. Down by the harbor, the island's inactive Coast Guard station looked as if it had been shuttered for three centuries, not half of one. Past the harbor, out in Vineyard Sound, whitecaps were building. Good thing Eller wasn't with them. He might not enjoy the boat ride back.

Beyond Cuttyhunk Pond, she spotted the Bourne boat chugging eastward, battling the waves. She'd dismissed the unit after Reddit was handcuffed. She hadn't actually needed them. They'd been redundant, not that Peabody would agree. Donnelly had assured her he would have shot and stopped Reddit if the man kept running.

She didn't doubt Donnelly. Reddit was lucky to be alive. He'd never know how close he came to being shot. It'd been four years since she'd had to pull the trigger, on a stakeout in Hyannis. The young man had died. She still felt sorrow, but not guilt. He would have killed her. Ashes to ashes. Turning away from the window, she searched Reddit's cottage.

Bourque left an hour later having found nothing but an old

shotgun. No dive gear, no VHF receivers, no knives, Strider SMF or otherwise.

## Chapter 36

### Vineyard Sound

Malley at the helm, the Back Cove departed Cuttyhunk Pond with Reddit secured in the cabin, guarded by Donnelly and Bourque. She took in Reddit's face at her leisure. He didn't appear to have a care in the world or, she decided, little he cared about. He raised his handcuffed wrists. "You can unlock these, Lieutenant. I'm not a risk to anyone."

She ignored him.

"Why did you shoot at me?" He sounded incredulous. "I was going to surrender."

She didn't reply.

"Why did you shoot?" he testily asked.

"I shot *over* you."

He shook his head. "Was I going anywhere?"

"When suspects run, Mr. Reddit, cops shoot them. Simple as that. You don't want to get hurt, don't run."

There were two things Bourque wished every citizen heeded: *Don't run from cops. Don't fight them.* Resisting arrest got you hurt, if not killed. Regrettably, occasionally, you were confronted by rogue cops. If rogue cops came at you, she told people who'd listen, yell like hell, get bystanders involved, snapping pics, making videos, anything. Rogues were an uncomfortable truth. Like Heaney said, evildoers did what they did to make themselves feel stronger. Unfortunately, they made everyone around them weaker. Years ago, her father's words had defined her role and given her resilience. In his view, detectives were society's dark angels. Her job was to seek out evil, not to shy away from it. To know it fully, but to choose the light.

"Here's the bigger question," she said to Reddit. "Why did you run?"

He smiled a Shatner-smile. "I'd rather make a last run than a last stand."

"What were you running from?"

He smiled again. "*That's* the question. I knew the guy at my door was a cop." He gestured out the cabin at Malley. "He'd look like a cop in his skivvies. You, Lieutenant, on the other hand, wouldn't. If I saw you in your skivvies, I wouldn't be thinking cop. Aren't you going to ask what I'd be thinking?"

Bourque didn't respond. The detainee was in a voluble mood.

"No offense, Lieutenant, but I can say what I want. I figure I'm going away for a long time." He shrugged. "My lawyer would tell me to button up, but it doesn't matter. You didn't come out here without solid proof."

She withheld comment.

"I'll tell you about Ruby. She was lovely. Don't you think so?"

Bourque nodded, playing along.

"Unfortunately, she didn't keep her end of the bargain. She fell for Fitzgerald. And she knew too much."

"How did she get involved?"

"I recruited her. I needed someone to get close to Fitzgerald and find out how radical he was. There she was, Winnie's old friend, showing up at the house every week or so. It seemed preordained. She was the perfect spy. Fitz the Fool didn't suspect a thing."

Bourque remained silent, letting Reddit continue at his own pace. She'd pegged him as not only voluble, but egotistical. He wanted them to know how clever he was. Her phone recorder was already on. He'd essentially admitted to committing major crimes: *I'm going away for a long time.* Having worked almost a hundred homicides, she'd made an observation. Most murderers were extremely self-confident. Reddit certainly was.

He shifted his weight.

Donnelly shot him a warning glance.

"Relax," the detainee said, then rolled both eyes and carried on. "Ruby told me Fitz was getting more radical by the week. That was in July. I knew I had to do something soon."

"Were you working alone?"

"Winnie didn't know anything. Not a thing."

Not correct, Bourque reflected. His wife knew more than he thought. "What about Winston Reddit?"

"Him either."

Bourque wasn't sure about that. She'd be calling on Reddit Underwriters' senior partner shortly. "You avoided my question. Were you working alone?"

"Yes. If you surround yourself with yes-men, you don't see

what's coming. One day, bam, you go down like the Titanic. Of course, there was Ruby, but she was never a toady. And she was the perfect mole. She set Fitz up for me. Informed me he'd be aboard the *Islander* on October nineteenth, making the last passage of the day. You see, Fitz told her in advance. The fool. Blind as a kitten."

"What did she set him up for?"

Reddit smiled. "Are you trying to get a confession from me?"

Bourque didn't answer. She was sure he'd keep talking. There was no need to push him.

"My dive club called to say a cop inquired about me, a female. It was you, wasn't it? You found out I was a diver."

She nodded. As often happened, someone at the club had squealed.

"I bet that got you thinking about me."

She didn't comment. "How involved was Ms. Halliday?"

"She was an assistant, nothing more. She told Fitz to be on the aft viewing deck when the disembarkation horn sounded, which he was. She said she'd meet him there." Reddit smirked at Bourque. "Which was a lie."

"Did she know you were going to kill him?"

Reddit ignored the question. He raised his chin and stared out the cabin as Cuttyhunk receded from view. A few minutes later, he was still staring back at the island.

Bourque debated if she should prod him, just a tad.

Eventually he spoke. "Ruby didn't know what I was going to do."

"So, you killed Daniel Fitzgerald?"

He nodded. "My lawyer will hit the roof, but yes, I killed Fitz."

"Why?" With many murder cases, an admission of guilt wasn't unusual. Nailing down the details was another matter.

"I couldn't ignore the truth. Day by day, he was stealing Ruby's heart. But that was only a small part of the story. He was about to destroy my family's livelihood, something we've worked centuries to build. Along comes Mr. Fitz. In a few years he undoes our past. And our future."

"There are dozens of activists out there. Why did you go after him?"

"He had the biggest megaphone," Reddit declared. "When you encounter an infected tree, Lieutenant, do you just lop off the branches? No, you eliminate the trunk. You chop the tree down."

"Why now?" Bourque asked.

"Simple. The clock was running. Ruby told me he'd stopped fighting Laker. He decided he was wasting his time on her. So he went all in on whales. That's when I knew I had to take him out. Ruby hid street clothes behind a loose panel in the aft stairwell. I changed into them. Couldn't walk up to Fitz in a dive suit, could I?"

"Did you dive off the ship after you killed him?"

"Yes. Swam north for five minutes, then into land. Left my gear and tank under some concrete rubble and walked home. Ruby retrieved everything later that night, except my knife and the street clothes, which I'd put in a waterproof bag and hid behind the panel." Reddit unleashed his Shatner-smile. "Bloody clothes and a murder weapon. Too dangerous to carry that around. Ruby came to the rescue again. She fished out the bag and hid it in her store in a box, then took it off the ship that night. Veins of ice. But no one stopped her or searched her."

A miss, Bourque admitted. Investigations were rarely able to plug all the holes. "When did you get the knife back?"

"I didn't."

Bourque didn't believe him. How could that be? The same knife had been used to kill Fitzgerald, Halliday, and Unger. "You're saying you didn't kill Ruby Halliday?"

"That's right."

Bourque took that with a large grain of salt. "You said you worked alone."

"I did. No one worked *with* me. But some people worked for me."

Bourque moved on. In time, the whole truth would come out. "Why did Ms. Halliday help you?"

He shrugged. "Funny thing," he ruminatively said. "I had money and connections, but I needed her. She knew that. While she was willing, she wasn't subservient, not in the least. In fact, she took advantage of me. Then she started going over to his side."

Bourque didn't respond. Reddit wasn't the first man to get fooled by a woman who seemed to embrace his vision. She'd fooled Fitzgerald as well. "Why did you kill her?"

"Like I told you, I didn't."

"Then who did?" Bourque asked.

Reddit didn't reply.

"Why was she killed?"

"Simple. She knew too much. She'd implicate me. Besides, she was a traitor. Not only did she fall for Fitz, she started talking about whale rights. She swallowed his madness, and then what did she do? She began taking his position against the real Cape Codders. The shippers, the longshoremen, the fishermen. Her own father! She betrayed her roots."

Bourque changed tack. "Did you try to steal a dry suit from a surf shop in Eastham?"

"Yes. I didn't want to use my own suit to nix Fitz. But the robbery failed, so I had to."

"The storeowner said the thief was bald."

"Diversion, Lieutenant. Always deploy it when you can. I notice you did. Your little team must have docked in Westend Pond. I used a bald-head disguise. Easiest trick ever."

"We know you also used a Strider SMF knife."

"How do you know that?"

She couldn't tell if something had changed in Reddit's face or if the shadows in the cabin were playing tricks on her. "Forensics, Mr. Reddit. It's foolproof. Where did you get the Strider?"

"Winston bought it at an auction. I *borrowed* it from his office. He never used it."

"What was Winston's part in your plan?"

"I told you, he had none. I betrayed Winnie, yes, but not him. And I let my boys down. That's the worst thing. You don't have to die to go to hell. Hell is letting your children down. You sink deeper each time you fail them."

Bourque heard remorse but didn't see any on Reddit's face.

"I had to kill Fitz," he insisted. "I had to. To give them a future."

She didn't comment.

"Do *you* know America?" he challenged. "I don't, not anymore. Everything goes now. Whales have rights, birds have rights. Trees, oceans. What about my family's rights? Fitz and his ilk are short-sighted fools."

Bourque sat back. Reddit didn't see the inconsistency of his words. In the supposedly lamentable Era of Everything Goes, he did what *he* wanted: lie, kill, further *his* interests.

Reddit seemed to have read her mind. "You want me to be law-abiding in a lawless time? It's like being a nudist among cannibals.

You're showing a lot of flesh. They eat you first."

"What about Paul Unger?" she asked. "Did you kill him?"

"No. Unger was a miscalculation. He should never have been involved. I paid him to take the heat, but he didn't take it. He could finger me. He had to go."

"How much did you pay him to confess to Halliday's murder?"

"Two-hundred-fifty grand. Forty was to erase his crack cocaine debt, and there'd be two-ten when he got out. Not much for doing time, but he was good with it. What addict wouldn't be?"

"Ex-addict."

"Same difference."

"Why was his penis cut off?"

"Again, simple. Unger was playing around with Ruby. Besides, the lowlife didn't do his job. A simple job. I paid him and he failed."

"How did you find him?"

"I didn't have to find him. I met him diving."

"Did you take wall hangings from his apartment?"

"No."

"Someone did."

"That's right. A few photos of him on boats."

"With you?"

Reddit nodded. "Me and other diving buddies."

*Buddies*, Bourque reflected. A man who killed buddies or had them killed. "Let's talk about your collaborators. Ruby wasn't the only one. There was Ruby's killer, as well as Unger's killer."

"It was the same killer. Cleaner that way."

"The law will go easier on you if you tell us who it was."

He shook his head. "I can't. My personal code. However, I'll point you in the right direction."

"I'll make that known."

"Doesn't matter. Look at the probable charges against me. One murder, an accessory to two more. Even with leniency, I could be ninety when I get out. If I get out."

Bourque couldn't counter that.

"By the way, I assumed the police would come for me eventually. You can't hide everything. I'm a ship insurance broker who's also a diver. Not that many of us."

She nodded. "Tell me the direction. Is it your wife?"

"Winnie!? Are you listening? What would happen to our boys? They'd be parentless. They'd be lost. It's not Winnie," he ranted, "it's not Winston. The boys need her, the business needs him!"

"The direction, Mr. Reddit."

"Think maritime."

"Maritime?"

"Think."

She stilled her mind. Maritime. The sea, the coast, ports, ships. *Open your eyes wider. Dispel the darkness.* Ferries, she thought The *Islander* connection? It could be someone on the *Islander.* "The *Islander?*" she asked Reddit.

He waved vaguely.

She interpreted his gesture as a *maybe, no; maybe, yes.* Captain Macey, she considered, or Balan. No, not likely. They'd both sworn to being on the ship during Halliday's murder window. Carson? Could be. What about the other ferry staff? Again, not likely. They'd also sworn to being aboard the ship. All the depositions had been cross-checked. However, only six of the ferry staff had been questioned about Unger's murder, the night of November 9th. The rest were due to be questioned in the coming days. That, Bourque acknowledged, was a big missing piece. At the moment, there was nothing she could do about it.

She told herself to focus on what she knew. During Halliday's murder window, Carson hadn't been on the ferry. She'd rechecked his alibi. He was at Cape Cod Hospital in Hyannis from roughly 1800 to 2200. However, the hospital report noted his gallstone attack was minor, suggesting he didn't need to come in.

Now, sitting in the Back Cove cabin, she reassessed that detail. It was possible to slip away from an Emerg waiting room and return in time to see the doctor. Carson had a four-hour window. She did the math. An hour would get him from Hyannis to Orleans and back and give him time to kill Halliday. She hadn't had the foresight to realize it. There was another angle. Forensics suggested Halliday and Unger were killed by an ambidextrous person or a lefty. Carson was a lefty. If Reddit was insinuating a ferry worker, the killer could be Carson. Not conclusive, but another possible strike against him. Bourque motioned for Donnelly to guard Reddit and left the cabin.

Outside, in the sharp wind, the temperature had fallen to twenty-nine Fahrenheit. The Back Cove was plowing through three-foot waves. Skeins of murky cloud intensified the darkness. In a few hours, the Cape had slipped into winter. The air was as brittle as old ice, the whitecaps relentless, the boat's antennae twanging in the wind. Off to starboard, over Martha's Vineyard, newborn snow issued from the sky.

She huddled in the shelter of the helm and pulled out her phone.

"Captain," she said when Peabody answered, "there's another possible suspect, Sam Carson."

"All right. What's the news on Reddit?"

"He admitted to killing Fitzgerald. We have him in custody."

"Since when?"

She didn't reply. "Keep Carson under surveillance. Suspicion of murder."

## Chapter 37

**DAY TWENTY-SEVEN: Barnstable. November 15th**

The following afternoon, Peabody led a Captain Verge from HQ to Rick Reddit's cell at Barnstable Unit. The suspect's lawyer was waiting. Eller had returned from Holyoke. He and Bourque viewed the proceedings from a shadow room. Observing Reddit's body language and impatient voice, she suspected it wouldn't be long before he was formally charged. He raced through the preliminaries, twice waving his lawyer aside. Twenty minutes later, Verge arraigned Reddit for the first-degree murder of Fitzgerald and charged him as an accessory to the first-degree murders of Halliday and Unger. Reddit didn't disclose their murderer.

Eller turned his back on the viewing console.

"One down," Bourque said to him.

"One to go," he replied. "Apparently."

She nodded. She'd requisitioned security camera footage from the Cape Cod Hospital Emergency Room on the evening of October 21st. Sam Carson had left the room at twenty-ten and returned at twenty-one-oh-eight. In the team's view, there was a high probability he'd murdered Halliday during that window. The timeline fit. However, did he have a motive? And did he murder Unger?

Now, Bourque watched a relieved Reddit leave the cell. As her academy trainers used to say, detective work wasn't rocket science. *Force perps into a corner. They'll break.* Reddit did, quicker than most.

She stood and walked away. Intuition had joined forces with forensics. Some would call the union "chemistry," but she knew better. Chemistry was logical and mathematical. Detection was more like alchemy, chemistry's arcane forerunner, with its roots in a mysterious rationale. In detection, unlike in mathematics, you couldn't rely solely on logic. You had to go beyond it.

Bourque and Eller headed out for a sandwich. Captain Verge had asked them to interview Sam Carson in three hours. He'd just been arrested.

"You did it again," Eller said as he and Bourque sat in the nearby diner. "You went in without me." He winked. "You could have waited for me to join the Cuttyhunk op."

"I would have, but it wasn't Kansas out there. Bit choppy for a flatlander."

"No prob," he scoffed. "Little trip to the islands. Seriously, you did a great job. Justice will be served. Not just for Massachusetts," he added, "but for the whole nation."

She raised her coffee cup. Eller clicked it. Even on Cape Cod, detective work could have a national impact. Gigi might come to see that.

"Did Reddit talk to you about Ruby Halliday?" Eller asked.

"Yes. I'd say she was simply a sidekick, an accomplice. It was inevitable, you know."

"What's that?"

"That Karri Laker was going to be a false lead. The obvious lead is usually false."

"Usually," he agreed. "No prob as long as one is true."

"Exactly."

□ □ □

Bourque and Eller entered Interview Room One to find Sam Carson sitting in the room's Slider, facing a possible multiple-murder charge. He'd shaved off his moustache. Other than that, he looked the same: short and strong with light brown hair. He also looked confident. He'd declined legal representation. His folly, Bourque reflected. Eller had insisted that she run the show but she felt no pressure. Her job was to get the best of interviewees, be they career criminals or neighborhood POIs. In most cases, she didn't go about it by being hardnosed, but by being approachable and, occasionally—when necessary—disingenuous. She'd start Carson with a few suggestions, not lies, but implications that the police knew more than they did, the main one being that Reddit had fingered Carson for the Halliday and Unger murders.

"Well," she offhandedly began, "here we are again."

Carson didn't respond.

She studied his face. His wide brow was unfurrowed; his pike-green eyes, steady. However, whether his expression was resistant or acquiescent, she couldn't say. "Are you ambidextrous, Mr. Carson?"

"No."

"Left-handed?"

He hesitated. "Yes."

"I understand you don't own a knife." Time for the first suggestion. "So you acquired one from someone. A Strider SMF, to be exact."

Carson didn't react.

Bourque would circle back to that later. Now for the next suggestion, followed by a little spin. "You were working for Rick Reddit. Don't worry about protecting him. He didn't protect you."

"What?"

"He confessed to killing Daniel Fitzgerald and hiring someone to kill Ruby Halliday and Paul Unger. That someone is you. Do you want a lawyer, sir?"

Carson shook his head. However, from her read of his face, his mind was churning.

"Okay. Let's continue to talk. If you want a lawyer, tell me."

Carson nodded.

"You weren't in the Emergency Department at Cape Cod Hospital for the full four hours you mentioned. You reported leaving Emerg just after ten p.m. You also left earlier. When?"

Carson shrugged.

"You don't remember when? Let me tell you. Eight-ten p.m.," she stated. "It's on a hospital security camera. You returned to Emerg at nine-oh-eight p.m."

He shrugged again. The message written on his face was unmistakable. He knew where things were headed. "I thought it was earlier."

*Game over*, Bourque thought. "No, it was nine-oh-eight." She evaluated the suspect. He looked like he was ready to confess, which wasn't unusual for murderers in Massachusetts. When the game was up, most local perps didn't drag it out. Carson's face showed sorrow for his actions, unlike Reddit's earlier that day. She'd leave Carson's formal confession to Captain Verge. She hadn't officially read the suspect his rights. Furthermore, she'd made implications, meaning the interview contents could be thrown out of court. In the interim, she figured Carson would keep talking. "We'll call a lawyer, sir. Do you mind if I ask a few questions while we wait?"

"A lawyer won't change anything."

"All right," she said. "Let's confirm your movements. After you left the hospital at eight-ten p.m., you drove to Orleans. Is that right?"

"Yes."

"How did you get into Ruby Halliday's house?"

"I had a key."

"The backdoor key?"

He shook his head. "The front door key. I opened it, relocked it, then went to the backdoor and unlocked it from inside to throw off investigators."

Bourque considered the answer. "Who gave you the key?"

"R. R.," he replied.

R. R.? Was Kane in the picture? "R. R. Kane?" she asked.

"No, Rick Reddit."

"Do you know R. R. Kane?"

"Never heard of him."

Bourque didn't see any indications of subterfuge. Nonetheless, although Reddit was a declared accessory, she'd be revisiting Kane's file. A case wasn't closed until all the loose ends were tied up. She addressed Carson. "Did Mr. Reddit also give you the Strider knife?"

He nodded and sat still.

"Where is it?"

"Bottom of Vineyard Sound."

"How did you meet Mr. Reddit?"

"We grew up in Plymouth, in the same neighborhood."

The Plymouth connection, Bourque reflected. Her mother Sarah would be horrified. In Sarah's eyes, Plymouth Rock was the Rock of Ages, the Bethlehem of America. She'd say the Rock of Ages had fractured. Bourque shook her head inwardly. It was still in one piece, although it might be grimier. Plymouth was the real America, dreams and all, warts and all. "Did you loosen panels in the ferry's fore and aft stairwells?" she asked Carson.

"Yes."

As Bourque suspected. Given the *Islander* continually switched loading ends, making the aft deck the foredeck and vice versa, someone would likely have loosened panels in both stairwells. It could have been Halliday, but Carson had been a more probable candidate. "Did you go to the apartment of Paul Unger on the night of November ninth?" she asked.

"Yes."

"How did you get in?"

"Rick Reddit gave me a key."

"Why did you work for Mr. Reddit?"

"Money. My boys needed money."

"Drugs? Debts?"

"No, school. Harvard. Both of them want to go to grad school. It was going to cost a fortune."

"How much did Mr. Reddit pay you?"

"Two-hundred-fifty thousand for each kni—" Carson stumbled on the word. "—each knifing. I didn't care if I got caught. My boys needed my help."

*My boys* again, Bourque reflected. A common bond. A common motive? Had Reddit committed murder to help his boys? Or to safeguard his business? He didn't appear to be psychotic. Carson's case looked simpler. He seemed to have done it for his boys, and perhaps his house, which spoke of money. As her father often said, a case was a series of facts waiting to be uncovered. Perhaps the perps' deeper motives would surface. She wouldn't lose sleep over them. Right now, she was pondering the saga of the Fitzgeralds, hoping the curse wouldn't continue.

□ □ □

After watching Carson formally confess, Bourque and Eller exited the shadow room and strode to the main door. "Back to Holyoke." He winked. "Not a Falmouth hotel."

"I'll tell Peabody."

"Nah, tell him I booked a week at The Inn." Eller chuckled. "I'll send him the bill."

"He'd blow a gasket."

"Or two. Til next time, Bourque."

"Next time. Have a cherry schnapps for me."

"You got it." Eller hesitated. "Look me up in Holyoke. Anytime."

She smiled and nodded. "I will." She knew Eller meant it; he didn't extend empty invitations.

Eller gone, Bourque walked pensively to her car, her mind on the murders. As always, there'd been a slew of false leads: Laker, Captain Macey and Balan, the Marine connection to the Strider knife, Irvine, Conti, likely Kane. Marty was right about Laker. The governor might want to hold on to power, but she wasn't in the killing game. Then there was the one-murderer angle. Bourque shook her head. One knife didn't equal one murderer. That had been a big mistake. She'd been as wrong as she'd been right. Every case turned on a collection of mazes, none more complicated than the human brains involved. Inside those brains, synapses had fired, propelling thoughts into the world, which in turn triggered three murders.

As she reached her car, it started to snow. Wide, wet flakes fell on her face. Looking up, she watched thousands of crystals tumble toward her. The moon appeared to be frozen, its force seemingly spent. She felt a strange sense of peace as though time had stopped and the moon had joined it. The snow intensified, its white crystals landing everywhere, on her eyes, her hair, the slumbering Cape, the dying yet living trees, the entirety of Massachusetts. The moon faded from view. The snow fell with abandon.

The End

# ACKNOWLEDGEMENTS

My deepest thanks to Stark House Press, especially to Greg Shepard, Mark Shepard, and Bill Kelly. Being the second novel in the Detective Bourque series, continuity loomed large. The book had to fit in the series. I'm indebted to numerous people for keeping me on track.

While there will be many 'repeat' characters in the series, Ivy Bourque is by far the main character. The stories are her stories. She's a prototypical New Englander, approachable and egalitarian. But that's not all she is. In this novel, I gave her leeway to become a more nuanced person, a person with her own hitches and quirks. Many people helped me get Bourque's second story right, among them Ken Haigh, David Hoath, David and Penny Hosken, Fairlie Dalton, Fran Walsh, Jim Poling Sr., Mike Potter, John and Mary Ann Potter, and, of course, Ninety-Nine.

Many thanks to all those readers who continue to reach out and tell me my writing entertains or intrigues them. Writing is a conversation. Your words inform mine.